PRAISE

PRAISE

Andrew McGahan

Winner Australian/Vogel Literary Award

Carroll & Graf Publishers, Inc.
New York

Author's Note

As far as I know, there is no Capital Hotel in Brisbane. All the other pubs and Brisbane localities mentioned in the book are real. However, characters who are described throughout as working in these establishments are entirely fictional. They are not meant to bear any resemblance whatsoever to people who work, or have worked, in any of these places.

Copyright © 1992 by Andrew McGahan

All rights reserved

Published by arrangement with Allen & Unwin Pty. Ltd., Australia.

First Carroll & Graf edition 1993

Carroll & Graf Publishers, Inc.
260 Fifth Avenue
New York, NY 10001

Library of Congress Cataloging-in-Publication Data

McGahan, Andrew.
    Praise / Andrew McGahan.—1st Carroll & Graf
ed.
      p.   cm.
    ISBN 0-88184-938-3 : $19.95
    I. Title.
  PR9619.3.M3234P7   1993
  823—dc20   92-46446
                                    CIP

Manufactured in the United States of America

For Sam

For Darwin

ONE

Things started with Cynthia in October.

It was three days after my twenty-third birthday. I'd just quit work at the drive-through bottle shop of the Capital Hotel. I'd been there three years, working twenty hours a week at serving the cars and stacking beer in the fridges. I had no fondness for serving cars or stacking beer, but even so it took an ugly dispute between the staff and the management to get me out. They didn't sack me, but they sacked everyone else, people who'd been there for years longer than me. I showed up for the evening shift and my name was the only one left on the roster. They wanted me to work the next four days straight, twelve hours a day, until they made up the numbers. I'd never worked four days straight in my life. If I'd been a man of strength I would've walked out there and then, left the customers waiting, the manager screaming. I wasn't a man of strength. I waited until the end of the shift. I closed up the shop. Then I resigned. Quietly. The manager asked me why. He asked me if it was something personal. There wasn't much

1

I could say. I was tired. I felt it was time to wind that part of my life down. Work wasn't the answer to anything. . .

This was in Brisbane. Throwing away the job, all I had left was a car, seven hundred dollars in the bank and a two-room rented flat in New Farm.

I lived there alone.

The flat was in an old house, not far from New Farm Park and the river. There were eleven other apartments, all two rooms. The toilets and showers were communal.

The other residents were old men. Single. Out of work. Living out their days on the pension. To occupy themselves they spent their time drinking cask wine, red or white, in each other's rooms. They went through seven, eight, nine casks a day between them. When the casks were finished, they inflated the empty bladders and threw them out to the back yard. There were hundreds of the things out there, silver and plastic and indestructible. The real estate agent who ran the house had given up complaining about it. We weren't worth his time. Nothing in the place was, the behaviour of the residents least of all. We were all on two-week leases and he couldn't understand why we lived there in the first place.

I lived there because it was the cheapest accommodation I could find. Twenty hours a week at the bottle shop didn't leave much of a wage. And also because the rooms on either side of me were empty, and because the old men up and down the hallway were mostly harmless. They fought with each other and stole off each other, but left me and my things pretty much alone. They liked me. I was young, I was going to inherit whatever sort of earth it was they left.

Some of them liked me more than others. One was an old black man named Richard. He had an occasional habit of watching me when I was in the shower. There were no doors on the booths. He'd drift up and bring out his smooth old penis and inquire if I would like to suck it for him. Or if I wanted him to suck me. Then, after I'd say no, he'd focus on my waist and masturbate until he came over the tiles. I let him be. He was no danger. He was weak and worn and bruised from the drinking, and from the periodic beatings the others gave him. They considered themselves hardened men. Several of them had fought in World War Two. They had no time for faggots.

After my resignation from the bottle shop I drove home and parked in the back yard, then walked up the back steps into the hall. It was getting close to midnight. Most of the doors were open. The old men were arm wrestling in one of the rooms. I looked in. Two of them were clasped fist to fist on the double bed. Three or four others were watching on, screaming. It was all hatred and need. 'Gordon!' they yelled, 'Gordon get *in* here!'

They were eyeing off the six pack I was carrying. I declined. I was in a thoughtful mood. I was unemployed again, there were life decisions to be made. I wanted the beers for myself.

My room was two doors up, and everyone's keys fitted everyone else's doors. I was always suprised that no one went into my rooms when I was out. I had a TV in there, and food, and very often beer in the fridge, but things only occasionally went missing. Mostly it was clothes. Shirts. I unlocked my door and closed it behind me. I put the six pack in the fridge, took one beer out, opened it and sat there for a time. The thoughtful mood went away. I reached over to the phone and called up Morris. He was one of the people who'd been sacked from the Capital. He worked in the bottle shop with me. He was young and quick and more or less ran the place. He was the only one who understood the stocking system. No one had thought *he'd* go.

3

'So what happened?' I asked him.

'What happened with what?'

'You've been fired.'

'What!? No one told *me*.'

'And I've quit.'

'Really?' He yelled the news to someone off phone, then came back on. 'Karen says hello and congratulations. So what'd they say?'

'They said they didn't like your attitude.' In fact, the manager had told me he thought Morris was an arsehole. It was partly true. Morris knew more about pubs than anyone else at the Capital. His contempt was fairly obvious. 'They also fired Lisa, Carla, Cynthia and Geoff.'

Cynthia was in there, but I didn't know much about her then. She was just one of the barmaids. A little sharper than the rest perhaps.

'Jesus,' Morris was saying. 'No one's told me anything. I was gonna go to work tomorrow. And you've quit?'

'It seemed a good time.'

'We've gotta celebrate this. You got anything to drink?'

'A six pack. I'm on the first now.'

'Okay. I've got some wine. I'm on my way.'

'Morris, you realise I didn't quit for your sake.'

'C'mon, I know you, it was solidarity. It was a *protest*. So what're you gonna do now?'

'Nothing. Not for a while anyway.'

I hung up and rolled a cigarette and turned on the television. I could hear voices arguing from up the hall. It was a Wednesday night. I thought about it. Doing nothing for a while. It sounded fine, but I'd been out of work before and it'd never lasted more than a week or two. Money was the thing. You needed at least a little. In the end there was always Social Security, and the dole, but bureaucracies and their systems depressed me. Work in many ways seemed easier. I thought about maybe, despite it all, getting up

4

and looking for work the next day. Bottle shop work, pub work, was always easy enough to find.

Then Morris arrived. He had four bottles of good white wine. Embezzled, along with several dozen others over the years, from the Capital. We settled in and drank. It helped. We justified each other, justified our positions. We didn't need the Capital. Morris caught a cab home when it was finished.

Next morning I woke late. Life was waiting there.

I got up and went down the hall to the toilets. I met one of the old men on the way. His name was Vass. I didn't know if it was his first name or last. He never said. He'd been living there longer than any of us, longer than even the agent remembered.

'The bastards stole my radio,' he told me.

'I've quit work,' I told him.

'Yeah? You gonna get another job?'

'Not today.'

And then I was on the bowl, letting the shit go

TWO

New Farm Park was just around the corner from the house. I went there after I'd showered. It was about midday. I sat at one of the tables overlooking the river. There weren't many people around. It was a grey day, drizzling from time to time. I rolled a cigarette and smoked it. I felt pleased with myself. It was definitely a better thing to be sitting there in the park than to be at the bottle shop. I'd got that much right.

I sat there about an hour.

The rain steadied, got heavy.

I walked home.

The afternoon moved on. There was nothing on TV. I prowled around the flat, wondering what to do with myself. There were no answers. Then the phone rang. It was Cynthia.

I knew almost nothing about her.

I'd always maintained a certain distance from the staff at the Capital. I liked them, I drank with them, but I didn't get involved. There were only a few, Carla and Morris, and maybe Lisa, that I bothered with outside working hours. Most of my friends came from other parts of my life. From school. University. Most of the sex came from there too, but there wasn't that much sex and what there was hadn't been much good. I was young and nervous and not very enthusiastic. I didn't have the libido I felt I was supposed to have. And I didn't expect things to improve. I relied on masturbation.

And Cynthia had only been working at the Capital for three or four months. We'd talked just the once, about a book I found her reading behind the bar one day. It was by Voltaire. It wasn't much of a conversation. I didn't know who Voltaire was.

'I heard you quit,' she said, on the phone.
   'I heard you got fired.'
   'I didn't get fired. I quit before they got round to it.'
   'Really? Why?'
   'I'm leaving Brisbane anyway. I *hate* this place.'
   That was understandable. I was happy enough in Brisbane, but it wasn't for everyone.
   She said, 'I was wondering if you felt like a few drinks?'
   'Sure. I've got the time. You mean going out? Or would you like to come over here?'
   'Well, my parents are away for a couple of weeks, if you'd like to come over here instead. It's a nice house.'
   So she lived with her parents. I wondered how old she was. She looked about twenty-eight, or thirty.
   'Okay,' I said. I wrote down the address. 'You want me to get you something to drink on the way?'
   'No, only for yourself. I've already got some beer here.'

I drove over. I stopped along the way for some beer. Twelve bottles of Fourex. Cynthia lived in St Lucia. Her parents' house was set back off the street. The yard behind it led down into a rainforested gully. I carried the carton up the footpath and knocked on the door.

'Who is it?'

'It's me.'

The door opened.

'Hello,' I said.

She had a cigarette in her mouth. I remembered her brand was Winfield Blue. She took the cigarette out of her mouth, blew out the smoke.

I held up the carton.

'Come on in,' she said.

I followed her into the kitchen and we stacked the beer in the fridge. There were several six packs of Tooheys Old in there as well. She already had a can open for herself, so I poured myself a beer and looked around the house. She was right, it was nice. Wooden floors and big rooms and a verandah overlooking the gully. We sat out there. The sky was still grey but the rain had stopped.

I said, 'So where are your parents?'

'In Darwin. Dad's in the Army. He's a major. He's being transferred up there. He's gone up with Mum to sort out a new house. Then they'll come back and get the furniture and get me and we'll leave.'

'You're going with them?'

'There's no reason to stay in Brisbane. I've only been here for six months. I don't know anyone here. I don't like the town. And I want to spend some time with Mum and Dad. It's the first time I've lived with them in years. They threw me out of home when I was fifteen.'

'How old are you now?'

'Twenty-three.'

I stared at her. Twenty-three? She didn't look it. Short dyed blond hair, a round creased face, big solid hips.

'You're kidding? Twenty-three?'

'I know. I look older. I've got a skin condition. Eczema. It's fucked up my face.'

I got up and had a close look at her face. She was wearing a lot of make-up, but under the make-up you could see that her skin was red and scraped and tough. I told her this. She said it wasn't tough. She said that it was in fact quite delicate. Just a touch could make it bleed. The problem was allergic reactions. She was allergic to things like wool, dust, soap, various foods, alcohol. She finished her beer and got herself another one.

I watched her gulp it down.

'So how old are you?' she said.

'Twenty-three.'

'You look older. You've got soft skin, but you still look older. Maybe it's the hair.'

'Maybe it is.'

My hair, at the time, was long. Unwashed. Down to the shoulders.

We sat there all afternoon. Mostly we talked about the pub and how good it felt to be out of it. I asked her if she'd been to Darwin before. She hadn't. I told her I'd seen Darwin and that I couldn't imagine her liking it any more than Brisbane. She shrugged.

I asked, 'How come you've moved back in with your parents after all this time?'

'I came up here to straighten out. I'd been in Sydney for a year on heroin. I got sick of it.'

'You still on it now?'

'No. It's easy enough to quit once you're away from the crowd. I was in love with this girl at the time and she was a dealer. I got it for free.'

'Are you gay?'

'No, but I've been with women a few times. The problem

9

with women is they don't have penises. I have a thing for penises.'

We drank on. Her parents had a dog, a cattle dog named Ralph. She threw it a tennis ball and he chased it around. It occurred to me to wonder why she had invited me there. I hadn't thought about it until then. Not that there was any way to tell. It was fine in any case, there on the verandah.

The dog ran around. She looked at me. 'So do you do anything other than work in pubs?' she said.

'Not really. I went to uni a few years ago but left half way through. I was studying Arts.'

'I'd love to go to uni one day, if I hadn't stuffed around so much at school. I heard you wrote poetry.'

'Who told you that?'

'Everyone at the pub.'

'That's strange.'

We started talking about writers we'd read. She seemed to have read far more than I had. I asked her if she wrote. She said she didn't. She said she didn't do anything.

Night came on and we dialled a pizza for dinner.

But she was right. I had been writing poetry for three or four years by then. And short stories. And a novel, when I was nineteen. But after the novel, poetry was the only thing I had much interest in. It was quick and easy and satisfying. I wrote mostly about sex and my deep disappointment with it. I didn't know much about sex.

It started to rain again. We moved into the living room and sprawled on the couches and listened to various records, some of which I knew, most of which I didn't. Cynthia talked. She was good to listen to. Generally it was about sex. Sex was important to her. She told me about her experiences with it, about all the men and women she'd slept with. I got the whole story. She started masturbating when she was twelve, getting off on the penetration. With odd things around the house at first, than vibrators, and then to sex with boys by the time she was fourteen. Which was why her parents had tossed her out of home. She'd disappeared one weekend, spent three nights at her boyfriend's place. When she arrived back at the family house her parents had her bags packed.

I'd grown up on a farm, three hours west of Brisbane, the ninth child out of ten, Catholic parents. I was masturbating by twelve as well, but I didn't sleep with anyone till I was nineteen.

I thought Cynthia's childhood sounded more interesting.

Finally the beer ran out. We were still thirsty, and it wasn't closing time yet. We decided more drinks were in order.

'You want to drive?' Cynthia said.

I explained that I wasn't comfortable about drink driving.

'Jesus,' she said. 'Okay, I'll drive.'

I wasn't so uncomfortable about drink driving that I wouldn't let someone else do it. We took my car, Cynthia behind the wheel, and drove to the nearest bottle shop. We pulled up and the boy came over. I felt for him. I know how hateful customers became after a while. They disturbed the peace.

I said to the boy, 'A dozen cans of Toohey's Old.'

He went away and came back with the beer. He did it slowly.

'It's okay,' I told him, 'I used to work in a bottle shop too. In fact I only just quit.'

'Yeah?' he said. 'Which one?'

'The Capital.'

'Never heard of it.'

We paid up.

'Poor bastard,' I said, as we pulled back out to the street.

11

We returned to her place. She was a good driver. Confident and fast. We settled back into the couches. We talked on. About her life, about mine. Hers was definitely more interesting. Then I started losing it to drunkenness and the need for sleep. She explained that there were only two bedrooms in the house, her own and her parents', and that she didn't think it'd be a good idea for me to use her parents'. I went in and looked and saw what she meant. The room was immaculate. The bed was covered with a plastic dust sheet.

'Your parents are paranoid about dust?'

'My *mother* is paranoid about dust. Don't worry. I've got a double bed, you can have half of that.'

I agreed. Cynthia wandered off to the toilet. I lay on the bed. I kept my clothes on. She came back. I watched while she undressed on her side of the bed. Her body was big and white and her back was sprinkled with the same allergic rash as her face. She climbed in and we lay there, side by side.

'You can take your clothes off,' she said. 'I won't rape you.'

I took off my jeans. We moved a little closer. Then we slept.

THREE

Cynthia woke me late next morning.

'What's wrong with your breathing? You sound like you're about to suffocate.'

I sat up and started coughing. The hangover moved in. 'It's asthma,' I told her. I reached for my jeans and went through the pockets for the Ventolin inhaler. She watched me puff away on it, sucking in the drug.

'And you *smoke*?'

I smoked. In fact I had only started smoking about a year before. I was living in the Northern Territory. It was the boredom that got to me. I started with Winfield Blues, two or three a day, then discovered menthols. Alpine Ultra Lights. I worked my way up to seven or eight packs a week. I struck problems. I was wheezing all the time, vomiting after only three or four drinks. I switched over to rolled tobacco and things got better. Not quite so many poisons. I got through one pouch maybe every three or four days. Any brand.

I explained all this to her as I rolled a cigarette. 'It helps in the morning, believe it or not.'

The Ventolin was working. I could breathe. I lit the cigarette and inhaled. The lungs caught, coughed it up. I inhaled again. This time it held. It felt good. The asthma wasn't a problem. Asthma could always be controlled.

Cynthia found her own pack and we smoked in silence for a while. The pillows had rubbed most of the make-up off her face and her skin was livid red. It was bleeding in places.

'Does it hurt?'

'It itches. I scratch my face in my sleep. That's why it bleeds.'

'Isn't there anything you can do for it?'

'Not really. The only drug that can stop it is cortisone, and cortisone is too dangerous to use for more than week or two at a time. It clears up the skin for a while, but in the long run it does more damage than the eczema does. I still use it, though, when my skin gets bad. That's why my face is all wrinkled. The cortisone does that.'

'Or you could avoid the things you're allergic to?'

She nodded. 'Or I could avoid the things I'm allergic to.'

We smoked. She rolled on her side and looked at me. 'Thought you'd at least try something last night,' she said.

'It didn't occur to me. No offence.'

'Do you like sex?'

'It hasn't worked out too well so far.'

'What's been wrong?'

'Who knows. It can all be very cold, sometimes.'

'You don't seem cold. You have a very warm laugh.'

We got up. Cynthia grilled us some ham and tomato for breakfast. I considered the cans of beer that were left in the fridge. They looked good, better than I felt.

'I don't know if I'm up to these,' I said.

'Have you ever tried Catovits?'

I hadn't.

'They're pills,' she said. 'They give them to old people in

14

hospitals to keep them alert. They're like speed. I get them on prescription for depression, but they're great hangover cures.'

She brought out a foil sheet containing round red pills. We took one each. We ate our breakfast. The hangover evaporated like magic. We opened some beer, moved out onto the verandah. The day was overcast and damp.

'You doing anything today?' she asked.

'Uh-uh. How about you?'

'No.'

We watched the sky for a while.

'And you've plenty of these Catovits?'

'Enough,' she said.

I stayed with her for the next six days.

We slept together all that time, but we made no bodily contact other than rolling against each other in our sleep. It was something new for Cynthia. She'd fucked a lot of men. Sex was taken very much for granted. But she didn't seem to mind. And I was content. I liked her conversation, but sex was something else all together. I masturbated occasionally when I was alone in the bed. From time to time she requested that I leave the bedroom so that she could do the same. It was a workable system.

On the sixth day I called one of my sisters, Louise. There were four girls in my family, and six boys. Louise was only a couple of years older than me. She was a doctor. She was about to move to Sydney to specialise in pathology. She wanted to cut up the bodies.

'Gordon? I heard you quit.'

'It's true. Work was killing me.'

'So what now?'

'I don't know. I've been taking it easy the last week.'

'Are you still coming to my party?'

15

She was throwing a party at her house, to say goodbye
to her friends.

'I'll be there. Is it okay if I bring someone?'

'Of course. Who?'

'A friend from the pub. One of the barmaids.'

'Oh? Anyone special?'

'Just a friend, Louise.'

'Okay . . .'

Cynthia took some time getting ready. She covered her
face with powders and creams. When she was finished you
couldn't tell about her face, not unless you looked very
closely. She went through this every time she left the house.
She hated her skin. Another thing she hated was her tattoo. She had a tattoo of a butterfly on her left breast. If she
was wearing a light coloured shirt she wore a bandaid over
the tattoo to hide it. Tonight though she was wearing a
black top and a black skirt. They were work clothes. She'd
been in pubs for so long that all the clothes she owned
were either black or white.

'I like it,' I said, about the tattoo.

'I don't. I don't know what the fuck I had in mind when
I got it done . . .'

'How old were you then?'

'Fifteen. I did everything when I was fifteen.'

We drove over to the party and walked in with a carton
of Toohey's Old and a four-litre cask of Lambrusco. There
were thirty or forty people there. I knew most of them.
Louise's friends. University graduates. Doctors. The gain-
fully employed. I wasn't sure what I thought of them.
I'd almost gone that way myself. I'd believed in things.
Dedication. Diligence. Direction. I'd even finished school
in the top one percent of the state. It was a cruel and
meaningless system, still, there I was at the top of it.

But things had changed since then. I was ashamed of it all now.

I introduced Cynthia to my sister and a few others. We put our drinks in the laundry sink, where the ice was, and sucked down the beer. The party developed. Cynthia took to it well. She was short and oddly shaped, but she had style. She moved around, talking, laughing, concentrating on the men.

I ended up on the couch, drinking and watching. The stereo was on, a few people were dancing. The rest were getting themselves wherever it was they needed to go. It was Friday night. Party night. It was beyond my conception, the importance of Friday night to those who worked a five-day week. It was always something to watch though, curious and a little appalling. All that desperate relief. Right across the country, in nightclubs and bars and restaurants, millions of them were at it. If I thought about it too long it became horrifying.

Cynthia came back to me some time after midnight. She was drunk.

'So when are you going to fuck me?' she said.

'I didn't know you wanted me to.'

'Of course I do. You're the one who's got all the hang-ups about it . . .'

I looked up at her. It was not a thing I understood. I had no sense of timing, of when things should or shouldn't be happening in a relationship. Of when a relationship had even started.

'Seriously?' I said. 'You think we should sleep together?'

'We've *been* sleeping together. I think we should fuck.'

'Okay then.'

'You mean I've been waiting all this time and all I had to do was ask?'

'I guess so.'

'Jesus. What is wrong with you?'

'I'm sorry. I just haven't thought about it.'

She looked at me, hard. 'How can you not think about it?'

I shrugged. The truth was I thought about it all the time, but not about it actually happening, not with anyone I knew.

She said, 'Tonight then?'

I said, 'Okay.'

But we didn't leave the party until our beer had run out and people were starting on the Lambrusco.

We caught a cab home, to my place. The house was lively. The old men were still awake, most of the doors were open and the radios were turned up high. Vass stuck his head out of his room and said good evening.

I introduced Cynthia. Vass bowed, all charm. He was tall and thin and black. Emphysema made him whisper when he talked. 'Hello little lady,' he said. Cynthia leaned against me.

'Hello,' she said.

Vass looked at me. 'You kids feel like a drink?'

'I don't think so, Vass.'

'Where you been all week anyway?'

'Away. Cynthia's place.'

'Ah. Well. You know you've got some new neighbours.'

'No. I didn't know that.'

'Right in the room next to yours.'

'I see.'

'They put out a welcome mat, for chrissake.'

'Have you met them?'

'Not yet.'

Then he was gone. Cynthia was curled up against me. She looked tired. I led her into my flat. Maybe we'd just crawl into bed and go to sleep. I wouldn't have minded. I was nervous. The only thing that was going to get me through fucking her was the alcohol, and I hadn't had that

18

much to drink. I wasn't sure what to do. Cynthia had fucked dozens of people. She'd been in love, she'd said, she'd fucked for love — what did I know about it? I'd had, at that stage, a total of five casual and unsuccessful sexual affairs. One of them was a brief encounter with a man, two of the others — with women — had only lasted one ugly night ... I had no rhythm, no grace. I couldn't even dance. How could you fuck if you couldn't dance?

But as soon as my door was closed, Cynthia came alive. She reached up, pushed me back against the wall.

We kissed.

There was no emotion in it. My eyes were open and staring at her face. Our mouths were stretched, our tongues jamming in and out. It was grotesque. I was not fond of kissing. Either it was like this, grotesque, or it was something terribly tender. Something far more than sex, something that demanded sincerity. And I had real problems with sincerity.

Why wasn't I a man? Why was I worrying about sincerity? Why couldn't I throw her down on the bed and be brutal?

My body was the problem. My prick had no guts. It couldn't take over my brain like pricks were supposed to. It couldn't subject everything to the whim of the Lord Penis.

It was too small, that was the problem. I had a theory. Desire was directly proportional to size! You needed something big to wave around, to inspire nausea and confidence. I had no chance.

And her body was the problem. Women's bodies were the problem. They did nothing for me, they were just flesh. It wasn't bodies I got off on, it was personalities, indulgent personalities, fucked-up personalities, ugliness, fear ... the *situation* of fear. But even then, when it came down to the sex, something seemed to be missing.

It didn't matter. Cynthia displayed no great interest in

kissing either. She pushed me over to the bed and threw me down. She might have been short but she weighed as much as me and was just as strong. We kissed some more and she wrestled me out of my jeans. I was erect, for what it was worth. I was operating, I was functioning, but the mind was still there, it wouldn't shut up: What do I do now?

But Cynthia was away. She didn't bother undressing. She reached under her skirt, pulled off her panties and jumped straight on me. She jammed herself down. 'Fuck,' she said. She thrust away. Her eyes were closed. All I could feel was friction and pain. She wasn't even wet. I grabbed her hips and held on. She threw her head back. 'Oh *fuck*.' Then she rolled off and lay there, curled up.

I touched her back. 'Are you okay?'

'I'm okay. I just came, that's all.'

It'd been no more than twenty or thirty seconds. My penis had barely even registered it.

After a while she uncurled. 'I'm sorry,' she said, 'that was almost rape. It's just that I haven't done if for so long with a boy. I've been thinking about it for days. I've been so horny.'

'I'm sorry, I didn't know.'

'I thought you must hate sex.'

'It's not that. I just haven't managed to enjoy it much yet.'

'I can't understand that.'

'It doesn't matter.'

She found her cigarettes and lit one. I took one of hers rather than roll one of my own. It was the first Winfield Blue I'd had for months and it tasted very good.

'One thing you should know,' she said, 'when I come, I have to do it alone. Don't try to talk to me when I'm coming, don't try to touch me or do anything to me. Just leave me alone. Okay?'

'Okay,' I said.

We smoked our cigarettes.

'Can we do it again?' she asked, after we were finished.

'If you want.'

FOUR

We woke late next day. There was an argument in the flat
next door. The new tenants. A man and a woman. The
voices were loud and angry but indistinct. I sat up and
began coughing. Cynthia watched me as I went through
the routine of sucking in the Ventolin and rolling the first
cigarette.

Her skin was bad again. It was my fault. I'd been explor-
ing it during the night, testing the limits. The disease was
all over her face, neck, shoulders and back. It made her
skin tender and wrinkled, covered it with hundreds of small
scabs that broke away with my fingertips. Now, in the
morning, her face was oozing blood. The bleeding woman.
If I'd rubbed my unshaven cheeks up against hers I could
probably have killed her.

She rooted through her bag to find some cream. She said
it didn't help much, but it was better than nothing.

The argument next door rose to screaming, cut off
abruptly.

'There,' I said, 'he's killed her.'

'She's probably in love. She won't mind.'

'I suppose that's why he did it.'

'Love is a dangerous thing,' she agreed. She curled up against me. She reached down, rolled my balls between her fingers. She did it gently. 'Your name *would* have to be Gordon.'

'What's wrong with Gordon?'

'All the great loves of my life seem to have been named Gordon. There were two of them. And they both left. Each time it fucked me up for years.'

'Oh.'

She rolled over on top of me, stared at my face. 'Never mind, you're beautiful. Your *eyelashes* are beautiful. And your skin. It's like a baby's. I'd kill for skin like that. It's a woman's skin.'

'I stay out of the sun.'

'So who were your great loves?'

'There was only one. And we were at school at the time. I wanted to run away with her, I wanted to marry her. It went on for years. I think it affected me permanently. It's a very significant time, adolescence. Significant and tortured. We never even kissed. We only saw each other at school. She lived out of town. We held hands a lot.'

'Poor baby. Are you still in love with her?'

'I haven't seen her for a couple of years. I probably am.'

'And no one else?'

'Not really. There's one other woman, perhaps. An *older* woman. But that's a little complicated. And otherwise things have been pretty slow.'

'But why? I couldn't believe it when the other girls at the pub said you were single. I said I *want* that boy, and they said they thought you must be gay . . . are you?'

'I don't think so. I've only slept with a man once.'

'Did you enjoy it?'

'Yes. I did. Still, I don't know. It was only the once, and I was very drunk . . . it's not much to go on.'

'Do you fantasise about men?'

'Sometimes. Not as often as I do about women. And there's always a certain amount of violence about it.'

'So why didn't you do it again?'

'The chance never came up. He moved to Adelaide. And there's never been anyone else that appealed . . .'

'What was his penis like?'

We talked penises for a while. Sizes and shapes and the uses of such. She pulled back the sheet and slid down my stomach and examined mine. 'They're such amazing things,' she said, moving it around, 'I wish I had one of my own, just to play with.'

I watched her over my stomach.

'It's not very big though, is it' I said.

'How long is it erect?'

'Five inches. Just *under* five inches.'

'Well . . . I wouldn't worry too much. It's enough to work. And the really big pricks can be horrible sometimes. As long as they're wide enough, as long is the shape is right, the length doesn't matter so much. The worst penis I ever had was about a foot long but it was so thin it hurt. It was like being fucked with a knitting needle. I like yours. It's cute.'

Cute. I didn't want cute. I wanted ugly. I wanted something huge and purple and bulging with veins. I wanted a *pole*. This life of mine was cursed with all the wrong attributes.

Cynthia meanwhile had started muttering and whispering to my cuteness. I watched her. She kissed it, sucked it. It rose up. She pulled back, considered.

'I think it wants to fuck me,' she said.

'I think I know what my own penis wants.'

'Bullshit. I'm the only one that knows.'

She came climbing back up, lifted herself and descended.

She was wet. I slid straight in. 'Another fucking Gordon,' she said.

'Gordon is a useful name. Not a single famous person has ever been called Gordon.'

She was pushing down, sliding back. 'What about Gordon Lightfoot?'

'Who's Gordon Lightfoot?'

'Forget it. And *move*.'

I moved. I did my best.

She rode me into the ground.

Later that day I retrieved my car from Louise's place, then drove Cynthia home. Her parents were due back and she wanted to get the house clean.

'I'll call you in a day or two, okay?'

'Okay.'

We didn't kiss goodbye. That was good. She closed the car door and walked up the path. She always moved fast when she walked. She was impatient.

I drove home.

FIVE

It was time to consider money. I still had about five hundred dollars left, but the idea of finding another job was becoming incomprehensible. I was destined for unemployment. I walked down to the Fortitude Valley C.E.S. I told the woman behind the counter that I'd like to register. This was the first step towards getting the dole. Once the C.E.S. had you listed, then you could register yourself at Social Security for unemployment benefits. She gave me a form. I looked at it, read it through, then filled it in. It was a surrender of sorts. She told me to wait for an interview. I sat down along the wall and waited.

The place was crowded. Bad times in the economic world. There weren't many jobs listed on the boards. People walked around, staring at the adds for assistant cooks, builders' labourers, service station attendants. . .and maybe they all *needed* the work. Maybe they had kids to support, maybe they had debts. I didn't need the work. I was young and single and male. Society was constructed for the likes of me.

But I was worried. My fear of bureaucracies was real,

and the C.E.S. and the Department of Social Security were reputedly monsters. I'd spent most of my life avoiding going on the dole, just to stay out of their grasp. They needed to know things. They needed to limit and define. They created motives where motives didn't exist. They assumed guilt, they searched for it, rooted it out and pinned it down. And I *was* guilty. Every form I'd ever filled out had told me that. I didn't have the right desires. The only safe course was employment. No one bothered you if you were employed. But then no one bothered you if you were dead either. Employment was death. Safety was death. These things had to be understood.

A man called out 'Gordon Buchanan'. I got up and followed him down a line of small cubicles until we came to his. He was middle-aged, round, balding. He was the monster personified, but there was no joy in it for him either. He was carrying the form I'd filled in. I sat down and he sat down. He read through the pages, typing the information into his computer terminal.

'So you're a barman?' he said.

'Well, I'm usually in the bottle shops, not behind the bar.'

'Okay. And you're capable and willing to look for full-time work?'

'Well . . . only part-time really. I've only ever worked twenty or thirty hours a week. It's all I need to get by.'

He typed it in. 'Of course we can't help you much with your job searching. Not with part-time work. Things are so busy these days we can only concentrate on the full-time stuff.'

'That's okay. Pub work is always easy to find.'

He nodded. I nodded.

We were agreed.

It was all bullshit for both of us.

'You realise,' he said, 'that you won't be eligible for unemployment benefits if you're only looking for part-time
work.'

'Oh.' That was a suprise. 'But I don't *need* a full-time job.
I'm happy with part-time.'

'Sorry. To be eligible for unemployment benefits you have
to declare that you are able and willing to look for full-time
work.' He gave me a look. Waited.

Which was fair enough. The game was there to be played.

'Okay,' I said, 'Put down that I'm after full-time work.'

He typed it in patiently.

'Now,' he said, 'I'll give you some forms, and if you want
to apply for benefits you fill them in and take them down
to Social Security and they'll take over from there. Okay?'

'Sure.'

'One more thing. Come and check and boards regularly.
We don't have the time to send any referrals out at the
moment. Okay?'

'Okay.'

He glanced through my forms again.

'Anything else?'

'No.'

He led me back to the waiting area. Then he picked up
another set of forms from the pile and called out a name.

I took my Social Security forms back to the car and read
through them. They seemed depressingly detailed. One
section asked for bank account numbers and stated that
anyone with an accessible fund of five hundred dollars or
more would not be immediately eligible for benefits. I
thought about that for while, then got out my car again,
went to the bank and withdrew all my money.

But Social Security could wait for a few more days. There
were several things I needed to gather up anyway. Three
forms of identification, for a start, which I wasn't sure I

28

had. And more importantly, I needed a separation certificate from the Capital, to prove I was no longer working there.

Cynthia had warned me about this. She'd been unemployed for several years all told, here and there. She advised that if possible I should get my former boss to fill in the form in such a way that it said he'd sacked me. A sacked worker was elegible for benefits much sooner than one who'd quit.

I didn't know if my old manager would do this.

He was an unpleasant person.

Still, I had to go and see him anyway. I had discovered, in the act of emptying my bank account, that the money owing to me for my last half-week's work had not been paid.

But that could wait too.

I was tired and hungover and more occupied with thoughts about Cynthia than I was with finances. I drove home, opened up the flat and went to bed.

I woke in the dim evening and got up. I showered, made a sandwich, turned on the TV. There was a knock on the door. Vass came in. He was red-eyed and smelled of old wine, but he was sober. His lungs sounded as bad as they'd ever been. Death was close. I always watched Vass carefully when his emphysema was in ascendance. It was my own future, after all.

'That was a nice girl you had here last night,' he said.

'Yes. She is.'

'I walked past last night in the hall and I could hear you going for it . . .'

'The walls are very thin.'

'You met the new people yet?'

'I heard them this morning. They were screaming at each other. What're they like?'

'They're nice kids. They just got up here from Sydney.

You wanna buy a car? They have to sell their car. It's an HQ Holden stationwagon. They need the money.'

My own car was an HZ Holden sedan, the last of the Kingswood series. I was very fond of it. There was something pure and humble about the lines, the wide-set wheels, the simple 3.3 litre engine. But there was no room in my heart for another one.

I said, 'No, one car is enough. How much do they want for it?'

'Eight hundred.'

Which might've been good value. I didn't know. The truth was I didn't even own my car. It had been the family vehicle, years before. It'd been handed down by my parents through the various sons and daughters until it came to me. It was still registered in my parents' name, and they still paid the registration, year after year.

They were very good, my mother and father, to a son who even at twenty-three hadn't shown much sign of getting his economic life in order.

'He's Spanish,' said Vass. 'His name is Raymond.'

'Is that a Spanish name?'

'How the fuck should I know? That's just what he said. And she's a nice little thing. Cathy. She's white.'

'Why'd they come to Brisbane.'

'I dunno.'

Vass thought everyone that moved in was okay at first. Generally he ended up hating them within a week or two.

'Did you get your radio back?' I asked.

'Huh? How did you know my radio was gone?'

'You told me. In the hallway. About a week ago.'

'Aaah. No. The bastards. One of them took it. They stole my TV and they stole my radio and now I've got nothing.'

Although I didn't know who had stolen the radio, I certainly knew why. It was a big old thing, with powerful speakers, and he played it loud, always on country music stations. Vass was mostly deaf. He refused to wear his hearing aid, even in private. We'd all gone through nights of hammering on his door and yelling at him to turn the volume down, but he'd stay in his room and pretend he couldn't hear. Still, I felt for him. He rarely left the two rooms he lived in, and without a TV or radio, all he had left was reading and drinking. I'd seen what he read. In his flat there were stacks of Louis Lamour western novels.

'That's pretty bad,' I told him.

He nodded. He seemed sad.

'You aren't working today?' he asked.

'No. I quit. Remember?'

'Aaah. So you did. You treat that girl nice, okay.'

'I will.'

'Don't hit her. There's too much of that.'

'I won't.'

And so we watched TV.

SIX

Next day I drove over to the Capital Hotel. I found the manager out in the bottle shop. Nothing had changed much, except I didn't recognise the boy working there. The manager's name was Simon. He was twenty-two. He hadn't been there long. He was the last in a long line of managers the owners had appointed to get the pub going again. The Capital had been running down steadily for the last decade or so. On his first day as manager Simon had assembled the staff and made a speech.

He'd said, 'There's only one thing I want you to remember. We're here to make this place a success. As long as everyone is working as hard as they can and as long as the hotel is bringing in as many paying customers as I know it should, everything will be fine. You'll be happy, and I'll be happy. Remember, we're a team, and if everyone puts a little extra effort in we can make this work.'

He was the youngest person in the room. It was no real suprise that everyone had left or been sacked within a month.

But he liked me, for some reason, and when I told him

about the certificate I needed and about how I hadn't been paid yet, he appeared genuinely concerned. He took me up to the office and counted out the money I was owed. Then he found a severance form and asked me how I wanted it filled out.

'Could you say you sacked me?'

He could. There were several options on those forms as to why an employer might discharge an employee. One was to do with incompetence on the employee's part, another was for excessive absenteeism and so on, and one was simply for lack of available work. He ticked the third. Looked at me. 'Anything else?'

'No. That's about it.'

'If you ever wanna come back, y'know, just give me a call.'

'Thanks.'

I didn't understand it. He was decent to me, but I still didn't like him. Some people you never did. Maybe it was just that he was fool enough to expect his staff to care about the hotel, and fool enough to *tell* his staff that he expected it. Working in pubs, or in any retail business, was at best a dreary and mindless existence. To be merely competent at it — to refrain, say, from abusing forty or fifty per cent of your customers — often took a soul-destroying effort. To have *enthusiasm* demanded of you, that was more than the job was worth.

Back home again I found visitors knocking on my door. Molly and Leo. I knew Leo from university. He was an Agricultural Sciences student. He lived on study benefits and worked part-time as a cleaner in a department store. He was short and wiry, with long stringy red hair. His movements were nervous. Molly was his girlfriend of three or four months. She was a modern-day love child. In a sense they both were. They were striving for a peaceful

33

existence. Molly worked as a nurse. Part-time. Very few of my friends had passed into that netherworld of a full-time career.

I invited them in.

'You feel like a smoke?' Leo asked. He was already rolling one. I didn't smoke a great deal, in this particular sense, but there was nothing else happening for the afternoon. Leo lit up and we passed the joint around. It wasn't very strong, which was good. If it'd been strong I would've been useless for conversation for the next hour or so.

'I hear you quit work,' Molly was saying.

'Uh-huh. I registered at the C.E.S. yesterday. I'm going on the dole at last.'

'What will you do with all that time? Will you write?'

Molly wrote short stories and poetry. I'd never read anything of hers. I had, once, in a bad and drunken moment, shown her a few of my own poems. She hadn't liked them. She thought they were crude and pointless.

'I don't think so,' I said. 'I think I'll just sit around here for a few months.'

'Sit around? How can you just sit around?'

'It's easy. You just have to keep your expectations under control. Expectations are the problem with everything.'

'You have to have expectations about something.'

'No. No, you *don't*.'

Leo and Molly had no plans for the afternoon either. In the end we walked down to one of the local pubs, the Queen's Arms. We sat in the public bar and drank, then moved into the private bar where a band was starting up. They were doing ironic covers of songs from the sixties and seventies. It seemed appropriate enough, considering the company.

Molly and Leo were a strange couple. For all their peaceful intentions, there was a lot of hatred between them, from Molly in particular. She was possibly the most commercially attractive women I'd ever met, but she was the coldest too.

34

She wore purple sarongs, talked to flowers, but there was nothing of the earth mother inside her.

That was part of Cynthia's attraction. She was very much earth mother material. Big and warm and chaotic.

I told them about her.

'A woman,' Molly screamed. 'You've got a *woman*?'

'Only for a few more days. She's leaving soon.'

'I thought you were never fucking anyone ever again?'

The poems I'd showed Molly happened to have been some of the blacker ones, written in moments of deep sexual despair.

I said, 'Neither did I. Cynthia sort of snuck up on me.'

'Who is she?' asked Leo. 'You've never even mentioned her.'

'I met her at the Capital. She works behind the bar.'

'A barmaid?'

'Yes. A barmaid.' I looked at him. 'And barmaids, Leo, are to be respected.'

Molly said, 'So are nurses.'

We drank on our beers.

'Well, agricultural scientists,' said Leo, 'have it hard too.'

We stayed until closing time, got ourselves solidly drunk, then wound our way back to my flat. The house was alive with violence and noise. The old men were going for each other. I introduced everyone round and we drank on for an hour or two. We were in Lewis's flat. Lewis was fifty or fifty-five, but looked less. He had bright silver hair slicked back in a fifties style. He was a Vietnam veteran. He survived now on an unexplained invalid pension. Whatever the problem was, it gave him a sour outlook on the world. He wore tight-fitting T-shirts with the sleeves rolled up to the shoulder, and terrorised the rest of the house. Except for me. I had the only car in the place. I was useful to have on side.

'Where the fuck've you been lately?' he said. 'I hear you got a woman. This her?' He was looking at Molly, who was next to me at the time.

Molly shrieked. 'Me? With *Gordon*?'

Finally we retired to my place. Leo rolled another joint and we smoked it. It seemed stronger now.

'I can't drive home,' said Leo.

'You can stay here.'

'Where?'

'In the bed. There's room for three of us. It's a very large bed.'

'I'm not sleeping next to you,' said Molly.

'Leo can sleep in the middle.'

It was agreed.

We smoked one more joint. I was tiring. So was Molly. We decided to sleep. Leo wasn't tired. Smoking always gave him energy. He said he was going back to the old men. After he was gone, Molly and I went into the bedroom.

'Don't you dare try anything,' she said.

'Trust me. I won't.'

The bed — which I had acquired by sheer luck some years before — was indeed huge. It may have been what they call Emperor size. I turned off the light and we undressed, climbed in. I didn't watch Molly undressing. I had no desire to see her naked. I didn't think her body would fit in with my idea of the rest of her. We pulled up the sheet and lay there, a foot of empty mattress between us.

'So you did it with Cynthia, in this bed?'

'Yes. We did it in this bed.'

'What'd you do?'

'Not much. Cynthia got on top and jumped around. That was about it.'

'Did you go down on her?'

36

'No.'

'Do you like going down on women?'

'I don't have much experience really, but yes, I like it.'

'Leo never goes down on me. He says he hates the taste.'

'That's a shame. Do you do it to him?'

'I have to. He makes me. But I don't let him come. No one's coming in *my* mouth.'

'You might be missing the point.'

'No. Penises are horrible things.'

'Penises are fine. Penises are beautiful.'

'Not Leo's. It's big and it's ugly.'

'It's big? How big?'

'Oh, big. Big and circumcised. And it has a blister right on top.'

'A *blister*?'

'A blister. And he says it itches. He uses me to scratch it. We only fuck to scratch. He has orgasmic scratches.'

'That really sounds like something. Why does he have a blister? Is it a disease?'

'He swears it's not. It better fucking not be.'

'A blister. Jesus. It'd make coming *worthwhile.*'

'What do you mean, worthwhile?'

'Just because a man ejaculates, Molly, it doesn't mean he enjoys it. Ejaculations can be pretty empty things. They aren't enough on their own. The fucking has to be good in spirit if it's going to be good anywhere else.'

'I didn't think it was like that for men.'

'It might not even be true . . .'

'Why don't you enjoy fucking?'

'I don't have any spirit. I'm a beaten man. At twenty-three.'

'I don't believe that.'

'I know. I only say it for the sympathy. Women treat you better if they think you're incapable of sex.'

'Is that true?'

'I don't know. But you're being nice to me.'
'Maybe . . . but the last thing I want is a man with hangups. I've got enough of my own.'
'Yes. It's always the way.'

I fell asleep.

I woke up some time later, struggling with asthma. I reached for the Ventolin and sucked it in. Leo was in the bed, asleep on the other side of Molly. The sheet had fallen off. There was light coming in from the next room. I looked at Molly. She was lying on her back with her limbs spreadeagled over Leo. Her long black hair was pooled all over the sheets. I looked at her breasts. They were much bigger than I'd realised. Then I looked at her lower half. She had a round stomach, and a tight small bunch of black pubic hair. Somehow it looked incomplete. Neutered. I found it depressing.

Leo was lying on his side, towards Molly. His penis hung down over his thigh. It was big all right, but I couldn't see the blister.

I covered them up with the sheet, lay back down.

I woke up again. I needed to piss. Leo and Molly were fucking beside me. Softly, but not that softly. I didn't move. I peered at them out of half-closed eyes. Molly was riding him. Her big tits rolled as she slid back and forth. Her eyes were open. Leo's eyes were open. They were staring at each other. I couldn't pick the emotion. I closed my eyes. It seemed polite.

I wondered if I'd missed anything. Who'd gone down on whom? Had anyone? They made it seem political, a battle of the sexes. As if there was something degrading about their respective organs. They knew less about it than I did.

Leo came. He made a long satisfied sound. Maybe it meant he'd won. Good for him, I thought. Him and his blister.

I lay there for a while longer. Molly rolled off him and they settled back down to sleep. I got up, wrapped a towel around my waist, and made off down the hallway to the toilets.

SEVEN

Two days later I called Cynthia. The moving was going faster than expected. That night she and her parents were due to shift into a hotel at the Army's expense. The third day after that, they'd be on the plane to Darwin.

'I've got my own room,' she said, 'with a double bed. I made sure about that, and free room service. Why don't you come round?'

It sounded good. I drove over that evening. The hotel was a luxury affair overlooking the river at Toowong. The Army treated its majors well. Reception told me the way to Cynthia's room. She came to the door with a can of Toohey's Old in one hand, a cigarette in the other. 'Quick,' she said, 'get in.'

I slid in. 'What's wrong?'

'My parents' room is right across the hall.'

'Aren't I supposed to be here?'

'Well, I didn't actually tell them. They won't mind, but I don't feel like going through all the introductions yet.'

I explored her room. It was huge. Two double beds,

couches and chairs, a view across the city and a monster
TV/video system. 'Impressive,' I said. 'And we can call
anything on room service?'

'Yep. Only problem is they don't stock Toohey's Old. I
had to go out and buy these.'

'Fourex will do me.'

'You're staying the night?'

'How can I leave?'

We dialled room service, and they sent up a dozen cans
of Fourex. Cynthia signed for it at the door.

We settled. Talked. Watched TV. Finally Cynthia pulled
out her camera and tripod and began setting them up in
front of the bed.

'I want some photos of you before I go.'

She was an amateur photographer. She'd already shown
me some of her photos. They were mainly still-lifes of plants
or buildings. She didn't do many people.

I said, 'I'm not likely to enjoy this.'

'Shut up. We're doing it. Sit down.'

I got up and sat on the bed and stared at the camera.

'I should have told you to bring your leather jacket.' She
was peering through the lens.

'It's summer.'

'Undo you shirt.'

'I'm not posing naked.'

'I didn't think you would. Undo your shirt.'

'No.'

'Fucking hell.' She came around the camera and started
wrestling with me over my shirt. 'C'mon, I want you just
in your jeans, with your hair down. It gets me all horny.'

'You've never even seen me like that.'

'I know how it'll look.'

She got the shirt off and went back to the camera. She
looked through the lens. 'Go on, untie your hair.'

I usually wore my hair tied back. I undid it.

She snapped a few shots. 'Now lie back.'

'C'mon Cynthia.'

'Lie *back*.'

I reclined back on my elbows. 'I hate this.' She clicked a few more off.

'Now, just stay like that,' she said, and came around the camera again. This time she reached for my zip.

'No!'

'Don't move. I just wanna undo it a little, okay?'

'Okay, okay.'

She undid the button and pulled the zip right down. 'Mmm . . . no underwear.' I stared at the ceiling. 'And how's your little penis?' She dug into my jeans and found it. She pulled it out. 'Hello,' she said.

'Cynthia . . .'

'Will you shut up?' She kissed it and patted it. Then she set back admiringly. 'Isn't that sweet?'

'You are not going to photograph it.'

'But you could just leave it like that. It doesn't even have to be erect.'

'No!'

'All right, all right.' She tucked it away and pulled the zip halfway back up. She took three more shots. Then she put the lens cap on and crawled up over me. 'That *has* got me horny.' We kissed for a few moments, then between us we tugged my jeans off and she lifted her skirt. She wasn't wearing any underwear either. She was already wet. She lowered herself and I slid in.

We started moving. It felt good. Then, very suddenly, I was about to come. I couldn't stop it. I pumped away, holding it back, and then it was there.

Cynthia sat up. 'You *bastard*.'

'I'm sorry.'

'Well, quick, get it up again.'

'I can't, not straight away.'

42

'But I want it hard!'

'There are other things I can do, Cynthia.'

'No way. I want an erection.'

I often came very quickly. It could be depressing. If the woman was patient about it, it just made it worse. Cynthia understood things. Don't get patient, get angry.

We rolled around for a while and my penis rose. She jumped on me again. And again, within a minute, I was ejaculating.

'Jesus *Christ*. What are you doing?'

'I'm sorry. Really. It just happens.'

'Then tell me to stop and wait a while, okay. Don't just do it without me.'

'I'll try.'

She got off. I began playing between her legs with my hand. She had an open, pliable vagina and the largest clitoris I'd ever seen.

'Why is this thing so big?'

'It's the steroids, maybe. I've taken so many of the fucking things for my skin, they've deformed the rest of me.'

'It's a useful sort of deformity.'

'That's not all, though. Steroids affect your moods too. When I'm on the cortisone I go crazy. I get aggressive. I get violent.'

I rolled my finger around. She lay back. I rolled my finger around some more. I was crouched between her legs, watching my hand. I thought I should probably use my mouth, but that hadn't worked so well the last time I'd tried it on a woman. I stayed with my finger. Her legs clamped tight around my hand. I picked up the pace until my wrist started to hurt.

I stopped. I kept my hand curled around her cunt for a while. Then I slipped my index finger in. She arched up, 'Not that, not now.' I persevered. She lay back again. I kneeled up in front of her and began fucking with just the

43

one finger, then two. She started to roll and moan. I shifted up to three.

'Roll over,' I said.

She rolled over, lying flat on her chest with her big arse lifted in the air. I set to with three fingers and finally she came, clutching the pillow over her head.

I sat up and watched her.

'Hand fucking is wonderful,' she said, after a time. 'Hand fucking from behind is especially wonderful.'

It depressed me. I was beginning to suspect that Cynthia's orgasms came not so much from anything *I* did, as from her ability to turn herself on to things, to anything, and anyone. I could've *been* anyone. Maybe that was the way it would always be with sex, and maybe there was nothing so surprising about it, but I felt the need to do something more. I had to prove my existence. I needed power. I rolled her over again and applied my mouth to her clitoris.

'Jesus.' She sounded tired. Her thigh closed around my ears. She held my head there a while. Nothing happened. I stroked away with my tongue. Then her legs opened again. I sat up and looked at her. She looked back.

'I'll show you something,' she said.

She took my hand and placed it over her own. Then with both our fingers she began manipulating her clitoris. 'See? Push it one way until it sort of stretches, then roll your finger over it and let it snap back, then push it the other way.' She showed me for a few moments more, then pulled her hands back under her head. I carried on. I could see what she meant. 'It hurts just a bit,' she said, 'and it takes a lot longer to come, but then when you do . . .'

I nodded. I was interested. These were the things I needed to know. I slid two of the fingers of my left hand into her and began moving them very slowly, in time to my right hand. I picked up the pace. I concentrated on it, coordinating things. It wasn't sex, it was vectors, speed, mathematics.

44

And maths was something I *was* good at. I worked and worked and she squirmed and shuddered and then came, jamming her cunt up against my hand. It was a victory for science.

We lay on the bed for a while, smoking and talking. Then I got up, went to the toilet, and opened us some beer.

'You hungry?' I asked.

It was early still, so we dialled room service. The menu was extensive. We chose pizza.

We ate and drank and smoked, and watched TV.

Cynthia said, 'You don't mind me showing you how to do things, do you?'

'God, no. I can use the help.'

She shook her head. 'Don't be so down on yourself. You're no natural, you don't do anything right, but there's still something about you.'

'I'm glad.'

'Maybe it's just the looks.'

'What about them?'

'You're that close to being ugly, you know, you're *that* close.'

'But?'

'But you're beautiful.'

'Maybe to you.'

'It's not just me, Gordon. I'm sure there's others.'

'It's not true, Cynthia. Women like to think that other women find their man attractive, that's all.'

She laughed. 'You don't know a fucking *thing*.'

We finished the pizza and drank some more beer and watched TV. Then we climbed back into bed. She slid down my belly and took me in her mouth. I got hard. Her head moved up and down, her tongue was pumping. I grabbed for her legs and dragged her lower half around. Her cunt was over my face. I nuzzled my way in. She had light brown pubic hair, lots of it. I sorted my way through, found her clitoris. We worked away at each other for a while. Cynthia started making noises in her throat. I felt the pressure building in my erection. It was always a strange thing, that *pressure*. Sometimes it was hateful. Too much depended upon it. But then at other times . . .

I was nearly there. My tongue was aching, it was losing its rhythym against her cunt. Then Cynthia pulled her mouth away. 'Stop it,' she told me, 'I want to concentrate on this.'

I stopped. She went back to it with her mouth. Her finger was between my legs and nudging at my arsehole. It all still felt good, but the pressure had dwindled away. I didn't think I would be able to come. Ejaculations were fickle things. I moved my hips and tried to will the semen into her mouth. It wouldn't go. I tugged at her arms. 'Stop,' I said.

She raised her mouth and looked at me. She was rubbing the slippery knob of my penis with her hand.

I said, 'It's hard to come like that sometimes.'

She laughed. 'What is wrong with you?' But she slid up and mounted. We began fucking, slowly. In a few moments I was right on the verge again.

'Stop,' I said.

She stopped and shook her head at me. Then she lay down flat on my chest. She kissed me. Then she began moving again, very slowly. I felt more in control this time. We picked up pace. Cynthia reared herself up on her arms, then she was sitting upright.

'I'm gonna come soon,' I said.

'No, not yet.'

She began bucking her hips furiously. She was close. I grabbed on and pushed as hard and fast as I could. Cynthia

threw her head back. She said, 'Not yet, not yet, not *yet.*'
But there was no stopping things now — I came. She threw
herself back down on me, sweaty and panting and angry.
'Oh *fuck.*'

We lay there for a while.

'You didn't make it, did you,' I said.

'No.'

She looked at me with a flushed exasperated bleeding
face that I suddenly found deeply beautiful.

'We're going to have to do something about this,' she
said.

EIGHT

It was morning again. The phone was ringing.

Cynthia reached over and picked it up. 'Yeah?' There was a pause and then she sat up. 'Helen! Where are you? How'd you know I was here?'

I climbed out of bed and wandered into the toilet. I looked at myself in the mirror. I was pale and round and unshaven, with a head of long tangled hair. Not even enough fat there to look sleek. Just flab. What was the appeal? Cynthia's body was better. It was solid and strong and indulgent. I didn't feel comfortable with slim women. Somehow a well maintained body suggested a dubious preoccupation with good living. There had to be room in a life for drinking too much and eating badly and lying around in front of TV for days on end . . . fitness was a curse.

I pissed and went back out to the bed, curled up next to Cynthia. I waited for the phone conversation to end. She was laughing. When she finally hung up she said, 'I can't believe it! Helen is in Brisbane.'

Helen, it turned out, was an old friend of Cynthia's from Melbourne. They had shared a house for a time. Helen was up in Queensland for a two-week holiday, with her boyfriend. She'd tracked Cynthia down through the agents who were selling the house.

Cynthia was excited. They had arranged to meet in the City for lunch. 'You'll come, won't you? You'll like Helen and Dave.'

'Well, I should really get over to Social Security at some stage. Before the weekend. After that, though, I'll be free.'

Cynthia, knowing all about Social Security, predicted they'd keep me there for at least a few hours. We decided that she would bring Helen and Dave back to the hotel room after lunch. I could catch up with them then.

There was a knock on the door. A man's voice called out Cynthia's name.

'Shit,' she said, 'it's Dad. Quick, get in the bathroom.'

'Is he really going to mind that much?'

'No, I just don't feel like doing it now. Go on.'

I went and stood in the bathroom, feeling foolish. Cynthia opened the door. My clothes were still spread all over the carpet. There was a man in this room, any father could see that, any *major* could see that. The man was hiding in the shower, he was raping a major's daughter in an army hotel room. The major's daughter was raping *him* in an army hotel room. The major's daughter was taking *photographs* of it . . .

I waited. I could hear them talking in the doorway, but not what they were saying. There were no yells, no threats. Then she came back. 'They're going out for the day and wanted to see if I was interested. I told them about Helen.'

'Okay.'

'I'm sorry about hiding you.'

'It's probably for the best.'

We got dressed. I went out to my car. I drove back to my flat, had some toast for lunch, then gathered up the Social Security forms.

Social Security.

The *Department* of Social Security.

They made me nervous, they weren't like the C.E.S. The C.E.S. didn't care what you did. The C.E.S. had forty times more people on their lists than they had jobs. Eighty times more people. They knew they were losing it day by day.

Social Security, though, was different. They were dealing with money, they knew they were important. They wanted to know what you were up to. Their application form was five or six pages long. I filled it out. The questions were detailed and disturbing. I appreciated the necessity, but that was all. I told them I wasn't married, wasn't de facto, had no dependants, no disabilities, no savings, no investments, no hope . . . but I still didn't have the three forms of identification. This was a more serious problem than I'd expected. I couldn't prove who I was. A licence and a bankbook — I was only two-thirds in existence.

I started going through drawers and boxes around the flat. I found my tax file number. That was useful, but it didn't count as ID. I dug deeper. I found old poems, old stories, old letters. I read some of them, lost track of the time. I was there for a couple of hours. All I came up with was a copy of my senior year school results. Report cards. Why did I still have things like that? Why didn't I keep anything I needed? Where were my tax records, my rent receipts, a pay slip with a current address? I went back to the list. It was a miracle. There, at the very bottom, it said that academic results, while not preferred, were an acceptable proof of identity. I'd stumbled over the line. The years of education had meant something after all.

I packed it up and drove into the Valley.

The Valley Social Security office was in a big blue, almost windowless building. There were four or five people hanging around on the footpath outside, smoking and talking.

They were all under twenty. They watched me walk in with my paperwork. They had a bored, competent air. They knew what it was all about. They probably knew how to get by without any I D. I didn't. I was soft. I'd had it easy for the last six years.

Inside the place was crowded, non-smoking and partly desperate. Most people were there just to lodge their fortnightly forms, but there was a strong percentage, maybe a third, who were there to confront the system, to work it. There was money available. The system freely gave out a certain amount, but these people wanted more, needed more; you could see their minds working over it. And there were ways. There was provision in the Social Security code for Special Benefits above and beyond the standard payments. And these people knew that. The stories were running round in their heads . . . my money got stolen, I got robbed, they're kicking me out of my home, I need the money now, I've gotta eat, haven't I? I gotta *survive*.

None of it mattered. The only thing that mattered was proof. The Social Security staff weren't fools. There was a large sign over the counter. 'Normal living expenses — including rent and food — are *not* considered sufficient cause to be eligible for Special Benefits.'

I joined one of two queues, ten or fifteen back from the counter. It was moving slowly. Apart from the queues, there were twenty or thirty people sitting around in the plastic chairs. They were waiting for interviews in the booths. Being a first-time applicant I was destined for a booth, for my preliminary interview. Cynthia had warned me that this was where I'd be held up for an hour or two. I looked at the clock on the wall. It was already mid-afternoon. I was going to be late getting back to her hotel.

The queue shuffled forward. Most people just handed over the regular form and left. A few had more complex requests or complaints. They argued, listened, got rejected

51

or got waved over to the chairs to wait. They slowed things down.

Finally I arrived. The woman was waiting. I said, 'I'd like to apply for unemployment benefits.' I pushed the forms across to her.

She took them, glanced through. 'ID?'

I gave them to her. She looked at the licence, and the bankbook, and then at the school results. She looked at me.

'This isn't really much good . . .'

'Sorry. It's all I could find. It's on the list.'

'Haven't you got a birth certificate?'

'I lost it. I could get a new copy of it, I suppose.'

'New copies won't do.'

'Well?'

She drummed her fingers. She sighed. 'Okay. Look. Try to find something better before you come back for your interview. I'll make you an appointment for Monday.'

'Monday?'

'We can't fit you in today. Look at the place.'

'Oh . . .'

'Read these,' she said. She pushed some leaflets forward. Then another form. 'And fill this out if you think you need to. It's the Special Benefits form. Okay?'

'Okay.' I picked it all up. She filled out another card saying that my appointment was for eleven a.m., Monday.

I moved aside, walked back out on the street. The smokers were there, watching me, reading me. I still felt that they knew something I didn't. I hadn't walked out with any money. I hadn't even walked out with the promise of any money. That couldn't be good.

I got to my car, climbed in, and drove back to Cynthia's hotel.

NINE

Cynthia and Helen and Dave were all in the room when I arrived. Helen was a nurse and Dave was an unemployed mechanic. Helen was about thirty-five. Dave was younger, maybe mid-twenties. He rode a bike, a Ducati. The two of them were taking it up the east coast. The introductions were made. We settled down over some beer. Helen and Dave weren't terribly happy with the way their holiday was going.

'I can't believe this place doesn't have any beaches,' Helen said. 'I always thought Brisbane was a surfing town, a beach town, but all it's got is Moreton Bay. Moreton Bay and mud flats.'

I said, 'The Gold Coast is the surfing town. Surfers Paradise. Coolangatta. It's only an hour away. That's where the beaches are.'

'I know, we've already been there. It's disgusting. It's so commercial.'

'Yes. They've done very well.'

'Even *Melbourne* has better beaches than you do.'

'You might be right. Brisbane does have mangroves, though.'

'Mangroves? What can you do with mangroves?'

'You can walk through them. Have you ever done that?'

'No.'

'Well. Wait until late in the afternoon, just around sunset. And take lots of insect repellent.'

'Is it worth it?'

'You might like it more than Surfers Paradise.'

Time passed. I finished my second can of beer. The conversation got around to what we should do for the rest of the day.

'I could get us some acid,' said Dave. 'I've got some friends up here who might have some.'

Cynthia jumped up. 'Acid! I haven't had acid in *ages*. Gordon, you want some acid?'

'What exactly is acid?'

'You don't know? You really don't know? It's LSD. Haven't you ever tried it?'

'No. No one has ever offered me any. I've led a very sheltered life.'

'Well, do you want to? Tripping is one of the best things . . .'

'Sure. Yes.'

'I don't have the guy's number on me,' said Dave. 'We'll have to go back over to our place.'

Dave and Helen were staying at Helen's sister's house in Spring Hill. We all climbed in the Kingswood and drove over.

'Look at this city,' Helen yelled from the back seat. 'There's nothing happening. There's no one on the streets. How do you stand it?'

'Things are happening, you just have to look a little harder. At least no one bothers you. There's worse places than Brisbane.'

'There's *better*.'

'We almost had the tallest building in the world. That would've been something, don't you think?'

'What do you mean almost?'

'There was a huge public outcry when the government announced the proposal. People were terrified by the idea. It would've been three times the height of the other local skyscrapers. They thought it would ruin the balance of things — the rest of the CBD would looked ridiculous, the whole *city* would look ridiculous. And it would interfere with radio reception, and TV reception, and it'd put half the suburbs into permanent shade, planes were going to crash into it, the airport would have to be re-arranged, the land underneath would subside into the river . . . lobby groups were screaming, it was a nightmare. Finally the Supreme Court ruled the whole thing was illegal. The developers backed down. Now they're not building anything. They've just left a great big hole in the ground.'

'Christ. Queenslanders.'

'I agree with them up to a point. The city really *would've* looked ridiculous. But that, of course, is exactly why they should've built it. It would've been an appropriate statement. About Brisbane. About cities in general.'

We got to Spring Hill, found the sister's place. It was a renovated terrace house, overlooking the city centre. Inside it was dark and cool and sparse. The sister had taste. We had the place to ourselves, she was away for the weekend. We settled into the lounge as Dave made the call.

He waited for a while, letting it ring. 'There's no answer.'

'Damn!' Cynthia looked at us all. 'What now?'

'I know some people,' said Helen. 'I could try them.'

Dave handed her the phone, left the room.

I leaned over to Cynthia and said, 'They have a lot of contacts here for two people that live in Melbourne.'

'It's the drug crowd. You just get to know people. All over the place.'

55

'Do you know any dealers in Brisbane?'

'I might. But I came here to give that up. I didn't try to keep track of anyone.'

We waited. Dave came back in with a bottle of beer and some glasses. He filled them up. Helen got off the phone. 'No acid,' she said. 'We can get some smack though.'

'Smack?' I asked.

'Heroin,' said Cynthia.

'Oh.'

'Well,' said Helen, 'What d'you think?'

Dave was handing out the beers. 'Sounds okay to me,' he said. 'Cynthia?'

'No, I swore I wouldn't go back to it. But you guys go ahead if you want.' She looked at me.

I looked back. 'Well, I've never tried it — I wouldn't mind. But not if it's going to bother you.'

'No, I don't mind. Go on, it's certainly worth trying, at least once. I'll be okay.'

It was settled. Helen rang back and made arrangements to meet in a pub for the sale.

'How much will it cost?' I asked her.

'Well, if it's only your first time, you won't need much, probably only a third of a gram. Fifty dollars should cover it.' I took out my wallet, gave her the money.

Cynthia watched us. 'Oh fuck it,' she said. 'What the hell. Count me in.'

Helen looked at her. 'You sure you want to?'

'I'd go crazy watching you guys.'

'Okay. Oh, Gordon, can you buy syringes over the counter in Queensland, do you know?'

'You can. They changed the law just a while ago.'

'Great. You wanna come along, Cynthia?'

'Okay. We can take Gordon's car.'

'You want me to come?' I said.

Cynthia held out her hand for the keys. 'No. You'd look

guilty. You'd have *I'm buying heroin* written all over your face.'

I gave her the keys.

Dave and I were left alone. We sipped on the beer and talked some more about Melbourne and Brisbane, Victoria and Queensland, and how they compared. It was a pointless discussion, but it passed the time. I liked Dave. He was short and ugly, very softly spoken, with a rich quiet laugh.

'You only just met Cynthia, huh?' he asked.

'A couple of weeks ago. It's a pity she's leaving so soon.'

'Yeah. She doesn't sound so happy about it herself.'

'Darwin is no place to rush off to, if you think Brisbane is boring.'

An hour went by. We wondered about the girls. They had planned to buy two grams all told. I tried to remember what the laws were in Queensland about heroin. I knew they'd been strengthened at the same time that they'd legalised syringes. Mandatory life sentence for possession of a certain amount or above. I didn't think it was as small as two grams, but I wasn't sure. I'd have to front up to the major. I'm sorry sir, your daughter's been arrested. She was caught buying some smack. For me. Who am I? I'm the no-good bum she found out in the bottle shop. What's smack? Well, it's heroin, sir. Fifteen or twenty years is all she'll get, but then she knew the risks. She used to be a junkie, didn't you know?

The girls got back twenty minutes later. It'd all gone okay. There were no problems.

'But Christ, they were sleazy people,' said Cynthia. 'They looked evil. They made us play pool with them first. They really dragged it out. None of my dealers in Sydney were like that.'

Helen agreed. 'They were arseholes, they were cliches. Brisbane is a fucked-up town. No style at all.'

57

We went into Helen and Dave's room and sat on the bed. Helen brought out a small, folded square of paper, four syringes, a few vials of distilled water, a belt, and a shot glass. The equipment.

She made the preparations. She unfolded the paper and tipped the powder into the glass. She followed it with the distilled water. The powder dissolved. Cynthia drew the mixture into the syringes. Smaller doses for myself and her, about double that amount for Helen and Dave.

'Okay,' she said, laying the syringes out in a row. 'Who's first?'

Dave volunteered.

'Doing it yourself?'

'No. I'll let the nurse handle it.'

Helen got up off the floor and sat next to him. She wrapped the belt around his upper arm and pulled it tight. The veins on his arms bulged. She took one of the syringes, rubbed one of the bulges with her fingers. Then she slid the needle in. She pulled the plunger backwards, drew enough blood to satisfy her, then shoved it back down. It touched bottom. She pulled it out. Dave put his finger on the puncture and folded his arm up to his chest. Helen took the belt away.

We all watched him. He looked at his arm. He nodded. 'It's not bad.'

'Good.'

Helen did herself, and then Cynthia.

'I *love* this stuff,' Cynthia said, watching her arm. 'It's like coming and coming for hours.' She lay back, taking deep breaths.

Helen came at me with the last syringe. 'Your turn.'

'No, I'll do it,' said Cynthia, sitting up again. 'I'm okay.'

She wrapped the belt around my arm and stroked the veins until they rose. I watched her face, looked at the syringe.

58

'How long since you've done this?'

'It isn't that long.'

She slid the needle in. I watched my blood seep up into the syringe. It mingled with the heroin. I thought about chemical reactions. The blood would be buzzing, the blood was already stoned. 'Now look at me,' she said, 'and keep looking at me.'

'Why?'

'I want to watch your face.'

She depressed the plunger.

For a moment there was nothing. Cynthia unwrapped the belt. She was smiling. 'You feel it?'

And then I did. It rushed into my head.

'Oh, you feel it all right,' she laughed. 'Your pupils just screwed down to dots.'

I kept staring at her. It was rebounding down through my arms and legs. Finally I had to sink down on the bed. If this was what it was like for women when they came, then they had it a lot better than men. Cynthia bent over me and stroked my face and for a time we all lay there. Heroin.

After a while though the first rush faded. Cynthia began talking to Helen and Dave. Small talk. I didn't pay attention. I sat up again. I felt a little dizzy, a little nauseous. My mouth was dry.

We decided to go out onto the verandah. Helen cleaned up before we left. She capped the syringes and put away the other things. I stood up. My balance was gone. I reeled along the hallway. The others laughed.

'It'll go away,' said Cynthia.

We sat on the verandah. It was late afternoon. The sun was setting over the city and the hills and television towers. We sat and chatted, off and on, for an hour or so. The conversation wasn't important. It was good just to sit and look. Everything looked fine.

59

I rolled and smoked. I decided a beer was in order. I got up and moved down the hall. I was still dizzy. By the time I got to the kitchen I was feeling sick, and then very sick. Battery acid, I thought, washing powder. Overdose. Death. I bounced along the wall to the toilet and kneeled over the bowl. I opened my mouth, gagged. Nothing came. I put my finger down my throat. I gagged again. Nothing.

I felt a little better. I stood up and unzipped. There was pressure in my bladder, but I couldn't piss. I gave up and went back to the fridge. I got a bottle of beer and four glasses, then went back to the verandah.

'I can't throw up.'

They nodded.

'We should've told you,' Cynthia said. 'Sometimes you can't. It's the heroin. It does something to the stomach. It can also stop bodily secretions. Is your mouth dry? You won't be able to shit or piss either, not unless you really have to.'

So that was that. I was still nauseous, but nausea didn't seem so bad if you knew nothing could come from it. We drank the beer. It swilled around in my stomach. I had the feeling that nothing was being digested down there.

'How about a bath?' Cynthia asked me.

'Sure.'

'Not here though. Let's get back to the hotel.'

'Okay. But I don't think I can drive.'

'I'll drive. I know what I'm doing. I used to have four or five times this amount in a day, when I was using.'

'That much?'

'That's nothing.'

We said our goodbyes to Helen and Dave and climbed in the car. Cynthia started up and drove as well as she ever did.

'It's when I'm on acid,' she said, 'that's when things get scary. Traffic lights start talking to me.'

'We should stop off somewhere,' I said, 'and get some nitrous.'

'Nitrous?'

'Nitrous oxide. Laughing gas. You buy it in supermarkets. It comes in little cylinders that they use to make fresh whipped cream. The little cylinders also fit into soda syphons, so you inhale it from one of those. It's great if you're already stoned or drunk. But it only lasts a minute or two.'

'Minutes? Is that all? Why bother?'

'They're very weird minutes.'

But Cynthia wasn't interested. It sounded like kids' stuff to her. Like sniffing glue or petrol.

We got back to the hotel and snuck into her room, in case her parents were around. Cynthia filled the bath. She poured in some shampoo to make bubbles. It was a big tub, with taps at the side, not at the end. Built for two. I got us a beer each. Cynthia went through her bags and found some scented candles. She put a tape on the stereo and switched off the light. We undressed. Climbed in.

It was good. We sat with our heads at opposite ends, with our legs entwined. Mostly we talked, smoked cigarettes. My toes were playing with her cunt. Her hands were around my penis and balls. For long periods we kissed and stroked each other. I'd never enjoyed kissing, but this time it was everything it was supposed to be. Cynthia's lips and Cynthia's tongue and Cynthia's teeth — I could *taste* her. Nothing grotesque at all. This was a person, a good person that I liked a great deal. This was Cynthia. It was better than fucking.

My penis rose from time to time.

I lifted my hips out of the water so we could look at it.

'God,' said Cynthia, 'look at the circumcision scars. That must've hurt.'

'Yes, it's a nasty tradition.'

'Uncircumsised penises are great. You can play little

61

games with them. Poor things, they should leave them alone.'

It stood there between us. Not terribly proud.

'Show me how you do it when you wank,' she said.

I showed her, moving my hand and thumb the right ways. She watched me and then tried it herself. The sensations were distant. The heroin, I thought.

'You can do it a bit harder,' I said. 'You don't have to be all that gentle with it. I'm not.'

She pumped it. She said, 'A lot of men don't wank this way, y'know. They don't like using their own hand. They like to fuck things. Pillows and sheets and mattresses.'

'I've heard that. It's a matter of taste. I don't think I'm so much into the psychology of actually fucking something, I just want the sensation and the fantasy. The hand seems a lot easier. Maybe that's significant. Maybe if I was more into fucking pillows I'd be more into fucking women.'

'Maybe. Someone should do some research. A survey of the masturbatory habits in males, and their consequences as regards fucking ability.'

'Hey. We could do it. We could really be on to something here!'

'I'd say it's already been done.'

'Don't be so sure.'

After a while Cynthia stopped pumping. It was pleasant, but an orgasm was light years away. We went back to kissing. My hands moved over her face and her back, testing out the skin disease. It all seemed beautiful, even the little scabs and the bleeding. There were small spirals of her blood in the water.

Finally we crawled out of the tub. We'd been there for four or five hours. It was after midnight. Cynthia sat on the toilet and tried to urinate. I knelt between her legs and watched.

'Fuck,' she said, 'I can't.'

'C'mon, you can do it. Push.'

She pushed and the piss trickled out. She rose. It was my turn. I stood over the bowl. My penis was shrivelled from all the time in the water and very small. Eventually it came.

'Bedtime,' said Cynthia.

We went and lay on the crisp hotel sheets. We began fucking. It was hard work. I couldn't come. Definitely the heroin. But Cynthia could. As easily as ever. She clocked up the orgasms. She was getting me back.

'You arranged this!' I said.

'Why would I? My fanny *hurts*.'

I began fucking her again.

'You bastard,' she said, but she dug back. Pain wasn't enough to stop her, nothing was. I got angry. She swore at me. 'You prick, you prick, you prick.' We plied at each other until she came again. Then I started again. She came again. We sweated and hurt and it went on for hours . . . I was power mad. I was the ejaculation-less male. I had this woman under my control. I could do anything. I was merciless.

Dawn approached. My penis was bright pink and felt raw enough to bleed. By then we were trying other things, mouths and fingers. It wasn't working. We set to one long last time, grunting and swearing at each other, pounding the flesh. And I was close at last. I was gonna do it. Cynthia was below me and she deserved the pain. She started coming. 'I'm not gonna stop,' I said, 'I am not going to *stop!*'

'You bastard, you BASTARD.'

I came. It was magnificent. The fire ran through.

We collapsed. I rolled off. Lay there.

'It hurts,' she moaned. 'I won't be able to walk for a week.'

'Stiff,' I said.

The sun was coming through. We organised our various cigarettes and smoked.

We slept for a few hours. Then someone was knocking on the door. Cynthia climbed out of bed, wrapped a towel around herself and answered it. I heard a male voice. It was her father. I lurched out of bed and threw on my clothes. Then I sat on the bed and waited. Cynthia finally closed the door and came back. She saw me and started laughing.

'He's not coming in,' she said.

'Well what d'you expect? You've got me very nervous. One of the most decorated soldiers in Vietnam, and here's me sneaking into his daughter's hotel room.'

'You're hardly the first.'

'I know.'

Cynthia climbed back into bed. 'Just one day to go. What'll we do with it?'

'I'll get out of your way, if you want.'

'No! What gave you that idea?'

'Nothing. I was just offering.'

'You're not leaving until I'm on my way to the airport, okay?'

'Okay.'

'So how do you feel anyway?'

I stretched out on my back. I felt very good indeed. Tired and sore, but happy.

'Heroin is a wonderful drug,' I said.

'It's the best.'

We lay there, staring the ceiling.

'What d'you think,' I said, 'just one more time?'

'What the fuck. You gotta live.'

She got up, dialled Helen's number.

TEN

The deal was the same. About two in the afternoon we drove over to the house in Spring Hill. Helen and Dave were waiting. The girls went off to make the purchase. Dave and I sat watching TV and drinking beer. It was about an hour before the girls returned. There'd been no pool game this time, but they'd had to sit around and have a couple of drinks before the dealer felt comfortable enough to make the transaction.

Cynthia was still revolted. 'I can just tell with some people, y'know. I can pass someone in the street and I get this *feeling* inside. It's like I can recognise danger. And that guy today was dangerous. Crazy.'

'Do you get this feeling often?'

'No. But I got fucked once by a guy who made me feel that way. It was like rape, it was evil. I still have nightmares about it.'

We all went into Dave and Helen's room and made the preparations. The amounts were the same. So was the order — Dave first. Helen got him ready. 'So what did you guys get up to yesterday?' she asked.

'We sat in the bath all night,' said Cynthia, 'then we went to bed. How about you?'

'Yeah, we tried fucking. Tried it for hours. I couldn't come. Neither could Dave.'

'Never can,' said Dave.

Helen shoved the plunger in and Dave studied his arm.

My turn came around.

I knew what to expect now, and I was ready, I was turned on. There was something deeply sexual about the syringes and the blood and the rush, about having someone else *stick it in.* Cynthia wrapped the belt around my arm. I looked at her eyes. They were all colour. Pinheads for pupils. She put the needle up against the skin. I wondered what this would be like if we were naked and in bed and fucking. If I was already inside her. If it wasn't just Cynthia doing it to me, if we were both doing it, injecting each other, in unison. If we were right on the point of coming as we sank the needles in. Not into our arms, but into our hips, our thighs . . .

It pricked. She pulled up the blood and it swirled around the syringe. She was a succubus. I was doomed. She injected the heroin. It came flooding up my arm — who would've thought blood moved so fast — into my chest, streaming into my brain like molten gold. I lay back and let it go.

Later we went out onto the verandah. Dave got us all beers. I was dizzy and nauseous again, but it was better than the first time.

We sat there for an hour or so, mostly quiet.

Cynthia was holding my hand, playing with my hair. 'Well,' she said, 'What'll we do? Another bath?'

'I guess so . . . we could try the tub at my place. It's not as big, but it'd be something different at least.'

'Okay.'

We got in the Kingswood. Cynthia was driving. The roads were quiet. Sunday afternoon.

'We should get some lubricant,' she said. 'My cunt hurts enough as it is.'

'Where do you get lubricant from?'

She looked at me. Shook her head. 'You get it from a chemist.'

We found a chemist. I went in. Cynthia didn't want to deal with the counter staff. She was embarrassed about her skin. Her face. It was bad, all that contact the night before. Sex was lethal to her.

The brand she wanted was called K-Y Personal Lubricant. I went in and wandered around the shelves. I was feeling good. I looked at all the colours, all the boxes. I moved smoothly down the aisles. It was all going well. Eventually I found the stuff amongst the tampons and pads. It came in a blue and white tube, in a blue and white box. I took one up to the counter. The woman looked at me.

I said, 'I'll just take this, thanks.'

I flicked up my hand to show her the box. I was moving faster than I realised. The tube flew out, up into the air. I watched it spin there. It floated. The woman reached out and caught it.

We looked at each other.

'Fine,' she said.

I paid up. I saw that the shelves behind the counter were lined with boxes of condoms. Cynthia and I were not using condoms. She was on the pill. She admitted she wasn't all that regular with the doses. I thought, because of that, condoms might've been a practical idea. But Cynthia said she hated them, and practicality was such an odious thing to labour under . . .

I got back to the car and gave her the K-Y.

'They've got a million condoms in there,' I said. 'You sure I shouldn't get some?'

'No! You just can't do it with those things. I'm not going to get pregnant anyway. I've been fucking for years without condoms. I'm infertile, I must be. All those drugs I've been on, the cortisone and the smack and the speed... they've ruined me.'

'Okay.'

'God, what am I saying. I'm never going to have children. Fucking is all I've got left.'

'You've got much more than that, Cynthia.'

As for diseases, it was a bit late to be worrying. Anything one of us had, the other had it by now.

She started up and we made it home. The house and the old men were fairly quiet. We opened up my flat and got some towels and the radio, then went down the hall to the baths. There were two tubs, each one in a small grimy booth. The booths at least had doors. The tubs though hadn't been properly cleaned in months. Vass, as the permanent resident, received a deduction from his rent to keep the bathroom and toilets scrubbed, but his efforts were haphazard. It was a big step down from the hotel. Still, the tubs were long and deep, the water was hot, and there was a certain gloomy atmosphere that white tiles and soap couldn't match. We plugged in the radio, closed the door, undressed and climbed in.

Then we were kissing again. It was glorious. Heroin *did* something to the mouth, brought it to life. We each had our hands behind the other's heads, pressing our faces together, melting lips and tongues and teeth... face fucking, two cunts, two pricks... the way it should've been with Mother Nature, right from the start.

Someone came in to use the toilets. We stopped kissing and listened. It was one of the old men. We could hear him unzip, hear the piss streaming into the bowl.

'Hey,' he yelled, 'who's in the bath?'

'Me,' I said, 'Gordon.'

It was Lewis. 'You're having a fucking *bath*?' No one ever used the tubs, everyone showered. Cynthia had my penis and balls in her hands.

'I felt like it,' I said.

Our voices echoed around the room.

'Hey,' said Lewis, 'you met the new people yet?'

'No, I haven't been around. What about them?'

'They're arseholes. They stole my clothes off the line.'

'That's bad.'

'Fucking junkies is what they are. They're on methadone. They hit the clinic every day. You know that? Thieves and fucking junkies.'

Cynthia was now sucking my penis under the water, blowing bubbles.

'Do they work?'

'Course fucking not.'

He went out. Cynthia came up for air.

The hours passed.

From time to time some of the other residents came in to shit or piss. This was life in the toilet. We listened to the farting and belching and liquid gushes. The sounds of creation. No one else tried to talk to us. The afternoon passed into evening. Every half hour or so we let some of the cold water out, poured hot water in.

Finally I climbed out. I needed to shit. I wrapped a towel around myself, opened the door and went into one of the two cubicles. The toilets were worse than the tubs. Shit stains all over the bowl, piss and wet wads of paper all over the floor. I sat down and strained for a while, but nothing came.

Cynthia called out. 'What's happening in there?'

'I can't do it.'

'Hang on.'

I heard the water in the tub swish. A moment later she opened the door of my the cubicle and came in, dripping and naked.

'Get *out* of here.'

'Oooh, you look so cute. Like a little boy.'

'I don't need you, Cynthia.'

'Poor little baby, of course you do.'

She knelt down between my legs and felt under my balls around to my arsehole. 'So nothing will come out, huh?' She wriggled her finger in.

'Jesus.' I was squirming. My prick rose.

Cynthia took me in her mouth and dug her finger further in. I thought, someone *has* to come in now.

I said, 'All right. Let's do it, then.'

She stopped sucking and mounted. We began fucking, started sweating. It was hot in there. We breathed in shit. She lay flat on my chest, reached down and around, and got just the tip of her finger up my arse again. The fucking picked up, short quick jabs. There was no room to move. I pulled her own cheeks apart and wriggled a finger into her arse. She had the tips of two fingers in mine, I slid two into hers. We were both panting and grunting. Our arms were straining. Sweat pooled on the seat.

Then she was coming. I came with her. We jammed our fingers in as far as they would go. It was all cheap and low and satisfying. The toilet could be proud of it. Shitting was good but this was better . . .

Cynthia got off me.

'Coming back to the tub?'

'No. No, I think I'll stay here a minute.'

'Okay.'

I sat on the seat.

The shit was on its way.

Afterwards we went back into the flat. We switched on the TV and got into bed. I had a small amount of leaf. We smoked it, propped up on the pillows.

I made us some toast. We weren't very hungry. We followed a prime-time movie through, smoking and sipping on cask wine. Then we moved against each other and started kissing. We did it for a long time without pressing it. Cynthia rolled on her stomach and asked me to scratch her back. Even with the heroin, the itching still bothered her. I sat across her hips and ran my fingers up and down between her shoulders. I did it very lightly. I didn't want to draw blood. She told me that I had nice hands.

'They're not writer's hands, though,' I said. 'Look at them. Short fingers, big fat palms. Creative geniuses are supposed to have long, thin, supple hands.'

'So you're not a creative genius. You don't have to be a creative genius to be a writer.'

'True.'

We got more active, sucking and licking each other, and Cynthia went through her bag for the K-Y. She crouched over me and opened the tube and squeezed some of it onto her hand. She rubbed it over my erection. Then she squeezed out some more and reached down between her legs, slid her fingers in.

Then she climbed on and *I* slid in. The lubricant certainly made a difference. There was no pain. We didn't attack each other this time, we were tired, we did it slow. It took a little longer, but it worked.

We curled up, looking at each other. This was good. Everything about Cynthia was good. Things were going to be a little sad for a while when she left. I thought about the long empty weeks stretching out. I wouldn't be working, I wouldn't be writing, I wouldn't be doing anything...

71

how many more Cynthias were there out there? And where were they?

Cynthia said, 'We'd better not sleep here. Mum and Dad'll be wondering where I am. We should get back to the hotel.'

'Okay.'

'I don't want to go, y'know. To Darwin.'

'No?'

'No.' She was quiet for a time, then she said, 'I think I've fallen for you. I'm sorry. I swore it wouldn't happen, and I swore I wouldn't tell you about it. I can't help it. I certainly didn't need to fall in love again.'

'It's okay.'

'What about you?'

'I don't know about love, Cynthia. But I don't want you to go. It'd be very good if you stayed.'

She smiled. 'No, I don't think you do know anything about love. But that doesn't worry me. I don't think you'd fuck me around or anything, or have other women . . . I don't think you even know how to do that.'

'No. I don't.'

'I really could stay, I suppose. But Christ, if things went wrong . . . Are you sure it isn't just the smack talking? Do you really want me to stay?'

'It isn't just the smack. I mean it.'

She was quiet for a while longer.

'Okay then, I'll stay.'

I kissed her. The smack in fact had long since faded away. It wasn't a magic kiss, but it still felt good. I wasn't worried about her staying. I wasn't worried about anything. I hadn't known her long, but it'd been intense, there wasn't much we hadn't covered. Cynthia was *right*.

The kiss stopped. Cynthia rolled onto her back, grabbed for a cigarette. 'Jesus,' she said, 'why do I do these things to myself? The folks will freak. The plane goes in about twelve hours.'

72

'How bad will it be?'

'Oh, bad. But I've done it to them before, they won't be suprised, it won't kill them.'

'When will you tell them?'

'Tonight maybe. Or in the morning. Christ, Christ, Christ. Be good to me, Gordon. I'm taking a big chance here. If it all fucks up I can still go up to Darwin I suppose, but if it comes to that . . .'

'All we can do is give it a try, Cynthia.'

'I know. I know.'

She drummed her fingers across her lips.

'Should we go?' I said.

'Okay. Let's get moving. I just can't believe I'm doing this again. I'm gonna kill myself this way. And your name is Gordon. It's fucking *Gordon*.'

'Well, I can't help that.'

I got her out of bed, into the car.

ELEVEN

We got back to the hotel. Cynthia was opening her door. The door opposite, her parents' door, popped open. It was her mother. 'Cynthia, you're here. Quick, I think you father's been concussed.'

'Christ,' said Cynthia. 'How?'

We went in. Her parents' room was much smaller than ours, only one double bed and no couches. Her father was sitting on the bed, holding a hand to the back of his head. He was wearing shorts.

'Mum, Dad, this is Gordon Buchanan.'

Mrs Lamonde looked me over. She was much taller than Cynthia, and thinner, but she had the same instant grace. 'Hello, Gordon,' she said.

'Hello, Mrs Lamonde. Mr Lamonde.'

He squinted up at me. He looked very much like an army major. Big, solid and hairy.

'How'd you do it?' Cynthia asked him.

'I was soaping my toes in the shower. I slipped.'

'I heard this huge bang,' added Mrs Lamonde.

We discussed concussion. No one was sure how you could tell if someone had it or not.

'Can you remember your birthday?' Mrs Lamonde asked.

'Of course I can remember my birthday.'

'How many fingers am I holding up?' Cynthia asked him, holding up all four.

'Will you *stop* it, I'm not concussed.'

Mrs Lamonde wasn't convinced. 'Do you feel dizzy?'

'I'm fine.' He stood up, swayed, and sat down again. 'All right, just a little dizzy.'

'I really think you should go to hospital.'

'I'm not going to hospital.'

But Mrs Lamonde kept at him. Eventually he agreed. 'I'm only doing this for you,' he told her. 'I know I'm fine.'

We decided that Cynthia and I would take him, in my car. We drove to the casualty ward of the Royal Brisbane. The nurse took him away. Cynthia and I sat down to wait.

'Your mother seemed very nice,' I said.

'She is. They both are. Not that we get along any better for it.'

'You would've been a hard sort of daughter.'

'Maybe. They're a strange couple. I never would've thought the army life would suit Mum. And Dad, what's he still *doing* in the army? He could do better, they both could.'

'People have to settle somewhere, Cynthia.'

She was looking away towards the examination rooms.

'I don't want them to die, though,' she said. 'It'd kill me if they died.'

The casualty ward was busy and we waited about an hour without any news. It was a long hour. We both needed sleep. We'd only had a few hours in the last two days. We took turns at going outside for a smoke. Finally Cynthia went and asked at the desk, then came back.

'He's not concussed. They were just keeping him around for a while to make sure. They didn't realise anyone was waiting.'

Her father came out a few minutes later. 'Sorry,' he said. 'I thought they were keeping me in there for a reason. I told you it was nothing.'

We drove home. Cynthia was in the back seat. The major was up front with me. He was the highest ranking officer of the Australian Army I'd ever had in the front seat of my car.

'So what do you do with yourself, Gordon?' he asked.

'Nothing at the moment. Normally, though, I work in pubs. That's how I know Cynthia.'

'He writes poetry,' added Cynthia, for which I wasn't grateful.

'Poetry? What sort of poetry?'

'Not very poetic poetry. It's very bland poetry. It doesn't rhyme.'

'Any of it published?'

'No.'

He laughed. That was good. 'Ever thought of joining the Army?'

'I don't think I'm the type.'

'Why not? When I was young everyone thought they were the right type for the Army.'

'I don't think young people think that way any more.'

'No, they don't. You're right about that.'

He seemed all right. He knew I'd been fucking his daughter and that I was nowhere near the first. He'd fought in Borneo and Vietnam and he'd survived, somewhere near sane. Then he'd stuck it out with life in an army that no one gave a damn about any more, drank too much maybe, and got himself stalled for years at the rank of major. Who knew why. Maybe he could do better, maybe he didn't care.

He had as much right as anyone to laugh at poetry.

We got back to the hotel. One the way upstairs the major told us that the doctor had told him how to diagnose true concussion. You looked at the patient's eyes and if the pupils were dilated and didn't contract in bright light then it meant there was trouble.

I wondered about my pupils, about Cynthia's. How constricted were they now, nine to ten hours after shooting up? And was there a connection? Between injecting heroin and slamming your head against a bathtub? No doubt they both brought peace of mind . . .

We handed him over to Mrs Lamonde. Cynthia told me to go and wait in her room. She came in herself about twenty minutes later. 'I told them,' she said.

'How'd they take it?'

'Not so well. They'll get over it, I suppose.'

'Did you tell them about me?'

'I said you had something to do with it.'

'Do they like me?'

'They didn't say. They asked me where I was going to live.'

'Where are you going to live? With me? Or somewhere else?'

'I'll stay with you.'

'Good.'

'I could just see it on their faces, though. Cynthia's got another man. Cynthia's fucked it up just like the last time, just like the time before that.'

'How many times has it been? How many men have there been?'

She thought about that. She started counting them up on her fingers. One hand, the other hand, back to the first hand. She gave up. 'I can't really remember. Lots. Too many.'

I shook my head.

If I ever was going to fall for someone again, it was going to be her.

TWELVE

Cynthia's parents flew out mid-morning. Cynthia took the car to see them off. She dropped me at the flat. I had to prepare for my next rendezvous with Social Security. Money was becoming a serious concern. I'd been spending up big. A hundred and fifty in the last three days.

And there wouldn't be much coming in for a while. According to the forms, once my application for benefits was finally accepted there would be a period of one week before my first payment. That would be one hundred and thirty-six dollars. Every two weeks after that I would receive payments of two hundred and seventy-two. In other words, all I could expect from Social Security for the next three weeks was a hundred and thirty-six dollars. I added this to the money I had left. Then I took away what I owed for the rent, which was already due and which would be due again in two weeks time. And then there were bills. The quarterly phone, gas and electricity.

After subtracting them all, I had ten dollars left. Ten dollars to feed and amuse myself for three weeks.

That was it then. It was time to talk Special Benefits.

Of course Cynthia had money. And she would be sharing the rent as well. But Social Security didn't know that. I had the bills, I had documents. I had proof. I filled out the Special Benefits form, collected it all and walked down to the Social Security office.

Nothing had changed. The smokers outside may have been different people, but they looked the same. They stared at me. I stared back. I was feeling confident this time. I was beginning to understand the way things worked. I joined one of the queues and made it to the counter. It was the same woman as before. There was no chance of her remembering me. I'd read somewhere that this particular office was one of the busiest in the state.

'I have an appointment,' I said, handing over the card.

She looked at it. 'You've got the forms?'

I handed them over, along with the bills and the three identifications. She didn't look at them.

'Okay, I'll pass these on. Take a seat and we'll call you.'

I found a seat. Smooth enough so far. I looked at the TV. I hadn't brought anything to read. I'd been vaguely expecting that having an appointment card meant you wouldn't have to wait. There was a clock on the wall. It rolled round twice while I sat there.

I watched the crowd. Most of them were young — seventeen, eighteen, nineteen. They moved around. They fought, laughed, yelled. I picked up New Zealand and British accents. We had an internationally famous social security system. Anyone could get it. Three forms of ID was all it took.

The older people — the long-term unemployed, the invalid pensioners — sat quietly and watched the action with weary expressions. They had no time for youth. What did the young know? The young were the competition, the young were the enemy. They flowed out of school by the millions and got in the way.

Finally I was called up to a booth. It was the same woman again. She had my pile of documents.

'This I D is lousy.'

'Honestly, it's all I could find.'

She began stamping the forms. 'Well, it'll have to do.' I waited. She finished stamping. 'Now, we've approved you for the standard Unemployment Benefits, but I see you want the Emergency Benefits too. I have to tell you I don't think you're really eligible for it. These bills of yours aren't extraordinary.'

I was ready for this. I said, 'But they still have to be paid. That's not even counting the rent and just general survival. The money has to come from somewhere.'

'Well . . . it's not up to me. I'll pass your application on and we'll get back to you. I'll give you an appointment for tomorrow.'

'Today's okay. I can wait.'

'But it could take hours.'

'That's fine. I really need the money today. All those bills are overdue.'

She resigned herself. 'Fair enough. Look, in the meantime, here's your standard fortnightly application. Fill it out and bring it in before eleven tomorrow. We'll mail you the next one with your first payment, and then every second Tuesday after that you'll have to bring it in, in person. Okay?'

'Okay.'

I went and sat down again.

This wasn't so bad. All you needed was patience. I waited another hour, then I was called up again. I drew a man this time. He looked about my age. He was well dressed. He looked cool, together. He had all my forms. The pile was getting bigger.

'Okay,' he said, 'we've decided you're entitled to Emergency Benefits to the sum of eighty-seven dollars and sixty-three cents.'

'Thank you. That'll help.'

'Don't thank me . . .'

He stamped another form. I signed it. Then it happened. He wrote out the cheque. Eighty-seven dollars and sixty-three *cents*.

He handed it over. I put it in my wallet. There was still a couple of hundred dollars in there. He saw the bills, fifties and twenties. Money. I put the wallet away. Made for the door. I was in, the monster had welcomed me home. I was being taken care of.

I walked to the nearest bank and cashed the cheque, then headed for home. A bit further on I passed a TAB I thought about it. Eighty-seven dollars, twenty to one, an each way bet, no, to *win*. It all seemed too simple. You couldn't take this sort of money seriously. It was the right thing to do, the spirited thing to do.

I went inside. I looked at the cards. Looked at the punters lining the walls, watching the TV screens. It was Social Security all over again.

I walked out.

I was never going to make it anyway.

Cynthia was waiting in the flat.

'How'd you go?' I asked.

'Not too bad. Dad was still pissed off. I talked to Mum mostly. I told her more about you and me, she seemed to understand . . . how about you?'

'I got cash. Special Benefits. Eighty-seven dollars and sixty-three cents.'

'Is that all? They ripped you off. The first time I went for Special Benefits I got over a hundred and I didn't even have any documentation. I just told them I had nowhere to stay. Eighty bucks is nothing. You just have to stand there and scream till they give you more.'

'No. I have a conscience. Social Security are my friends. They're good to me. Anyway, what're you going to do for money?'

'I think I'll get another job.'

'Not the dole?'

'No ... I've done that enough. I'm sick of the poverty. Besides, if we both go on the dole Social Security will work out that we're living together. We'd get even less then. If I get a job I can give a false address, my old address, and it won't be a problem. You can't give false addresses to Social Security.'

'What'll it be? Bar work?'

'I guess so. It's all I can do.'

She unpacked. She didn't have much, just two suitcases and a few books and a pile of records and tapes. There was plenty of space. The flat had come furnished with two big wardrobes, and they were empty. I kept my clothes in laundry baskets.

The flat itself consisted of two big rooms. One had been partitioned into two segments, the bedroom and the kitchen. The other held a couple of couches, a desk, the TV and a table. The floor was linoleum.

'If you want to change anything around,' I said, 'feel free. You're paying half the rent.'

'No, it's okay. It just needs cleaning. And some new curtains. And the walls need washing.'

'The walls?' I'd never heard of anyone washing walls. I let that one pass.

We sat on one of the couches and watched TV. We had a couple of glasses of cask wine. Cynthia started rearranging my legs and arms. 'You sit all wrong,' she said. 'You could look so good if you wanted to.'

'I don't want to.'

'It doesn't matter what you want. I'm the one who has to look at you.'

It made a certain amount of sense. She made me lie back, unbutton my shirt, undo the top button of my jeans. She took my penis out and kissed it and looked at it, talked to it, then put it away. I'd never seen anything like her. Then she started studying my face and neck.

'You've got blackheads!'

'So?'

She pulled my head down into her lap. 'You can't just leave them there. They're dangerous.' She began pinching the back of my neck.

'Cynthia, stop this . . .'

'But some of them are huge!'

'There's nothing there.'

'Be quiet. I'm concentrating.'

I let her go. It was nice to be mothered, nice to be bossed. Maybe that was my problem, unresolved complexes. I needed someone to be in control. The difficulty was people kept offering me the opposite. They let me do whatever I wanted, as if I knew what I was doing, as if I had credibility. It'd ruined the few relationships I'd had. Sooner or later the woman had started asking meaningful questions and I gave meaningless answers, and somehow they'd got taken seriously. It occurred to me sometimes that women listened too much, they considered too much, they paid attention to the wrong things. They didn't just *look*. If a man was there with them, he was there with them. That was the most important thing.

Cynthia seemed to understand. She could see I was there with her. I was safely under control. What I *said* hardly mattered. That was just conversation. Underneath it all, she knew I had no worthwhile opinions. Even on blackhead removal.

So I suffered it for twenty minutes. She showed me the results. She'd picked out tiny bits of skin and blood. They were stuck under her fingernails.

I said, 'I haven't had a pimple on my neck for years. There was nothing there, you just wanted to make me bleed.'

'Bullshit. You don't look after yourself.'

The afternoon passed.

We started thinking about dinner.

There was no food in the fridge. Cynthia felt like steak. She was a big meat eater. Steak and chicken. I preferred sausages, or pasta, or Chinese. Things you didn't have to chew. We decided to go shopping.

We drove to a mall at Annerley, across the river. We parked and walked around, looking at all the food. Cynthia held my hand. I was her man now. We found a butcher and studied the selection.

I said, 'I think I'll have rissoles.'

'Rissoles?'

'I feel like rissoles.'

They had them ready made. Garlic, pepper and beef rissoles. Big and round. I bought three of them, Cynthia went for rump steak. Then we found some potatoes, broccoli, and beans. And some Gravox. You had to have gravy.

We drove home. We picked up a sixpack of Toohey's Old on the way. Cynthia said she'd cook. I drank beer and watched TV and wandered into the kitchen from time to time.

'Burn the fuck out of those rissoles,' I said.

Everything smelt good. I grabbed Cynthia from behind while she stirred the gravy. I ran my hands up under her skirt. I felt like fucking her there and then, over the stove. I was turning into a husband. After one day.

84

'Not now,' she said. 'This is important.' Maybe she was turning into a wife. She leaned back against me and we watched the gravy bubble.

'How long?'

'Not long.'

We served it on the dining table and turned the TV around. There was nothing much on, so we broke out the Scrabble set and started playing while we ate. Our plates were overflowing. Mashed potato, meat, beans, gravy — no class, but it was what we needed.

When it was finished we cleared the plates away and concentrated on the Scrabble. Cynthia was a good Scrabble player. Not many people I knew were. I played a lot of Scrabble. You had to believe in Scrabble to be any good at it. You had to be prepared to play strategically, to agonise. Most people couldn't be bothered, they put down the first word they saw just to end the pain. And they lost.

Scrabble, if I cared to think about it, was like a lot of things I could see about life. If you really worked at something, the chances were you'd pull it off. The problem was that the success never seemed that good in the end. The struggle robbed it of joy. There was no real gain, no satisfaction. I didn't want to work at things. What I really wanted was to win without trying, to throw down brilliant words without even having to think, to be a natural.

I wasn't a natural. I had a working class brain. It took me time. And then sometimes you just didn't get the letters, there was nothing you could do. And sometimes they fell into place like a dream. Luck was the real decider. Luck was what it all came down to. Scrabble was *exactly* like life. And when luck was on your side, when it was running your way, then it was a wilder and richer thing than all the hard work in the world could ever be.

Cynthia knew it.

I knew it.

For the moment, we had it on our side. We were riding it, right there over the Scrabble board.

The game was close. We sweated over it for about an hour and a half, but Cynthia got there in the end. It was my first defeat in months.

We set up the tiles and started another game. This time I won. Cynthia was genuinely angry. She hadn't lost much lately either. She took the pen and drew two columns on the inside of the lid of the Scrabble box. One column she marked with a C, the other with an G, then she put one stroke in each.

'This is going to be serious,' she said.

She settled down on the couch. I washed up.

'When do you write?' she said, when I came back in.

'Whenever. Mostly at night, I suppose. It's not very regular with the poetry.'

'Am I going to be in your way?'

'God, no. I'm not writing anything at the moment. Nothing has happened to me lately.'

'What about me?'

'That might come later.'

'Can I *read* some of your poems?'

'One of these days, I suppose. They're pretty negative. Especially about sex. I think you'd find them ridiculous.'

'I wouldn't make any judgements. I just want to see how you write.'

'Judgements aren't the problem. It's letting you know how I think that worries me.'

'Why?'

'It'd kill us before our time, that's why.'

THIRTEEN

Next day I filed my first official dole form. The day after that, Cynthia went job hunting. She took off in the Kingswood late Wednesday morning. I had a shower, ate breakfast.

In the hall I finally met the new neighbours, Raymond and Cathy. Raymond was thin and dark. Fine-featured. He did look Spanish, but there was no accent. Cathy was slim and blond. She had a long sharp face. A fresh cut ran from just below her left eye to the bottom of her chin. It was deep. It had stitches. She wouldn't meet my eyes.

Cynthia came back after about an hour.

'Two offers,' she said.

'Already? Which pubs?'

'The Queen's Arms and the Brunswick. They were the first two I tried.'

'Which one will you take?'

'The Queen's Arms, I think. The manager seemed nice enough. He knows you.'

'He knows me?'

'He said you used to work for him. At the Boundary Hotel.'

'A really old guy? Brian?'

'Brian.'

'That was years ago.'

'He remembers you.'

'We did get on well.'

'He said he could even find a place for you, if you wanted.'

'What'd you say to that?'

'I said I didn't think you were really looking.'

'And what'd *he* say to that?'

'He said he wasn't really suprised.'

'Well, he's good to work for. He'd like you. You've got the soul of a barmaid and he's got the soul of an alcoholic. He couldn't help but like you.'

'The soul of a barmaid?'

'That's *good*. As long as the beer and the scotch are running, Brian will keep off your back. He respects the profession.'

'Alcoholics do run the best pubs.'

'Indeed they do.'

'I'll take the Queen's Arms, then. The Brunswick is closer, I suppose, but to hell with it.'

'Why did the Brunswick like you?'

'They said I was the first well dressed applicant they'd had in months. They wanted me to start straight away.'

'Well dressed?' I looked at her. She was wearing the standard long black skirt and white blouse.

'Better than most,' she said.

We did nothing all week. We slept long and late, watched TV, drank occasionally. We spent the afternoon planning the evening meals. It wasn't much, but neither of us was an outdoor person. And it was hot. Brisbane that week was going through something of a heatwave.

88

We fucked every night and every morning. Cynthia
could've done it forever. She already *had* been doing it
forever. I was struggling to keep up. Even after a few nights
I was running out of stamina and ideas.

'You have to use your imagination,' she said. 'You can't
just get on top and thrust away all the time, it gets boring.'

'I don't have an imagination.'

'Pretend you have. Tie me up. Get mean. You're too nice.'

'Tie you up?'

'You've heard of it, haven't you?'

And I was coming too fast. Or not coming at all. Always
at the wrong times. Cynthia didn't mind so much. My body
wasn't going anywhere. She knew she could get whatever
she wanted from it in time. But it bothered me. It was even
harder to get imaginative with a prick that you couldn't
rely on.

Sunday rolled around. It was time we got out. The flat was
closing in on us and the old men were becoming cranky up
and down the hall. Sunday afternoon was never a good time.

'I want food,' Cynthia said. 'I want *steak*.'

We went to the Story Bridge Hotel, under the Story
Bridge, in Kangaroo Point. It wasn't far. New Farm was
one side of the river, Kangaroo Point was on the other, the
bridge crossed between. We drove over and parked in the
car park. Inside we got ourselves drinks, ordered lunch at
the counter, then found ourselves a table out in the beer
garden. It was a good beer garden. There was no sun, only
the bridge above us. You could hear the cars and trucks
thumping over the concrete slabs.

The meals came. Cynthia got her steak. It was big. She
had a plate of fat fried chips with it. She wolfed it all down.
She could eat. I was having fish. A delicate little fillet in
light sauce. With salad. It was all the wrong way around.
Cynthia was more of a man than I was.

'How did I ever find you?' she said. 'I always said I'd never meet the sort of man I wanted because the sort of man I want never goes out to meet people. He's always at home in bed, or watching the football, or just doing nothing. Just like you. And I *found* you. How did that happen?'

'You didn't ask me out for drinks, you asked me over to your place for drinks. That's how it happened. The difference is significant.'

'It took me a long time to make that phone call.'

'I'm glad you did.'

After lunch we settled down and drank. We talked. It became clear we weren't going anywhere. The bar and the beer garden filled up as the afternoon progressed. The normal mix. It was a popular place. Around three a jazz band started playing. We didn't like jazz, but we stayed on. We had a table and it was a warm afternoon and all the better places seemed a long way away.

Cynthia asked, 'You put the Scrabble set in the car, didn't you?'

'I did.'

I went out and brought it in. We set up, started playing. We played two games. We won one each. By then the score was seven games to five, in Cynthia's favour. It was important business. People came over and watched us play. We dazzled them with seven, eight, nine letter words. We drank.

At some stage someone called my name. A woman's voice. I looked up and there was Rachel.

Rachel.

I'd seen her only three or four times in the last couple of years. Lately I hadn't even thought about her. But from the ages of about thirteen to twenty-one, she was more or less all I *had* thought about. She was my past. More or less my only past.

'Rachel,' I said.

90

'Hello Gordon.'

She was smiling. She looked pretty much the same. Tall. Short cropped hair, blonde, a little more blonde than I remembered it. Square face, big-jawed. She had a few large pimples on her chin. Rachel didn't pick at her pimples. She let them grow till they burst.

'So how's it going?' she said.

'Fine. Good. Rachel, this is Cynthia.'

'Hello Cynthia.'

'Cynthia has just moved in with me.'

'Really?'

'Yes.'

'You're still in New Farm? I heard you moved.'

'I did, but I'm still in New Farm.'

'And what've you been doing?'

'I quit work not long ago. That's about it. I'm on the dole now. What about you?'

'Not much. Study.'

Rachel was studying Administrative Sciences at Q.I.T. It was her second attempt at a degree. Originally it was Psychology at Queensland Uni, but she abandoned that around the same time that my own studies were faltering. Then we lost track of each other. I was working here and there around the country and she was unemployed and neurotic and living on Social Security in Brisbane. There was a man. She was in love with him. Hopelessly. She wanted his child. He didn't love her. For that, at least, I thought he was a fool. Meanwhile Rachel and I still met from time to time, but it was never very good between us. I wasn't the one she wanted around anymore, and we both knew it. She was depressed, tearful, wildly irrational, walking the streets at night, alone and drunk. I had my own problems. I stayed away. Later she pulled herself out of it and enrolled at Q.I.T. I heard about it from friends. I didn't know what it meant.

'How *is* the study?'

'Terrible. Nothing new there.'

'Do you want a seat? Are you here with anyone?'

It turned out she was there with a lot of people. Uni friends. But she sat down and we organised more drinks. Beer. We all drank beer.

It took Rachel and me about half an hour to catch up. Cynthia sat mostly silent, drinking. Then Rachel got up and said she was going back to her friends. After she was gone, Cynthia turned on me.

'She wants to fuck you.'

'Rachel? C'mon, she's had the chance to do that for years. I don't think she's changed her mind just tonight.'

'Who is she?'

'I told you about her. She's the one I went to school with, back in Dalby. The one I was obsessed with. The one I only ever held hands with. The one I never kissed.'

'*Her?*'

'Her.'

'But she's *ugly.*'

'Cynthia, everyone I know is ugly.'

'Well, she's still in love with you.'

'She isn't. She never has been.'

'You wouldn't know. You never look at people. She's jealous. She hates me.'

'That's crap, Cynthia. We haven't even talked in months. Besides, even if she had changed her mind about me, I'd say no.'

'Would you?'

'Of course I would.'

It was true. Rachel wasn't for me, life had taught me that much. We'd met each other in the first year of high school. She didn't live in Dalby, she was from a farm in the mountains, about an hour's drive away. She boarded in town during the week, for school. Her parents wanted to give her a Catholic education. On weekends she went home again. I was in love with her. I wasn't sure why. She was a serious girl, there was something incorruptibly sensible about her. No one else at school had it. Throughout the three years that we were at the same school I begged her to stay in town for just the one weekend. There were parties we could go to, things we could do.

She'd shake her head. 'Gordon, I'm needed at home, you know I can't.'

Cynthia and I finished the Scrabble game. We packed it up and Cynthia brought her seat around closer to mine. She draped her legs over my lap. We drank and talked. She reached over and moved my legs and arms around, getting them right. Then she leaned back, surveying. She smiled at me. 'My beautiful *boy*.' She was my mother, all right. She was crazy. I wondered if Rachel was watching us, what she would think. There was something of the mother in Rachel too, but it was a very different sort of mother.

But to hell with Rachel, I thought.

I was with Cynthia now.

We sat there until closing time. The table was covered in empty glasses. We decided to walk home and leave the car. The police drink-driving teams often had the bridge covered on Sunday nights. We left the bar and climbed up to the bridge. The river was there, moving slow. It reflected the city towers and the lights. I liked this part of Brisbane. I liked the towers. Towers were okay. They were artefacts. The bigger the better. Like the pyramids. Just as long as you didn't have to work in them. The city, as a workplace, looked odious. In that respect, maybe the World's Tallest Building really hadn't been much of an idea. Ten thousand office workers, that was how many they'd been hoping to squeeze into the thing.

We took it slow across the bridge. We stopped to look down at the water. The bridge was just high enough to make jumping worthwhile. And people sometimes did, although there was one better, higher bridge to jump off in Brisbane. It was because the Story Bridge had class, it had age. It was all iron and rivets and arches. The only problem was, if you jumped off the highest parts of the arches, you didn't hit water, you hit solid earth. The high parts were over the river banks. Not that it mattered, once you'd got enough free fall behind you.

'Have you ever been suicidal?' Cynthia asked.

'Not yet. What about you?'

'No. Never. I'm terrified of dying.'

We got off the bridge and into the backstreets of New Farm. We paused every now and then and kissed, good kisses, leaning up against trees and fences. Life was strange. Only a few weeks earlier I'd seen people doing exactly this and I'd hated them for it. And now here I was. Doing it myself. And it didn't feel as ugly as it looked. Or as beautiful.

'Let's find a park,' I said. 'Let's fuck on the grass.'

'Not in New Farm. People die in the parks around here. People get their heads cut off.'

Which was true. We went on home.

When we got there, we found Leo and Molly sitting in the couches, watching TV and sipping on beer.

'How'd you get in?'

'The old guy up the hall opened it for us. We told him we were friends of yours.'

Leo and Molly seemed as drunk as we were, or maybe they were stoned. We sat down and watched TV for a while. Leo wanted to know all about the heroin. He was annoyed

I hadn't told him about it, brought him in on the deal. I described it as best I could. Molly offered the opinion that heroin was a dangerous, evil drug. It wasn't *natural*. She was only into natural drugs. Marijuana and sometimes mushrooms.

I started drinking Leo and Molly's beer. Over the TV we could hear a fight building in the flat next door, the new neighbours again. Mostly it was a woman's voice we could hear. Cathy's voice. Raymond's was indistinct. They were arguing about money. I told the others about the cut on her face.

'It'll be a good-looking scar, though,' I said, 'when it's healed.'

Things next door began to get violent. Something heavy smashed against the wall. Cathy was screaming.

Vass came running into the room. 'You gonna call the police?'

'Is there any point?'

Raymond was yelling now. There was another crash on the wall. It sounded like the phone. The bells rang.

'I don't think he's hitting her yet,' Leo suggested.

We all listened. There were muffled sounds, but no more yelling or screaming.

'He's a mean bastard,' said Vass, 'and he steals too.'

'So I've heard.'

'I'd do something about your door, if I was you. It's the easiest to open in the whole damn place.'

He went out.

'He's the one who let us in,' said Leo.

Things quietened down. Leo and Molly stayed on. I mentioned that Cynthia and I had seen Rachel.

'I saw Rachel not so long ago,' said Leo, 'she was depressed. Her life isn't going too well. I think she misses you.'

'Me? Why?'

'Jesus, you guys were friends for years. And then you just stopped seeing her.'

'It wasn't just me. What's wrong with her life, anyway?'

'Men, mainly. She keeps falling for arseholes.'

So some things hadn't changed.

Leo and Molly left about two in the morning. The house was quiet. Cynthia and I undressed and climbed into bed.

'I like them,' Cynthia said. 'I thought you were going to ask them to stay, but I'm glad you didn't.'

'I wouldn't ask them to stay. They'd end up in bed with us. And I'd have to watch them fucking again. It wasn't much fun the first time.'

'No. God. Leo fucking. Leo *coming*. It'd be evil.'

'Everyone looks evil when they come. The animal is out.'

'You don't look evil. You look like you always look. Your face doesn't even change.'

'Really? That's alarming.'

'Yes. It is. Do you have any porn around here?'

'Magazines, you mean?'

'That's what I mean.'

I explained that porn of any extreme sort wasn't legally available in Queensland, except by mail order or on the black market. I didn't have any black market connections. Nor did I ever have the twenty or thirty dollars the mail order firms were asking. I did, however, have a friend called Harry in Sydney, where certain magazines at least were legal. Non-violent erotica. Harry was a porn fanatic. He toured the shops regularly and collected hundreds of volumes. And sometimes he'd mail me three or four issues that he was tired of. He thought I needed them. And they were always in mint condition. Crisp and clean. If he'd ever masturbated over them, he'd done it very carefully.

'So you've got some? Here?'

96

'Yes. I do.'

'Well, c'mon, let me see.'

I climbed out of bed, turned on the light. I dug the magazines out of a box. There were about twenty of them. Things like 'Teen Sex', or 'Cum' or 'Anal — Volume Three'. I wasn't like Harry. I used them to masturbate all the time. I hadn't treated them well. The covers had fallen off and the pages were bent.

Cynthia sat up and started going through them. 'I love these things,' she said. 'Some jerk offered me a role in a porn film once. The money was good, but not *that* fucking good.'

'No. And you were a serious actor.'

Cynthia had been involved in theatre at one stage. Amateur productions. It'd gone on for three or four years. She secured an Actors Equity card. She made it as an extra in a film called 'Windsurfer'. She auditioned for 'Neighbours' and missed out. Then she gave it away. Her skin hadn't been so bad in those days, she said, and she was a lot thinner.

'Problem is,' she said, turning the pages, 'if I think about this sort of thing too much I get turned off. The exploitation and all that. The thing with porn is not to think too logically. You just have to look. And make up your own fantasies.'

We kept going through the pages, taking in all the big pricks and open cunts and jammed arseholes. We didn't bother with the print. The stories were laughable. At least the pictures were just pictures. And they did what they were supposed to do. We pushed the magazines aside and started on each other. It was violent, pretentious sex. We were trying to match the photographs. Trying to make it hurt.

I ended up behind her, slamming it in. It wasn't that good, but in our way we were better than the pictures.

Pictures didn't have sound or smell. They missed out on the farts and the bad breath and the wet sucking noises . . . all the things about sex that you remembered.

And I was coming, despite all the alcohol. 'Not yet,' Cynthia said, 'not yet.' I held on. It never worked. 'Stop,' I said. Cynthia refused. She slammed her hips back. Then it was flooding through. Cynthia pounded her fist against the mattress. 'Damn, damn, damn!' I kept on as long as I could, then it was just pain. I stopped. Pulled out. Collapsed.

Cynthia stayed there, face down.

I said, 'No good?'

'No.'

She coughed, sniffed. Rolled over to me.

'We're *really* going to have to do something about this.'

FOURTEEN

Cynthia started work. Twenty-five, thirty hours a week. Usually she took the car. Sometimes she walked. It was only ten or fifteen minutes on foot. I picked her up if she was finishing late. I'd sit in the bar and have a beer or two while she closed up. I didn't see much of the manager, Brian, not at that hour. He generally started his drinking around ten in the morning. Scotch and water at first, then straight scotch.

Cynthia set about straightening out the house. The first problem was the lighting in the toilets and showers. The agents supplied new lightbulbs every few months, but the other residents usually stole them to replace their own. At night it was a matter of picking your way through the shit and piss in the dark. I'd given up. I pissed in the sink. It wasn't so easy for Cynthia. So she bought a new set of bulbs herself, marked them with red X's and installed them. She went from flat to flat threatening the old men with violence if she ever found one of her bulbs in their rooms.

They were impressed. The bulbs stayed. I stopped pissing in the sink.

We washed the walls of the flat, and went shopping for material to make curtains. We played Scrabble, cooked meals, watched TV and kept trying to work it out in bed. It was a pleasant life. And it'd come from nowhere. Luck was still with us. An eight letter word on a triple word score.

We saw a few people. Went out. Helen and Dave came over a couple of times before they went back to Melbourne. No one suggested heroin. We didn't have the money any more, neither did they. Cynthia and I did buy some grass from Leo. We smoked it at night, fucked on it. It was better than doing it straight.

Cynthia's skin got worse. It was all the alcohol and the dust in the flat. At night she rolled over and I scratched the disease on her back until she slept. She was a restless sleeper. As soon as I stopped the scratching she curled up against me and clung around my chest. I couldn't sleep that way. I needed to roll around. After a while I'd pry her arms off and push her away. She'd come back, time and time again through the night.

She had nighmares. I woke up one night to find her moaning in her sleep, terrified.

'Cynthia? Wake up. What's wrong?'

'Gordon?' She was still asleep. She reached for me.

'I'm here.'

She grabbed me, held on. 'Gordon,' she sighed. Her breathing relaxed. Her face was jammed up hot against mine, still sleeping. A little girl face. And my name, just my name had the power to fend off her bad dreams.

One night I too had a nighmare. I woke up screaming her name. Cynthia leapt up and started screaming back. We

were thumping each other in the dark. Cynthia got to the
light switch, flicked it on. We looked at each other.

'Jesus, Gordon . . .'

A door opened, someone moved in the hallway. 'You okay
in there?' It was Vass. Hearing aid switched on.

'We're okay,' I yelled.

'Sounded like someone was *dying*.'

'Nobody is dying.'

'Okay then . . .'

'What were you dreaming about?' Cynthia asked.

'You'd fallen in front of a train. I was watching and I
couldn't get to you in time.'

It didn't sound like much, but the train had been huge
and ugly and evil. It was screaming down on her. Her legs
were across the tracks, they were going to be sliced right
off.

'So you *do* love me,' she said.

'I don't know about *that*, Cynthia. I don't want to see you
die.'

We lit cigarettes. Left the light on for a while.

'This is pathetic, isn't it,' she said.

'Who knows, Cynthia, maybe it was a warning.'

'Yeah?'

'Maybe *I'm* the train.'

'You? Don't panic, Gordon. I think I'm capable of getting
off the tracks.'

On other nights Cynthia couldn't sleep for the itching.
Scratching her back wasn't enough. She was in real pain.
She clawed at her face and her shoulders and raised blood.
I took her hands and held them behind her back just to
stop it. She twisted and swore and cried. We struggled. We
fucked for the sake of distraction. Next morning her face
would be raked and livid. She kept her fingernails cut down
to the quick just to blunt her fingers, but it only helped a

little. She'd leave out the alcohol for a day or two. Leave out the soap when she showered. Take aspirin and panadol and chain smoke to occupy her hands...

On one of these nights she sucked my toes, and four or five days later, rashes erupted on my feet.

'That's really some disease you've got there,' I said.

'It can't be the eczema, it's not contagious. I told you. eczema is not even a disease. It's a condition.'

The skin was peeling away between my toes. I rubbed tinea cream into it. It didn't heal.

'What *is* that?'

'Talk to the old men,' she said. 'They're the ones you share the showers with.'

Sickness was in the air. We talked about all the diseases we'd ever had.

'What about venereal diseases?' I asked. 'Have you ever caught one? You must've at some stage. All those men.'

'No.'

'Have you ever checked?'

'No.'

And I had to admire that. She was heading for death a lot faster than I was.

FIFTEEN

A couple of weeks passed. One of my brothers, Charles, was getting married. My invitation said 'Gordon and friend'. I invited Cynthia. I said, 'Are you ready to meet the family? All of them this time?'

She was.

The wedding was in a church in the Valley. The reception was in one of the Valley hotels. Cynthia wasn't so sure about going to the wedding itself. It was a Catholic wedding, with an accompanying mass.

'But you aren't even Catholic any more,' she said.

'Charlie is — or even if he isn't, that's the way they're getting married. Have you ever seen a mass before?'

'No.'

'You'll love it, then. You'll find it interesting. Catholicism can be very weird to the outsider.'

'Okay, okay.'

We went. It was at St Patrick's church in the Valley, three o'clock on a Saturday afternoon. I liked weddings. Not so much for the ceremony, and not necessarily for what they stood for, but the receptions were good. Free drinks,

free food. I'd been to a lot of weddings. Charlie was the
sixth member of the family to go, with two more already
engaged. And if people were happy enough to get married,
then I was happy enough for them to do it.

We started walking down at about two thirty. I was wearing
the best suit coat and pants I owned, and a white shirt.
Cynthia had tied my hair back with a black bow. It would
pass instead of a tie. Cynthia herself was in her least worn
black and white outfit.

'We need new clothes,' she said. 'I'm sick of these clothes.
I've been in pubs too long.'

'New clothes? From where, and with what?'

'You've already got an account at Myers, haven't you?'

'I don't think they like me there any more. Besides, how
often do we go to weddings?'

We arrived. The crowd was waiting around outside the
church. We felt shabby.

All the family was there, a few of them from interstate.
I introduced Cynthia around. To Anne (my sister) and her
husband Mitchell and their five children. To Mary (my
sister) and her husband Edmund and their four children.
To Stephen (my brother) and his wife Renee and their three
children. To James (my brother) and his wife Ruth and
their two children. To Elizabeth (my sister) and her husband Kevin and their two children. To Joseph (my brother)
and his fiancee Pamela. To Louise (my sister) and her
fiancee Patrick. To my younger brother Michael. Then to
my parents, Tom and Margaret Buchanan, which only left
Charlie himself, and Lucy, his prospective wife, but that
introduction would come later, after the wedding.

Cynthia lasted through it all. We didn't bother with the
uncles and aunts. Three o'clock rolled round and we went
in.

It was small church and a big crowd. Cynthia and I sat at the rear of the family group. The children played, hung over their parents' shoulders, made faces. Cynthia made faces back. She loved kids. I wasn't so sure. I followed the mass. Sixteen years of Catholic upbringing were still in me.

Cynthia watched me from time to time. She leaned over. 'Stop it,' she whispered. 'You don't even believe in any of this.'

'Maybe not. But it's difficult. If you ever want to torture me, Cynthia, all you have to do is tie me up, stand in front of me and say "In the name of the Father, the Son and the Holy Spirit, Amen" — and watch me struggle to cross myself. The ritual dies hard.'

'Great. Thanks. I'll remember *that*.'

After an hour it was over. Charlie and Lucy were married. We filed out of the church, gathered for the family photographs, then hurried off to the pub.

'Is that what Catholic masses are always like?' Cynthia asked, on the way.

'More or less.'

'Jesus, no wonder you're so fucked up.'

'Maybe. I don't know. Catholicism might have a lot to answer for, but then so do I.'

It was a good reception. Charlie and Lucy were a relaxed couple. No formal seating, just food being carried around by waiters and an open bar. I started up on bourbon and Cynthia settled into vodkas and soda. Double nips for the first few. I lost Cynthia in the crowd and various members of the family swooped in.

'So who is she?'

'I met her at work.'

'But a heroin addict, Gordon?'

'Who told you that? Anyway, she's given it up.'

'Yeah? For how long?'

'Long enough.'

'She's pretty abrupt. You can't talk to her.'

'C'mon. She's nervous about meeting everyone.'

'Is it serious?'

'I don't know.'

'Where's she living?'

'With me.'

'With *you*. Do Mum and Dad know?'

'More or less.'

'So they don't know you're sleeping together.'

'It *is* a one bedroom flat.'

'Did you have to ask her to move in?'

'Look, I like her. I might even *love* her.'

'Love, Gordon? Love?'

'I know. It's a terrible thing to say . . .'

I wandered to and from the the bar. The night dissolved into drunken conversations. The family drank well. They were a good family. They'd get used to Cynthia.

The next thing I remembered I was sitting next to the piano, listening to one of the guests sing a long and involved song about women. He seemed to know what he was talking about. Cynthia appeared, swaying and smiling. She said, 'It's time I took you home.'

I looked around. There were only about a dozen people left.

'Okay.'

We staggered home, clutching at each other and kissing.

She said, 'I heard what you said tonight. You said you loved me.'

'You heard that? I'm sorry. I don't know how it happened.'

'I don't care. I believe you.'

'You shouldn't.'

'But it sounded so *good*.'

I didn't have the heart to argue. Maybe it was true. We got home and discovered that Vass had found his way into the flat and was watching the TV.

106

'Christ,' said Cynthia. 'We come home for a fuck and there's always someone here. Don't you have a home?'

'Hey,' said Vass, 'you can wait, can't you?'

'No!'

We sat down. Vass explained that there'd been a movie he wanted to watch, and he hadn't thought that we'd mind. I said it was okay. Cynthia curled up, her head on my lap. I took off my shoes.

'I made a rash comment about love tonight,' I told Vass, 'Cynthia thinks she's got me now.'

'I *have* got you. No one else is getting a chance.'

'I can't live up to it. You'll kill me.'

'Oh bullshit.'

Vass watched us. He had his own theories about women. I tried watching TV. I could barely focus. I rolled a joint and we smoked it. It made things worse.

'I'm going to bed,' said Cynthia. She got up and went.

I shrugged at Vass. He seemed to understand.

'She's a nice girl,' he told me again. 'You look after her.'

I nodded and we stared at the TV for ten minutes or so. Then I said, 'I've gotta go to bed.'

'All right,' he said, 'I'll go. I shouldn't have been here anyway.'

'It's okay, really.'

'No. This is your place.'

He left. Cynthia came out. She was still dressed. 'Look out,' she said. She got down on her knees in front of me. 'I've been wanking myself in there.'

'No kidding . . .'

She undid my zip and took my penis in her mouth. I was too stoned to move. I watched her, I watched my penis grow. Once it was erect she climbed up and lifted her skirt. She was naked underneath, and already wet.

She thrust away. The angle was strange. The sensations were coming from miles away. She started crying. 'God I love you, God I love you.' Then she came. She lay on my chest.

Yes, I thought, this woman could be dangerous.

She looked up. 'I want you to come in my mouth.'

It wasn't an offer she often made. Erections were rare and valuable things, they were for *fucking*. I nodded.

She slid down. She tugged my pants away and her mouth moved in, started working. She took my balls and pulled and stroked them. She had a strong grip. Then her mouth left the tip of my penis, worked its way down and engulfed one testicle, then the other.

'Are balls like breasts?' I said.

She pulled back. 'How do you mean?'

I wasn't sure what I meant. The joint seemed to be piling up on me. 'Forget it.'

She started again. There was an orgasm waiting in there somewhere. She moved back up to my penis, sucking and curling her tongue around the tip of it. The sensations became stronger. My erection felt long and thin and cold. Her teeth grated down the shaft. I reached my hands down, stroked her hair, pulled my hands back. She grunted, her mouth full, and rammed it deep into her throat, once, twice. It was a strangely delicate thing. I slid sideways down onto the couch. Things happened. I groaned, long and loud. I came. My hips thrust up into her mouth. She coughed, gurgled, took it in, then kept on sucking.

'Stop, Cynthia. It hurts.'

She let go. She came crawling up over my chest and kissed me. I opened my mouth and her tongue moved in. Her mouth felt loose. Slack. Stretched. But there was none of the salty taste I might've expected. There never was. One of the mysteries of sex.

'I could just eat you,' she said.

And women always said that, too, about men.

Another mystery.

108

SIXTEEN

Friday night Leo and Molly came over for drinks. Around ten o'clock Cynthia and Molly decided they felt like hitting a nightclub in the city. Maybe the Orient Hotel. Cynthia was up. She was on a two-week cortisone course. It made a difference. The itching was gone. Her skin was glowing.

Leo said he wasn't in the mood for a nightclub. I was drinking cask red. It was making me ill. Plus the asthma was bad. We both said no. The girls called a cab and went alone.

It was one of the few times Cynthia had ventured out without me, excepting work. I was glad she'd gone. I was glad she liked Molly. Cynthia had no one in Brisbane but me.

Leo and I drank and watched TV. I didn't feel any better. Leo became more animated with the wine. He started talking about going to the nightclub after all. I said that'd be fine. I'd just go to bed.

The phone rang. It was Cynthia. She sounded drunk. 'Come down,' she said, 'it's great.'

'Leo was about to go anyway. I don't know about me though . . .'

'C'mon, I'm bored.'

'Okay, then. We'll be there in a while.'

Leo and I decided we'd walk. The city was only about twenty minutes away by foot, but it was a mistake. Leo walked fast, and between the asthma and the alcohol, I was labouring.

'I might try and pick someone up tonight,' Leo said. We were about halfway there.

'What about Molly?'

'Oh, she'd cope. We've been going out for a long time, after all.'

'What, four months?'

'Well, you know how it is.'

I didn't. Four months didn't sound very long, but it was longer than I'd ever lasted with anyone. Anyone since Rachel, at least. And that didn't seem to count. As for Cynthia, there was no point wondering about the future. It'd come on its own.

We walked on. I was in serious trouble by the time we arrived. Breathless and sick. I needed to sit down. We paid four dollars at the door, and went upstairs. I didn't go to nightclubs often. I didn't like dancing, the drinks were expensive and the noise was constant. But I had been to this particular place before. It was a small, wedge-shaped room. There were cages on the walls behind which go-go girls sometimes danced. The music was sixties and seventies. It was the theme.

It was crowded when we walked in. Young people mostly, eighteen or nineteen, pale-faced and dressed in black. I felt depressed. I looked around for Cynthia. I couldn't see her. Leo went off to make a sweep of the corners. I reeled over to the bar. There were no seats. The music was very loud. I thought a drink might help. I dug into my pocket. All I had left were a few two-dollar coins. I pulled them out. They spilled from my hand, onto the floor.

'Shit,' I said. I couldn't even hear myself.

I dropped to my knees. There was no light. Legs and feet everywhere. The floor looked black. I began feeling around with my hands. Nothing. I felt like throwing up. Someone tapped me on the shoulder. It was Cynthia.

'What're you doing?' she yelled over the music. She looked as drunk as she'd sounded. Her face had the blank and brutal expression it sometimes got when she drank heavily. She could be frightening then. Singleminded.

'I dropped my money!'

'Forget it! I've got money!'

I stood up.

'Come to the toilets,' she yelled, 'and fuck me!'

'What?!'

'C'mon, let's go fuck!'

I remembered what the toilets were like. Small and shit-stained and jammed with people.

'No, Cynthia! Not now! I can't! I feel sick!'

Her eyes were unfocused. She wasn't even considering the possibility that I might refuse. 'But all you've gotta do is *sit* there!'

'I wouldn't even be able to get it up! No, really, no!'

She got angry. 'You won't ever do anything different! You're so fucking boring!'

We stood there.

This is great, I thought. This is fun.

She said, 'Do you wanna dance then?'

'No. You know I hate it.'

'Well, fuck you, I'm not gonna just stand here.' She went off through the crowd. I went after and caught her arm.

'Can I have some money?'

She looked at me. This is it, I thought, she's gonna hit me and it's gonna *hurt*. But then she went through her bag

111

and handed me five dollars. It was enough for two cans of beer. I went back to the bar, bought myself one, then threaded my way over to the wall and found a vacant window sill. I sat down and looked out and gulped in fresh air. After a while I began to feel a little better. Unwell, but tolerable.

I tasted the beer. It went down okay, which it often didn't, after wine. I shifted around and checked out the club. Everyone looked as bad as I felt. I spotted Cynthia. She was dancing with a long-haired boy in tight black jeans. They shouted words in each other's ear from time to time. I'd never seen Cynthia dance before. It was violent and impressive. The boy was watching. He was more or less just standing there, watching.

I started thinking about her life before she'd met me. I hadn't considered it as a real thing until this point, seeing her with someone else. And there'd been — at a guess — over twenty men before me, two of them serious. What was it she saw in them? What was it she saw in me? Was I any different? Was I *that* different?

Leo came wandering by. I caught his eye and waved him over. I wanted to talk to someone.

'Where's Molly?' I yelled.

'She's around. Where's Cynthia?'

'Dancing!' I pointed her out.

He shrugged. 'I gotta go. I'm looking for someone.' He headed off. I sat and watched and drank. Cynthia had disappeared. I finished the first beer, went and bought the second, then went back to the window sill. I was looking at the women. Most of them seemed unattached. Young. Some of them looked at me. I wondered what sort of image I made, sitting there. I felt old and badly dressed. At twenty-three. It was going to be a long life.

A woman was leaning on the wall beside me. She was

older than me, long black hair, thin white face. She was watching the dance floor, her eyes half closed.

I nursed my beer and thought about talking to her. There didn't seem much reason. I had nothing to say.

She leaned over to me and said something. I didn't catch it. I tilted my ear to her mouth. She said, 'Things can't be that bad.'

That was how I looked, then.

'They might be,' I said.

'You wanna dance?'

'I don't dance.'

'Then what are you doing here?'

'I don't know.'

She leaned back against the wall.

Where could you go from there? After a while she walked away. I finished the second beer and waited. I thought I might try vomiting.

Cynthia appeared. She was sweating. 'Having fun?'

'Who was that you were dancing with?'

'Just some guy. C'mon, let's go home. If you won't do it here, maybe you'll fuck me in bed.'

I thought of the long walk home. I knew I wouldn't make it. 'Let's get a taxi.'

'I don't care.'

We went downstairs into the street. We were out of the noise. My ears were ringing. There weren't any cabs. And there were a lot of other people around, waiting. We started walking, watching the street just in case.

Cynthia was still going on about sex. 'We'll go home. I'll lie down and spread my legs. You'll start pumping away. It'll be so fucking dull.'

Fine, I thought. Really fucking fine.

I spotted a cab coming towards us with its light on. I yelled and ran to the kerb, waving my arm. The driver saw me. He swerved over to pick us up. I opened the front door. Then from nowhere someone darted under my arm and into the front seat. It was a kid of seventeen or eighteen. His head was shaven. 'Thanks, man!' He pulled the door closed.

I stared at him for a second, amazed. Then I lost it. 'You prick,' I said. I grabbed his arm. 'You fucking *prick*.'

'Hey . . .' He tugged at my hand. 'Fuck off, man. I got the cab.'

The taxi started moving. I held onto his arm. 'Get the fuck out, get the fuck *out*.' I pulled the handle and the door fell open. I yanked him out onto the footpath. He went down. I kicked, caught him on the leg. He back-pedalled away. I went after him. I was screaming. 'What the fuck's wrong with you?'

He got up. 'What's wrong with me? What's wrong with *me*? Jesus, take the fucking the cab . . .'

I nodded. He was right. This was pathetic. 'C'mon,' I said to Cynthia. I sat in the front seat. Cynthia got in the back. The cab pulled out and moved.

'Sorry about that,' I said to the driver, after a while.

'No worries. The little shit had it coming. You're the one I was stopping for.'

'Yeah.'

Not that it had stopped him driving off with the wrong passenger.

Still, I felt better. Not quite so ill, not quite so pissed off with the world. There was only so much, after all, that you could take in one night. And in my case, maybe it wasn't so much at all.

We drove home in silence. Cynthia paid the bill and we got out. The taxi drove away. We stood there for a moment.

Cynthia was looking at me. 'I've never seen you get angry before.'

'I know. It just happened.'

114

She stepped in close, put her arms around me. 'It's got me all excited. I thought you were going to kill him.'

I shook my head. I couldn't believe her.

'You would've liked that?'

'You *bet*.'

So that was all it took.

We went up to the flat and we fucked and it was good.

'It was weird, you know,' she said, 'seeing you like that.'

'I don't often do it. I'm no good with anger. I get embarrassed.'

'I think sometimes it's like crying. Women cry to relieve tension, and sometimes they get angry, but men never cry, men just get violent. It's socialisation.'

'That doesn't justify anything, even if it's true.'

'I know. I'm sorry about before, about going to the toilets.'

'I only said no because I was sick.'

'I know.'

We lay there.

Then she said, 'Don't ever get angry like that with me. I don't wanna see it. You're *ugly* when you're mad.'

'I won't,' I said. 'I swear.'

I kissed her.

I was making a lot of promises.

SEVENTEEN

The weekend passed. On Wednesday night we went back to the Story Bridge Hotel. It was poetry night. There was a stage set up in the bar and anyone who felt so inclined could get up and read or recite their works. There were always plenty of takers. I'd been to the poetry night maybe seven or eight times by then, and had heard maybe two or three decent poems in all the time. Generally it was terrible.

It didn't matter. The crowd liked a victim. And for my part, it was good to know I wasn't any worse at it than anyone else. I'd never got up there myself of course. I wasn't a good speaker. I stuttered, spoke way too fast, lost track of my sentences. And then there were the poems themselves. I didn't read them aloud. I told myself they were written for the page.

But the crowd this particular Wednesday night was small and indifferent to the poets. Everyone was talking, drinking, wishing there was some music playing instead. Cynthia and I, and Leo and Molly and Rachel, were camped down one end of a table, ignoring the poets along with everyone else.

It was a bad time for Rachel. She was in the middle of exams at uni. She was getting ready to fail. I was the one who'd invited her. I'd called her up. She'd said 'Gordon! I didn't expect to hear from *you*.'

But I'd been thinking about her.

I was fifteen when I left Dalby, left her. I was being sent to a boarding school in Brisbane. I'd already been in love with Rachel for two years by then. A terrible, confused, adolescent love. I dreamed of eloping, of taking her away. She held my hand, she said that she cared for me more than anyone else in the world . . . but she wouldn't call it love, and she wouldn't come away with me. When we said goodbye I said, 'Do you think we'll still be together after all this? In ten years time?'

And she said, 'Of course. We'll always be friends.'

'I love you, Rachel.'

'Don't say that, Gordon, please.'

And she was right. Eight years later here we were.

We were talking, at the table, about love.

'Love . . .' Molly was saying, 'y'know, my mother once told me that I'd never know what love was. She said I was too cold. What a thing to say to your daughter.'

I knew very little about love. The word itself seemed vague to the point of meaninglessness. From what I could tell it covered sex and infatuation and obsession. In the early stages of a relationship. Then there was affection, and practicality, convenience, security, tolerance, owner-ship, responsibility, trust, friendship, hatred, danger, hu-miliation, pain, addiction . . .

All of us there at the table had our memories and inter-pretations. And we called them all the same thing. What could we be left with but confusion?

'It's about communication,' said Rachel. 'That's what's

important. You have to understand the other person's perspective. What you mean to them. And what they mean to you.'

And I could see that it was true. It was a typical thing for Rachel to say. And she had her reasons. But I couldn't agree with it. I couldn't feel it. Sometimes it sounded too much like work. A contortion. Where was the grace, where was the natural flow?

Cynthia and I had it. At least for the moment. We'd slid together and it'd fitted. It'd happened in a matter of hours. There'd been no decisions and no questions and no effort. It was barely even up to us. It was just there. A divine treat. A question of fate, not love.

The whole thing with Rachel had been different. There'd been no fate involved there, we'd never fitted together the way Cynthia and I did, but I'd still been *in love* with Rachel all those years. And I'd worked at it, tried to break through, but I'd never known why. I had no idea what that love meant, or where it came from. And it hadn't mattered to me that I didn't know.

Rachel, in any case, hadn't felt the same way about me. But even if she had, she would've wanted to know why. It was the way she was. And she would've wanted to know why I didn't know why. And I wouldn't have known. And that would've been it. It would've killed things between us. And if I had worked it out, that would've killed it too.

Because maybe it *could* be worked out.

And what was life, after all, without the mystery ?

The conversation rolled on. I lost interest. It was fine to know you were right, not worrying about what love meant, but it was no good being right and being alone. People insisted on expectations. Not that I was alone. I got up and went to the bar for another beer.

I was drunk. I was worried. Seeing Rachel again was affecting me badly. It was all coming back. Stay away from

Rachel, I told myself. It'd fuck me. It'd fuck her. And then there was Cynthia. *Cynthia.*

I took my beer and wandered into the next room. I was getting depressed. It was no time for listening to the poets. The next room had a pool table, another bar, and a much bigger crowd. It was mostly men. No one was playing pool. They were all watching the TV that hung above the bar. I found a seat, sat down, and looked up.

The TV wasn't on a regular station. It was Sky TV and tonight there was a talent show called 'Best Chest in the U.S.'. I picked up the format after a few minutes. There were six categories in which a woman could compete, based on the size of her breasts. The first heat was for the smaller women, then the categories went up by bra sizes, until up in the sixth it was for the 38Ds and above. Or something like that. I knew nothing about bra sizes. I only knew that the breasts got larger and larger as the show progressed. There were six entrants in each category. It was held before a live studio audience, with a panel of judges. Each contestant had about twenty seconds to get on stage, dance around, and rip off her top. Then the judges gave a score.

The crowd in the bar loved it. They whooped and roared. They grew frantic as the tits got bigger. Every face was staring up. They were howling at the women.

'I love you baby,' they screamed. 'I LOVE YOU!'

EIGHTEEN

My parents still lived on the family farm. It was nearly three hours west of Brisbane, ten miles from Dalby. I went out there for a few days every six weeks or so. The next time it came up, I asked Cynthia if she wanted to go. She said she didn't. She was working seven days straight at the time. It was getting near Christmas, the pub was busy.

'Okay, I'll go myself.'
'But I don't want you to go.'
'It'll only be for a few days.'
'I don't want to be alone. What'll I do?'
'You'll be working.'
'I don't want you to go!'
'You're not being reasonable, you won't even notice I'm gone . . .'
'I'll *notice*.'
I went.

The Buchanan farm was six hundred and sixty acres of black soil cultivation. It was almost perfectly square, perfectly flat and perfectly treeless. No hills, no creeks, no

120

scrub. Just dirt. All the other farms around were the same. I liked it. You walked out the back door and there was almost nothing to see, no matter which way you looked. Except for in the east. There was a range of high hills on the horizon. They were faded blue. Remote. I'd spent a long period of my life staring out at them. It was a hopeless thing. Rachel, and her parents' farm, lay just on the other side.

I lazed around the house for a couple of days. Twelve of us had lived there at one stage. Now there were just my parents and me. It was quiet. The food was good.

I rang the flat a couple of times. There was no answer.

I drove into Dalby and walked up and down the main street. I didn't recognise anyone and no one recognised me. I hadn't really lived there for seven or eight years. I had a beer in one of the pubs. I was the only one in the bar. The old woman behind the counter watched me drink. I left. I got back in the car and drove back to the farm.

I rang Cynthia. This time she answered.

'It's me,' I said. 'I'll be home tomorrow.'

'Good for you.'

'How's it been?'

'What d'you care.'

Then she hung up.

I arrived back in Brisbane about two the next afternoon and went straight to the flat. Both the rooms were shut up and hot. Cynthia was lying in bed, face deep in the pillow. I sat down beside her.

'Cynthia, I'm home.'

'I'm not asleep.'

She rolled over and sat up. She wouldn't look at me. Her face was puffy and scratched. She looked ill. She'd been crying.

'You okay?' I said.

She nodded and lit herself a cigarette. Then she folded her arms across her chest and stared at the foot of the bed. Really stared. It was something crazy people did.

'So did you do anything?' I asked, 'How was work?'

'I didn't go.'

'Cynthia, I'm sorry, but it was only three days.'

She looked at me. 'I don't know *anyone* in Brisbane, Gordon. There's nothing I can do if you're not here. Three days is a long time to be alone. Work's no good. There's no one I can talk to at work.'

I said nothing.

'I lay here for two days,' she went on, 'listening for cars in the driveway, just in case you decided to come home early.'

'I called . . .'

'I didn't want to *talk* to you. I wanted you here.'

She got up and went off for a shower. I opened all the windows and waited. When she came back she went back to bed. She started crying.

I lay down beside her.

'Cynthia . . .'

'I'm sorry. I don't mean to be such a bitch.'

'It's okay.'

'It's not just that. I lied. I did go to work one night.'

'So?'

'I don't want to tell you this.'

'Tell me what?'

She didn't answer.

I said, 'Did you spend the night with someone?'

She nodded. She was still crying.

'Cynthia, it doesn't matter. I don't care about things like that.'

She lifted her head and looked at me. 'I was just *so* mad at you.'

122

I kissed her. Her face was hot and wet. The little girl face.

'So who was it?'

'Just a guy from the pub. No one you know.'

'Did you enjoy it?'

'It was okay. It was a fuck.'

We lay there. I rolled myself a cigarette. 'Are you gonna do this every time I go away?'

'Don't laugh at me.'

'Look, Cynthia, you're crazier about sex than anyone I've ever even heard of. I'd be a fool to expect you to limit yourself to me.'

'It's not that, it's the *reason* I did it that gets to me. It's so childish.'

'Maybe. But don't kill yourself over it.'

We started kissing. It built up. I slid down to her cunt, parted the lips, and peered in. I thought, a lot of men have lost it in here. And the thought peered back, who had he been?

And what did he have?

Forget it, I told myself.

In went my tongue.

NINETEEN

Next day we received a phone call from Leo. 'I can get hold of some acid,' he said. 'You want some?'

'What's it cost?'

'Twenty-five dollars a tab. You only need the one.'

'Cynthia,' I said, 'Leo can get some acid. You interested?'

She came running in. 'Yes. Yes yes yes.'

'She wants some,' I told Leo, 'so I guess we'll need two.'

He said he'd be over in about an hour.

Cynthia was gleeful, moving round the flat. 'I haven't had a trip in years.'

'He's getting us one tab each. Is that enough?'

'You're sure it was tabs, not microdots?'

'Tabs.'

'Good. Dots are useless. One tab should be okay, as long as the stuff is good.'

'What *is* a tab anyway?'

'You really don't know anything, do you. A tab is a little square of paper that's been soaked in LSD. A microdot is a tiny little pill. Tabs are usually stronger.'

'Wait,' I said, 'this time, we have to get some nitrous.'

'Why?'

'You don't know what it's like Cynthia. This is the one and only drug I can introduce you to.'

I got dressed and drove to the nearest K-mart. There it was. On *special*. Two ninety-nine per box. There were ten little bulbs in a box, ten little trips. I picked up four boxes and took them to the checkout. The checkout boy looked at the boxes.

'Hey,' he said, 'having a party?'

'I'm whipping cream.'

He laughed. 'I've never seen anyone over thirty buy this stuff. Whipped cream my arse.'

I paid the money.

'Y'know what?' he said, 'you can get this stuff in big cylinders if you know where to go.'

'Yeah?'

'Yeah. I've got a brother who races stock cars. They use it in the pits, I'm not sure what for. But this guy in my brother's team just goes along to the chemical companies and buys it by the ton.'

'Thanks. I'll remember that.'

'A whole cylinder, man. Think of it.'

'I will.'

I drove home. On the way I stopped off to get a carton of VB cans. Leo arrived just as we were packing the carton away in the fridge.

'You get it?'

'I got it.'

Molly was with him. Cynthia gave Leo fifty dollars and we all sat down at the table. Leo took out four small packages of foil, and handed us one each. 'Now be careful,' Cynthia said. 'Don't touch the tabs with your fingers.'

We unwrapped the foil. Inside was a small square of paper. I watched Cynthia. She lifted the foil and tipped the paper onto her tongue.

125

'Should I swallow it or suck it?' I asked her.

'I always suck it for a while, but some people say you should just swallow. I don't think it really matters.'

I tipped the tab onto my tongue and held it there long enough to see if there was any taste. There wasn't. I swallowed it. Leo and Molly had already done the same.

We sat there.

'How long will it take?'

'About half an hour,' Cynthia said. 'Drugs like this are great, y'know. No matter what you take, smack or acid or ecstasy, once you've actually taken it you don't have to worry about the day any more. The drug'll handle it for you. You don't have to make any *effort*. It's like handing your life over to someone else for a while.'

'Sounds good to me. The less I have to do with this life, the better . . .'

We waited.

We drank beer and turned on the TV. There was a one-day cricket match on. We watched it. We all liked the cricket. After about twenty minutes the tips of my fingers began to go numb. I looked at my fingers, flexed them, lifted my arm. It felt light, almost weightless. I watched the screen for a few more minutes. The conversation had stopped. The screen seemed brighter than before, the movements of the players more subtle, more profound. Then Cynthia started laughing.

'Oh shit,' she said.

Things got blurred. We watched the cricket, talked, paced around the room, listened to music. My body felt invulnerable, easy and smooth and fast. I didn't have my usual stutter. I talked with style. Real style.

Then my vision was tunnelling. Whatever was directly in front of me was huge and intricate and I understood it completely, but on the peripherals, shadows loomed. It got

126

worse. The room was getting bigger. Our voices echoed around it. The ceiling started moving down. I could hear it breathing. I could see it breathing. 'Come outside,' said Cynthia. I followed her out into the back yard. Trees were exploding from the ground.

'Jesus,' I said, '*look* at that.

'What?'

'The trees, the trees. And oh fuck, the *sky*.'

We sat out there for an hour or so. Then Cynthia said, 'Let's go for a drive.'

We went back inside to get some more beer. Leo and Molly were lying together on the couch. Molly's top was mostly undone. It all looked much better than the last time I'd seen it.

'We're going driving. You wanna come?'

'You kidding?' said Leo.

'Cynthia's driving. It'll be fine. She knows exactly what she's doing.'

Molly shook her head. Leo shrugged.

Cynthia and I went out to the car. Cynthia got behind the wheel. 'Where to?'

'There's a park, I'll give you directions.'

We drove.

'We've gotta fuck on this, sooner or later,' I said

'There's plenty of time.'

My eyes roved. It was late afternoon. There was a huge sunset building in the west. From where I sat, it was looking dangerous. People were running away from it, ducking their heads, making for home.

The park I was aiming for wasn't far. We'd found it and piled out with our beer. A police car cruised past, checked us out, drove on. We climbed up the hill.

And suddenly we were on top of the city. We were alone. On three sides the hill dropped away to nothing. We wandered from view to view, laughing at each other. A couple of kids. Hippie clichés. On the edge of the hill were some swings. The city and the warehouses and the river spread out below us. We started swinging, beers in hand. We got them right up high. The chains shrieked. It was terrifying and good. We swung into the sunset.

'I love you!' Cynthia screamed, way up in the air.

Eventually we stopped swinging.

'What now?' I asked.

'We drive.'

We headed south along the freeway for a while, then swung off east into the suburbs and onwards along the bush roads towards the coast. It was dark by then. The headlights were on. Cynthia picked up speed. Eighty, a hundred, a hundred and twenty, a hundred and forty — it was as fast as the old Kingswood could go. We were on a road that rolled up and down the hills. We bounced along. I stuck my head out the window. Sucked in the air.

Cynthia said, 'Watch this.'

We hit the top of a hill. I could see the road stretching down. Then Cynthia flicked off the lights. She floored the accelerator. We roared down in pitch darkness. I screamed. Cynthia screamed. The car bottomed out and started climbing. Cynthia flicked the lights back on. We were on the wrong side of the road, verging on gravel. Cynthia righted the car and we breasted the hill.

She pounded the wheel. 'This car has *wings*.'

Down we went and out went the lights. This time the road, in the moment I'd seen it, hadn't looked so straight. It curved. It curved ninety degrees.

'Turn the fucking lights on!' I screamed.

Cynthia laughed, a banshee laugh. I looked at the speed. A hundred and fifty.

'TURN THE FUCKING THINGS ON!'

She did it. We were off the road, two wheels in dirt.

'Shit!' said Cynthia. She braked, swung the wheel. The

back slid out. We were spinning. I felt the car tilt, *knew* it would roll. I clutched onto the door. We went round once, twice. We started round again and then it stopped. We were on the road, facing back the way we'd come, clouds of dust billowing past us.

Cynthia was laughing, shrieking. 'Did you see that, did you *see* that!'

I let go of the door.

'You crazy bitch. You crazy fucking bitch.'

'Oh shut up, we're all right.'

'All right?!'

She turned the ignition, hit the accelerator.

By the time we got back to the flat the acid was running down. We went inside. Leo and Molly were smoking, drinking and watching TV. I went into the bedroom. The sheets were all over the place. 'You guys have been fucking in here.'

'So hey . . .' said Leo, 'where've you been?'

'Driving,' said Cynthia.

We all looked at each other.

The problem with going up was coming down.

I remembered the nitrous.

'I've got some nitrous,' I said.

Leo sat up. 'You've got some nitrous?'

'I do. I have some nitrous.'

I brought out the four boxes. I put them on the table. Then I went and found the soda syphon.

It gave us about ten minutes each, off the planet.

TWENTY

Cynthia's period was late.

She liked her periods. She liked the flow. It was smooth, it was deep. It turned her on. When she was a week overdue, she went to the Family Planning clinic in the Valley.

She came back after about twenty minutes. 'I couldn't see anyone today. They made me an appointment for tomorrow. I made one for you too.'

'For me?'

She handed me a leaflet. And there it was, in big bold letters. PREMATURE EJACULATION. I looked at it.

I said, 'Do you think they could do anything?'

'It couldn't hurt.'

'No. It couldn't.'

I read it through.

'Right,' I said, 'get undressed.'

'Now?'

'Now.'

We were on the floor. I was on top. I moved in.

'One,' I said. 'Two. Three. Four.'

'*Gordon.*'

'Five. Six. Seven. Eight.'

'What are you doing?'

'I'm counting the thrusts. The doctors will need some numbers. They can't help me without information. Nine. Ten. Eleven.'

'You can't count! You can't count and fuck. It's evil.'

'*Sex* is evil. Twelve. Thirteen. Fourteen.'

'You bastard. You won't make it past fifty.'

'Fifteen. Sixteen. Seventeen.'

'You won't make it past forty!'

'I'll make to one hundred. I'll make it to one hundred and twenty.'

'Bullshit.'

'Eighteen! Nineteen! Twenty!'

She was pumping back. 'You're gonna come! You're *hopeless*. You're not even gonna make it to thirty!'

I pumped back. 'TWENTY-ONE! TWENTY-TWO!'

'C'mon, fuck me, fuck me.'

'TWENTY-THREE! TWENTY-FOUR!'

'You're losing it, I can feel it.'

'Bullshit. You're losing it. You're gonna come first.'

'No chance.'

'You can't help it. You can't stop yourself. Thirty. Thirty-one. Thirty-two.'

We ground away. I lifted her legs up around my neck. I leaned forward. I was driving straight down. Nudging her bowels. 'Thirty-nine. Forty. Forty-one. Forty-two.' I was in control. I had her. My prick was working for once.

'FIFTY. FIFTY-ONE.'

'You bastard, you bastard . . .'

'SIXTY!

'SEVENTY!'

'EIGHTY!'

'NINETY!'

Cynthia threw her head back on the linoleum. 'Oh *fuck* you.' She drove it in. She was coming. I slammed out the last ones.

'ONE HUNDRED AND NINE! ONE HUNDRED AND TEN!'

'Stop!'

'No.'

'I've come! I've finished!'

'No. One hundred and eleven. One hundred and twelve.'

'It hurts . . .'

'I don't care.'

'Fuck. *Fuck.*'

'You're gonna do it again, you're gonna do it again before I do.'

'Try it.'

'I'm gonna make two hundred. I'm gonna make three hundred.'

I ground and sweated and pumped. I could feel it building. Cynthia was past the pain, she was grinding back. Her teeth were bared. She was snarling at me. It built and built and built. And then it was there.

'ONE HUNDRED AND EIGHTY FUCKING FIVE!'

TWENTY-ONE

We sat in the Family Planning waiting room, holding hands. I was the only man there. The women looked at me. Looked at Cynthia. Back to me. The air was hostile. What've you *done* to her?

Cynthia was called first. I sat there alone in enemy territory. Then I was called. The doctor ushered me in. She took down my name and particulars, then asked me what the problem was.

'I'm coming too fast.'

'I see. Exactly how fast do you mean? Before penetration?'

'No, but not all that long afterwards.'

'Could you say exactly how long?'

'Well, we counted it yesterday. It wasn't a very good indication. It went on for a hundred and eighty thrusts . . . but I'd say usually it's about half that. Or less than half, maybe a third.'

Thrusts? What was I doing, talking about *thrusts*? This was ludicrous.

She wrote it down. 'A third, you say. And it's usually like that?'

133

'Well, often enough to be annoying. Sometimes it's better the second or third time. And sometimes it's not a problem at all. Especially if I've been drinking. That tends to slow things down.'

'Mmm. So you drink, do you? How often would you say you drank?'

'Oh, three or four nights a week.'

'And you get drunk on these nights?'

'It depends. Mostly, I suppose.'

'Do you think you'd have more than forty-five drinks a week?'

'Probably.'

'You realise that's considered heavy drinking?'

'I suppose so.'

'Why do you drink?'

'I enjoy it.'

'Do you need it to socialise?'

'I enjoy socialising more if I'm drinking.'

'Why's that?'

'It's just more fun. But like I said, I don't come that fast when I'm drunk.'

She nodded. 'The level of your drinking could become a problem, you know. Does your partner drink as much as you do?'

'More or less.'

'Well, you both could have problems.'

We looked at each other.

'So what do you think I should do about coming?'

She sighed. 'Well, it doesn't sound that severe, but if you want, you can enrol in a programme we have. We'll teach you ways of developing control through manipulation of breathing, better understanding of your own reactions, co-operative movements from your partner and so forth. The course we run is for couples, so your partner would have to come along as well. You can sign on at the desk.'

134

'That's it?'
'Cut down on the drinking.'
'I'll think about it.'

I went back into the waiting room. Cynthia wasn't there.
I waited for a while then wandered out onto the street. I
saw a newsagent up on the corner. I walked up and bought
a paper. I browsed through the magazines. I saw Cynthia
coming and went out.
'There you are,' she said.
'How'd it go? Are you pregnant?'
'Nothing. The test was negative. But they're not sure
why my period is so late.'
'But you're definitely not pregnant?'
'They said if it didn't come within the next week to go
back for another test. Sometimes pregnancy doesn't show
up on the first test.'
'Well, we should celebrate.'
We started walking back to the car. Cynthia said, 'How
did things go with you?'
'I'm not sure. The doctor didn't seem to care much about
my ejaculations. She just wanted to know about my
drinking.'
'Your drinking?'
'She said we were drinking too much.'
'We don't drink that much. We're not professionals, that's
for sure. What did she say about fucking?'
'She didn't say anything, just that we could join a train-
ing programme if we wanted to. It's for couples. You'd have
to come along too.'
'Oh.'
'Not interested?'
'No. Fuck it. You'll do.'

TWENTY-TWO

A week went by. It was now only a few days to Christmas. Cynthia was working almost every day at the Queen's Arms. Christmas parties. She collected big tips. We drank them away.

I was planning on spending most of Christmas Day with the family. I invited Cynthia along. She said no. She was working late on Christmas Eve and all day on Boxing Day. She planned to spend Christmas Day in bed. I went shopping and bought her a Christmas present. I got two books. Elias Canetti's *Auto da Fe*, and Russell Hoban's *Riddley Walker*. I'd already read them, but I'd lost my own copies.

Cynthia's period did not arrive.

'I can't be pregnant,' she said. 'I'd know. I'd *feel* pregnant. Something must be wrong. I bet it's cancer. Cervical cancer. All that fucking around when I was a kid.'

'Which would you prefer? Pregnancy or cancer?'

'Christ. What sort of question is that?'

On the last working day before Christmas, we went back to Family Planning. This time Cynthia went in alone. I waited in the car.

Half an hour went by. I got out of the car, walked up to the newsagent, bought a newspaper, went back to the car and read it through. Now it was an hour. I was parked beside a boarding house. I watched an old man walk back and forth along the verandah. He had a wet butterfly-shaped stain on the front of his pants.

I thought about bowel cancer. There were three doctors in my family. I'd heard a lot about it. Then I remembered that during birth, a woman shits all over the place. Her anus could dilate to the size of a cricket ball. Not to mention what her cunt is going through. I thought about tearing. About the vagina and the anus ripping open into one huge crevasse. I rolled a cigarette. The time passed.

Then Cynthia appeared. She was walking down towards me. I tried to read her expression. It didn't seem bad, it didn't seem good. I leaned over and unlocked the passenger door. She opened it.

'How'd it go?'

'Six weeks pregnant,' she said. 'I'm due in July.'

She got in, closed the door. We drove home.

We went to bed and fucked.

Then we lay there, smoking.

'So what'll we do?' I said.

'I don't know. They gave me the number of Children by Choice, if I want an abortion.'

Abortions, technically, were not available on demand in Queensland. The legislation was loose, though — if the mother was deemed to be in any physical or emotional danger from the baby, she could go ahead with a termination. I knew there was at least one abortion clinic in Brisbane, and another one down across the border in New South Wales.

'What d'you think?' Cynthia asked.

'I don't think I'd be any use to you with a kid.'

137

'Would you leave me if I had the baby?'

'I'm not sure. I'd try not to, but in the long run, I couldn't say. Look at my life, Cynthia. Where would a child fit in?'

She was silent for a while.

Then she said, 'So I have to choose between you and the baby?'

'I don't know. Do *you* want it?'

'In some ways, yes I do.'

Silence.

I was thinking about a poem I'd written when I was fifteen. It was about abortion. I was against it then. I considered abortion to be murder. Legalised murder. And my opinion hadn't changed so much. I still thought that it was legalised murder. But now legalised murder didn't seem so bad. Self-defence was legalised murder. And an abortion seemed like self-defence for Cynthia and me, there in the bed. The baby was innocent, perhaps, but it could still be a killer.

Cynthia got up and went into the next room. I heard her pick up the phone, dial, talk, then hang up. She came back.

'What was that?'

'I called Children by Choice.'

She climbed back into bed. We lay side by side. Our hips and shoulders were touching.

'If I have to choose,' she said, 'I'll take you.'

TWENTY-THREE

On Christmas morning I gave Cynthia the books. She gave me a black shirt and three pairs of red underpants.

'Cynthia, I can't wear these.'

'But you'd look so cute. I hate those things you wear.'

All the underpants I owned were dark blue. I didn't bother with wearing them much anyway.

'I like the shirt, but I am not going to wear these things.'

She sighed. 'I'll wear them. You're no fun at all.'

'Look, would you wear a garter belt and stockings if I bought them for you?'

'Of course I would.'

'Bullshit.'

'You never *would* buy me garter belts and stockings.'

'No, that's very true.'

She looked at me. 'It would've been a nice kid, you know, between you and me. It would've had your skin.'

'Somehow I think your genes would've dominated.'

'It would've been nice, all the same.'

'You can still have it, y'know.'

'No. It's funny, though. I was so sure I'd be infertile. It's good to know I can at least have kids when I want them.'

We ate breakfast. Then I went off to be with the family. Cynthia went back to bed.

The family was gathering at the house of one of my brothers and his wife. Everyone was there. My parents, the ten original children, the six in-laws, the two prospective in-laws, and the sixteen grandchildren. Presents were exchanged. Unwrapped. Then it was into the champagne and beer. It was good. Everyone got along. We'd done pretty well to manage that, considering.

And then, after a long lunch, we removed ourselves to a nearby park to play cricket. Cricket was always a serious thing with the family. The teams went along hereditary lines. The ten Buchanan children formed a team called the Originals. The eight in-laws formed a team called the Outlaws. And the four grandchildren who were old enough to hold a bat formed a mercenary squad called the By-products. Three of them served with the Outlaws. The fourth partnered with the Originals to make up the eleven.

The Originals won the toss and elected to bowl. I wandered out to deep mid-off and found a tree to sit under. I had beer, and my pouch of tobacco. I sat down. I looked at the sun and waited.

'Gordon, are you ready out there?'

'I'm ready! I'm *keen!*'

Not that it mattered. Nothing came my way all afternoon. I bowled a few overs. Drank beer. Watched the wickets tumble. The Outlaws were all out for seventy-nine. Then it was our turn.

We started badly. By the time I fronted up we were four for twenty-seven. The light was in decline. My partner and I conferred mid-wicket. It was my younger brother Michael. Our last recognised batsman. He actually played club cricket occasionally, but only in the lower grades, and even then

140

as a bowler. And not a very good bowler. Still, he was all we had left.

'Farm the strike,' he told me.

I faced up. I was drunk. Everyone was. At least one of the milder in-laws was bowling. His first ball to me was gentle. I danced up. I swung. I missed. The keeper missed. The ball trickled away.

'Run!' Michael screamed.

We swerved down the pitch. One of the slips fielded. Threw. Missed. The ball scooted away to the boundary. Four overthrows. Five runs. I picked up my beer from behind the stumps. Not so bad, I thought, for a number six.

We conferred mid-wicket.

Michael looked at me closely. 'That was pathetic.'

'I know.' I drank from my beer. 'So now what?'

'Okay. Here's the plan. We don't take singles. Just run when I tell you.'

'That sounds fine.'

We returned to our respective ends.

Of the next thirty runs scored, I was responsible for four. Then Michael edged one to second slip and it was five for sixty-two. The next man in was Louise. The pathologist.

We conferred mid-wicket.

'Farm the strike,' I told her.

We were all out for sixty-seven.

An hour later I called Cynthia.

'I'm drunk,' I said. 'Do you wanna get a cab over here?'

'You said you wouldn't drink too much.'

'But we played cricket.'

'Okay. I understand. I'll be over.'

She was there not long afterwards. She had a couple of beers, played with some of the younger grandchildren, then looked at me.

141

'We should go.'

'Okay.'

On the way home she started crying.

'What's wrong?'

'You're so fucking lucky, having a family like that.'

'I know. It can be a bit much sometimes, but still, I know.'

'I wish I was in Darwin. I rang Mum and Dad before. They were having lunch with some friends. They were happy.'

'I'm sorry. I really am.'

She drove in silence for a while.

Then she said, 'Has anyone in your family had an abortion?'

'I don't know. Someone might have. I wouldn't necessarily be told about it.'

'Are you going to tell them about ours?'

'No. What about you and your parents?'

'Christ, no.'

We got home, cooked spaghetti for dinner, and watched TV.

Cynthia said, 'I didn't get any sleep today. I started reading *Auto da Fe* and couldn't stop. He does terrible things to the reader.'

'Wait until you get to the end.'

'I don't think I want to. I've cried enough already.'

I couldn't stay awake. The day's drinking was catching up. I went to bed.

Cynthia came in some time later and woke me up. I looked at the clock. Three hours had gone by.

'What've you been doing?'

'Watching TV,' she said, 'I've been watching the Christmas specials.'

TWENTY-FOUR

We were lying in bed. It was late afternoon.

Cynthia had visited Children by Choice. The abortion was booked for the first working day after New Year's. The Tweed Heads Clinic. In the morning, ten thirty. We'd have to be on the road by nine to make it.

We were reading the leaflets CBC had given her. She would be having a general anaesthetic. It would be her first time.

'What if I die?'

'You won't die.'

'But people do, all the time.'

'You'll be okay . . .'

'And look, I can't eat the night before. I can't even smoke. How the fuck can I not smoke?'

'It'll be bad, Cynthia, I understand that.'

'And no sex for two weeks afterwards!'

'You'll hardly feel like it, surely.'

She looked down at me.

'Well,' I said.

I was lying with my head on her stomach. There was a foetus just inches away from my ear.

It's tough, I thought.

Cynthia was still looking down. 'Oh God . . . they're gonna scrape the poor little bastard out.'

She gripped my head and forced it down into her belly.

I was trying not to think about it.

The phone rang. Cynthia got it. 'It's someone called Maree,' she told me.

I looked at her. She was holding the phone to her naked, pregnant belly. I got up and took it.

'Maree?'

'Hello, Gordon. How've you been?'

'Good. Good. What's up?'

'What're you doing for New Year's?'

'Nothing yet. Why?'

'We're having a party at the beachhouse, New Year's Eve, if you're interested. Cynthia too. Was that her who answered?'

'That was her.'

'I'd like to meet her. You can sleep over if you want. There's plenty of beds.'

'You feel like a New Year's Eve party?' I said to Cynthia.

'Whose?'

'Maree and Frank's. Friends of mine. It's at the coast. Down at Broadbeach.'

'That sounds okay.'

'Okay,' I told Maree, 'we'll be there.'

She gave me the details.

I climbed back into bed with Cynthia. 'You sure you're okay to go to something like this?'

'Yeah. I mean, what the fuck. It doesn't matter what I do, if I'm getting rid of it anyway.'

I nodded.

She said, 'So who are Frank and Maree?'

'I knew them at uni. Those two and Leo and Rachel and me, we all hung round together. I had a thing with Maree

144

for a while. She was a lot older than the rest of us, about ten years older. I was very impressed. We slept together a few times. But then she was in love with Frank and Frank was a friend of mine . . .'

'It got complicated?'

'It got complicated.'

TWENTY-FIVE

New Year's Eve. We'd had trouble getting organised. By the time we left Brisbane it was already ten thirty. Leo and Molly were with us. Leo and I in the front, Molly and Cynthia in the back. There was a carton of beer back there as well, a four litre cask of wine, a bottle of bourbon, some Coca-Cola and four tabs of acid. It seemed like enough.

By the time we finally made it to the beachhouse it was twenty minutes to midnight. The first person I met walking in was Rachel. She was drunk.

'Gordon!' she screamed. 'Where've you been?'

'Delayed.'

'I'm drunk.'

'I can tell.'

'I'm so fucking drunk.'

'How's the party going?'

'Oh it's going just great.'

There were maybe forty or fifty people there. Some older, Maree's friends. Some younger, Frank's friends. We organised a place for our drinks. I found Frank and Maree and introduced them to Cynthia.

'You're too late,' said Maree. 'The party is already dying.'
'But it's not even midnight yet. And we've got acid.'
'When are you going to take it?'
'Soon.'

There was beer and bourbon in the meantime. I wandered out onto the verandah. The beach was there. The wind and the surf were up. There were bonfires here and there. Other parties.

Maree appeared at my side. She was swaying and staring at me.

'So what've you been drinking?' I asked her.

She smiled. 'Vodka.' She tossed her head. Laughed.

She was always dangerous on vodka.

Then it was midnight. People started counting down the last ten seconds. I didn't count or yell. I looked at Maree, she looked at me. 'Happy New Year, Gordon,' she said. She leaned over and kissed me. 'Come outside.'

I followed her out. I couldn't see Cynthia. Or Molly. Or Leo. Or Frank. Maree and I wandered down along the beach. We passed the fires, made it into the half-light. Maree lay down in the sand. I lay down beside her.

'So how've you been, Gordon, really?'

'Good. Really.'

'You're still very special to me, y'know.'

'You are to me too.'

I rolled on to my side and looked at her. She was looking back. Her body was outlined against the fires. I remembered her body. Her breasts. They were large and freckled, with two or three thick red hairs around the nipple. Mother's breasts. But things had changed. I felt much older. My heart wasn't there for Maree any more. I was thinking about Cynthia. I was thinking about Rachel. I wondered what they were doing. Who they were with.

Maree said, 'What a year, what a fucking year.'

147

I didn't know what she meant.

'How've *you* been?' I asked.

'I think things might be over between Frank and me.'

'Really? Why?'

'I don't know. Maybe he's outgrown me. It was always going to be like that, I suppose.'

We lay there. The sounds of various parties drifted down.

'You love Cynthia, don't you?'

'I think so.'

'What about Rachel?'

'Indeed. What about Rachel?'

'I think she's having second thoughts about you.'

'That's the last thing I need to hear.'

After a while we got up and went back to the party. People were already going home or crashing in the bedrooms. Maree said she was going to bed. I'd forgotten my tobacco. I went out to the car to find it, and ran into Rachel. She was wandering up and down the street. She clung to me.

'Help me,' she said, 'I don't know what I'm doing.'

'Do you think you should go to bed?'

'Yes. Please.'

I took her back into the house, found her a bed and lay her down in it. I almost kissed her, stopped myself, left. Then I went into the kitchen. Frank and Leo and Cynthia and Molly were seated round the table. They were already half-way through the bourbon. I sat down next to Cynthia.

'What about this acid?' I said.

Leo brought out the tabs. We gulped them down with the bourbon. It was almost one in the morning and there were only a dozen people left, other than ourselves.

We had half an hour to wait. Cynthia and I went for a walk along the beach.

'You were out here with Maree tonight, weren't you?'

'Just for a walk.'

'Sure. Look, Gordon, I don't care anyway, not tonight. Fuck who you want.'

'I'm not going to fuck anyone.'

She shook her head, looked at me. 'You can't even cheat on me properly.'

We went back inside to the kitchen. The bourbon and the acid were starting to work. The kitchen began to swell, expand. Leo and I retired to a corner, laughing at each other. I lost track of everyone else. Suddenly a woman was there. It was Sophie. Another one from my university days.

'Sophie,' I said, 'I didn't know you were here.'

'I just arrived.'

She sat on my lap. Her face was flushed and sweating. It looked like mine felt.

'I'm on acid,' I said.

'I'm on ecstasy. It's better.'

'I've never tried it.'

'You should.'

She stroked my neck.

'Come outside,' she said.

'Why?'

Leo watched us.

'I want you to fuck me,' Sophie whispered.

'What?'

'I want you to *fuck* me. Wouldn't you like that?'

'No . . .'

She sighed. 'You're so boring.'

'So I keep hearing.'

'Well then, I'm going to dance!'

She was big and uncoordinated. There were other people dancing too. I hadn't even noticed. Leo got up and started dancing with Sophie. He grabbed her, tried to kiss her. She swung away.

Jesus, I thought.

149

I got up and started looking for Cynthia. It took me a long time. The acid slowed me down. I went from room to room. There were bodies sleeping all over the place. I went out onto the verandah. There was no one there. I looked over the edge. The whole beach seemed to be writhing. Bodies everywhere. There were two, quite close. On a blanket. I stared. I was hallucinating. There was no one there. Then there was someone there. They were naked. Entangled, half wrapped in clothes or rags or a sheet. I couldn't tell. I couldn't see. I decided it was Cynthia and Molly. It made sense. I leaned further over the railing. I felt like I was falling towards them.

'Gordon . . .'

It was Sophie. Leo was with her. His arm was around her shoulder. He had to reach up to get it there.

'I'm heading off,' she said. 'There's other parties.'

Leo looked up at her. 'You want me to come with you?'

She looked down at him. 'I'll be fine.'

Leo removed his arm. She disappeared. I heard noises coming from behind me, down in the sand.

'C'mon, Leo,' I said. 'Let's go for a walk.'

We went back through the kitchen, collected the bourbon and some of the beer, then went on into the yard. We stumbled around for while, looking for a way through the fence. 'Where's the fucking gate?' screamed Leo.

We panicked. It was the acid. We ran back and forth. We couldn't find the gate. We were stuck there. We'd never get out.

Then suddenly we were through. We plunged down onto the beach, to the water. It was black. Thunderous. We were terrified.

'Don't fucking leave me here, Buchanan.'

'We're lost. We're doomed.'

We stopped and pulled from the bourbon bottle.

I told Leo what I'd seen from the verandah.

'No fucking suprise there,' he said.

'No. No fucking suprise.'

We went on. We found a deserted stretch and sat on the sand. We lit up cigarettes, swilled the bourbon and struggled to keep rational. The hours passed. We finished the bourbon and the beer. Things went from black to grey. The wind was still driving in. Dawn was about an hour away. The horizon was piled with storm clouds. They glowed. Golden.

'This is amazing,' I said. 'We've gotta show someone else.'

We ran back up to the house. We looked for Cynthia and Molly. There was only the blanket lying there. Maybe it hadn't even happened. I went inside and started searching through the bedrooms. I came across Rachel.

'Rachel,' I said, shaking her, 'Rachel.'

She woke up. 'Gordon?'

'Come outside. You've gotta see this.'

'But it's cold.'

'Come on.'

She got up and followed me onto the verandah. It was all still there. She hugged her arms around herself. 'Beautiful,' she said. 'Can I go back to bed now?'

'Rachel!'

'I'm tired, Gordon. It really is beautiful, and I appreciate the thought of you waking me up, but I'm going back to bed.'

I wandered back out into the yard. No one was around. I sat down on the blanket. The light grew. The clouds were dazzling towers. The sun rose behind them.

Some time later Cynthia and Molly came walking back along the sand. 'Did you see that sunrise?' Cynthia yelled.

'I saw it.'

'You seen Leo?' Molly asked.

'I think he's inside somewhere.'

She went on up to the house. Cynthia sat down beside me.

'So. Did you get to stick it in last night?'

'No.' I put my arm around her. The acid was in decline. I felt very drunk and very tired. 'Of course it went better for you.'

'Of course.'

'I saw you, y'know.'

'I know you did.'

'I thought I was hallucinating.'

I gathered the blanket around us. We held hands.

The world brightened, lost its mystery. The sun emerged above the clouds. People began moving about in the house behind us.

We got up, brushed the sand off the blanket.

Then we went inside.

Cynthia went off to find Leo and Molly. I sat on the verandah. Frank came out. We surveyed the world.

'How's Maree?' I said.

'Pretty sick. She's asleep.'

'She said last night that things might be over between you two.'

'Yes. They might be.'

'Why?'

'I don't know. There doesn't seem to be anything to talk about anymore.'

'Well . . . you have been going out for a long time.'

'Yes. We have.'

Over four years, in fact.

What was there to say.

I met the others at the car. This time Leo and I took the back, Cynthia and Molly took the front. Molly had volunteered to drive. 'Wait a minute,' I said. I ran back inside and looked through the fridge. There was some beer left. I took four cans and went back to the car. 'Here you go,' I said, passing them around.

We drove.

The beer made my stomach inflate like a balloon. By the time we got home I was in pain. We opened up the flat and climbed into bed. Cynthia wanted sex. I wasn't up to it. I ached all over.

'Wasn't Molly enough?' I said.

'It was nice, but we didn't do that much really. She wants to fuck you, I think. She kept asking me what you were like.'

'You're wrong, Cynthia. Not everyone wants to fuck me. Certainly not Molly.'

'Maree, then.'

'That was years ago.'

Cynthia rolled over. I scratched her back for a while. Then we slept.

TWENTY-SIX

Next day was termination day, abortion day. We were up at eight in the morning. I ate some toast and drank some orange juice. Cynthia watched me eat. Her ban on food was in effect. She was still smoking, though.

We were in the car by nine and made our way onto the southern freeway. I was driving. We didn't talk. Cynthia smoked, and lit cigarettes for me when I asked.

'I wish we'd fucked yesterday,' she said, finally.

'Why?'

'I might die today. It would've been our last time.' She started crying. 'I don't wanna die without fucking you one more time.'

I put my hand on her leg.

'I'm sorry, Cynthia. But you won't die.'

'I might,' she whispered. She stared out the window. She looked small and afraid. It was strange. She was a stronger person than me, but she was afraid of more things than I was. Especially of death. I kept my hand on her leg.

We made good time. We crossed the border and followed the map Children by Choice had given us until we found the clinic. We parked. There was still half an hour to go. We sat in the car.

Cynthia said. 'I don't want to do this.'

'You don't have to. We can go back.'

'No, I have to. I just don't want to.'

We got out of the car and walked up to the clinic. In the doorway Cynthia stopped and took off her ring.

'Here.' She handed it to me. 'I'm not supposed to wear any jewellery.'

I took the ring and put it on my little finger.

We went inside. There was a large waiting room and it was full. We went to the desk and Cynthia checked in. The nurse took down a long list of details, then we went and sat down with all the others.

The place was busy. Every fifteen minutes or so one of the women was called. Others emerged from the recovery rooms. They picked up their men, or their friends, or their mothers, and left. Then it was Cynthia's turn

'Goodbye,' she said.

I kissed her The nurse took her away. Then the nurse came back. 'You can wait here, if you want, or you can come back in about an hour and a half.'

I decided I'd go out for a while. I went back to the car, and started up. I could see a hill up behind the town, and what looked like a park on top of it. I drove around until I found a road that took me up there. I parked and walked the last hundred yards up to the top. There was a bench. I sat down. I could see up and down the coast. The day was hot, with big white clouds moving slowly out to sea. It felt like it might storm, later on.

I looked at Cynthia's ring. It would be happening by now. I could see, down below, the building that contained the clinic. I rolled cigarettes and smoked. There was no one else in the park. The time passed.

I drove back down, parked, went into the clinic. I sat,

read magazines and waited. Then a nurse brought Cynthia out. 'Here she is.'

Cynthia didn't look at me.

'Let's go,' she said.

I followed her out. I put my arm around her.

'How'd it go?'

She was lighting a cigarette. 'I dunno. They knocked me out, I woke up. I was crying when I woke up.'

'Does it hurt?'

She shook her head, blew out smoke. 'It just feels empty.'

We got in the car. I said, 'What'll we do now? You could get something to eat, if you wanted.'

'No. Let's go home. I think I'll just go to bed.'

We drove home. The clouds were thinning out. It was turning into a splendid, sunny day.

I opened up the flat. Cynthia went straight to bed and curled up in a ball. I lay down beside her. I rubbed her back.

'Are you okay?'

'It doesn't hurt, but I feel terrible.'

'I'm sorry.'

We stayed there for hours, not talking.

I was still wearing her ring. I took it off, handed it over.

The next couple of days were quiet. We watched TV, drank, ate big meals. Cynthia didn't say much. I did what I could. She seemed to appreciate it. She wasn't in any pain, at least, and the bleeding was light.

Then on the afternoon of the third day she started getting cramps. They only lasted a few minutes, but they came once or twice every half hour. They hurt. We went to a chemist and bought some of the painkillers she used when her periods were bad. She took double doses and they seemed to help. The bleeding got worse.

By next afternoon the cramps were severe. She took huge doses of the painkillers. They didn't work. By ten that night she'd used them all. The cramps were hitting every ten minutes. She was curled up on the bed, holding her belly and crying. I massaged her stomach. The pain kept coming.

About midnight I said, 'There must be *something* that'd help.'

'We could ask a chemist. Do you know any late night chemists?'

I thought I knew of a couple, out in the suburbs. We got in the car and drove. Cynthia doubled up on the way. 'Oh fuck,' she said, 'Fuck fuck fuck!'

We made the chemist. It was closed. I drove to the other one I knew. It was closed too. What was wrong with this town? We'd been in the car for half an hour. Cynthia was curled against the door.

I found a phone booth and looked up chemists in the book. I rang five or six of them that were listed as late night. None of them were open.

'Jesus fucking *Christ!*'

I rang a hospital. I said, 'My girlfriend had an abortion a few days ago, and now she's having bad cramps. They're really hurting her. Could we get anything for it?'

'We couldn't just hand out medication. We'd have to examine her, and if she was bad enough we might admit her . . .'

'Hang on.' I ran back to the car. Cynthia was breathing hard. I said, 'I can't find a chemist. I rang the hospital. They'll examine you, if you want.'

'No. I don't wanna go near a fucking hospital. I'll be all right. Just take me home.'

I went back to the phone. 'She doesn't want to come in. Are you sure we couldn't just get something for the pain?'

'I'm sorry, not unless we can examine her . . .'

'Well do you know of any late night chemists that'd be open?'

'Gee, at this hour, I don't think so.'

I hung up. *Damn* Brisbane.

We drove home. I stopped at a Seven Eleven and bought some Panadol. Cynthia took six of them and went back to bed. The cramps continued. I kneaded her stomach. She was tiring, half delirious. It was hot. We were lying naked on the bed. Cynthia wasn't wearing any sort of pad. There were blood stains on the sheet. The latest set of cramps hit. She curled up.

'Help me,' she said. *'Fuck me.'*

'I can't.'

She grabbed my prick and pumped it with her fingers. *'Fuck me.'*

'You know I can't.'

'I don't *care*.'

She started sucking me, jamming her mouth up and down. She rubbed her cunt against my legs. I didn't know what to do. She was mad with pain and exhaustion.

She slid off me, rolled onto her stomach.

'Fuck my arse,' she said.

'Cynthia . . .'

'It's better than nothing!' She was crying. 'Please.'

I sat up between her legs. She reached behind and grabbed my penis, pulled it towards her.

'Put it in. Put it in *now*.'

I was hard. I nudged it against the hole, pushed. There was no lubrication. We needed time. We needed the K-Y.

'Oh *fuck*,' she hissed. It was hurting her.

I pulled away.

'No! Put it in.'

I moved in again. Pushed. I felt her arsehole widen and the tip of my penis was in. Cynthia buried her face down in the sheets. I pushed more. It went right in. I started fucking. Cynthia's hands were balled up into fists. She made sounds like pain. I kept going. I had her arse bunched up in my hands. I moved faster. Cynthia was choking, retching. 'Fuck, *Fuck*.' I came, ramming away.

I pulled out, rolled off.

Cynthia lay there.

'I'm sorry,' I said. I didn't know why. I felt helpless. This was worse than giving birth. This was worse than anything. Whatever you did with a pregnancy, it seemed, you paid.

And then the next set of cramps began.

Somewhere towards dawn we both fell asleep. When we woke next afternoon, the cramps and the bleeding had stopped. There was black blood all over the bed, all over us.

Three days later Cynthia went back to work.

Three days after that, four days ahead of schedule, we started fucking again.

TWENTY-SEVEN

Two or three months passed.

Cynthia worked at the Queen's Arms. Four days a week. I sat around at home all day and picked her up at night. It was good. We fought occasionally, but our lack of ambition, for ourselves, for the relationship, for anything, kept us going smoothly. We went out, drank with Leo, Molly, Frank, Maree, Rachel. Not much happened. Life was calm.

I travelled out to the farm twice more. Cynthia came with me the first time. She smoked the weekend nervously away in front of my parents. We slept in separate rooms. The second time she stayed in Brisbane. I arrived back and found her curled up in bed, sleepy and bored. She'd picked up another man. Someone she met over the bar. There was no malice in it.

Around us the house carried on. The old men drank and fought and some moved out and some moved in. Vass remained. Lewis remained. Cynthia's lightbulbs disappeared. She screamed in the hallway. They didn't reappear.

Raymond and Cathy were still there. They walked to the

methadone clinic every morning. When they came back, Raymond would change into a white bathrobe and saunter up and down the hallway, smoking. The old men hated him. There was no real reason, they just needed someone to hate. The bathrobe singled him out. They swore they only suffered his presence for Cathy's sake. They all liked Cathy. She was quiet and submissive and she had that scar . . .

Some time late in March we all received a letter from the agent about the power bills. We all paid for our own electricity. Each flat had its own meter. But the hallway lighting, the bathroom lighting, the hot water system for the showers, and the washing machine downstairs, were all on a general circuit. The agent was responsible for the running costs. Now, the letter said, this particular expense had abrubtly doubled. The agent was unhappy. He was threatening to transfer the costs over to us, if things didn't improve.

The old men were disturbed. They saved a considerable amount of money with the current scheme. None of us had our own hot water systems turned on. We all got our hot water from the hot water taps in the bathroom, the agent's hot water. We used buckets. Vass went from door to door, discussing the problem. No one understood why we were suddenly using more power. The hot water stealing had been going on for years. The letter gave us a month.

A few days later, Vass came to my door. 'Come downstairs,' he said, 'there's something you should see.' I followed him downstairs, under the house. There was plenty of space there. Mostly it was full of old furniture. Wardrobes and broken beds. We threaded through them, down to the far end. The ground rose. We had to duck our heads.

'Look,' he said, pointing.

161

I looked. There was an electrical socket on the wall. An extension cord was plugged into it. The cord ran up the wall and vanished into the floor above. Someone had drilled a hole there.

'I've never seen this before,' I said. 'How'd you find it?'

'I was looking, I had my suspicions. You see where it goes?'

I looked up again.

'That's Cathy and Raymond's room,' he said. 'The bastards have got all their stuff running off this point here. You ever been in their place? There's leads all over the place. For the TV, the lamps, the toaster, the stereo.'

'Ah.'

'You see? He's the prick that's stealing the electricity. This socket runs off the general circuit. They're gonna up our *rent* because of him.'

'So what are you gonna do?'

'I'm gonna tell the agents, that's what. Get the arsehole thrown out. First, though, I'll tell everyone else. I'll call a meeting. Tonight.'

'A meeting?'

'We gotta *punish* the bastard.'

'It's only a few dollars worth of power, Vass. We haven't paid anything for it yet. Just tell him to stop it.'

'No, the prick has gotta learn.'

Cynthia was working late. I wandered around the house. The old men were gathering in Vass's room. Bill and Douglas and Harry. Lewis. They drank their cask wine. Vass explained about the socket downstairs. The mood turned ugly.

'The prick.'

'The fucking bastard.'

'The fucking little piece of shit . . .'

I went back to my place, switched on the TV.

162

About an hour later it started. The old men were yelling in the hallway. I could hear Raymond yelling back. It went on. Cathy started screaming. I got up, opened my door.

They had Raymond outside his room. Five of them, everyone except Lewis. The old men were wild, howling, sinking in their bony fists and elbows. Raymond couldn't believe it. He was backing away. They kept him surrounded. They could all move fast, the old men, when it came to it. He put his arms over his head. 'Fucking old *cunts!*'

Then he just stood there. He went down on his knees. The old men kicked and cursed. Cathy went on screaming at them. It was grotesque, ludicrous. The old men were zombies. They were gonna tear his throat out, drink his blood. It was Night of the Living Dead.

Then Vass pulled out of it. He was coughing and spitting. The others gradually lost interest. They moved away. Raymond was left kneeling on the floor. His arms were still up around his head. He looked like he was waiting for the final bullet. He looked like Christ.

Cathy was standing in her doorway, her hand over her mouth, crying. 'We didn't fucking *know*,' she screamed.

The old men wouldn't look at her. Her scar gave her character, power, they couldn't face it. They were moving back down the hall, shaking, grunting, examining their knuckles.

Lewis was waiting there for them.

He saw me. Winked.

I shut my door.

Raymond and Cathy unplugged their lead. There were no lights in their flat the next night. Cynthia went and spoke to Cathy. It turned out their own power wasn't even connected. They couldn't afford the deposit. I thought about them sitting in there with nothing, in the dark. Vass meanwhile reported them to the agents. The agents agreed not to raise the rent, but they refused to evict Raymond and Cathy.

It didn't matter. A few nights later Cynthia and I were woken by more screaming and fighting from their flat. It sounded like four or five people. It sounded like people were getting killed. Cynthia got up and dialled the police. The police said they'd already had reports, a car was on its way.

We sat up in bed and listened. More voices. More screams. Then there were people in the hall. Yells. The fighting stopped. Someone was crying. Someone was talking on a two-way radio.

We waited. Finally I got up and opened my door. There were police in the hallway and two ambulance officers with a stretcher. A black man with his hands handcuffed behind his back was sitting on the floor. The police looked at me.

'What happened?' I asked.

'Did you make the call?'

'We made one of the calls.'

He nodded. 'You can go back to bed. Nobody died.'

Next morning there was only Cathy in the flat. Raymond was gone. Cathy packed all their gear into boxes. A man with a station wagon came and helped her load it all on board. Then she too was gone.

The old men went back to their business.

TWENTY-EIGHT

Saturday night. Cynthia and I were drinking over at Maree and Frank's house. Rachel was with us. I was drinking with the same people week after week, on the same nights, in the same places. It was comfortable, but it had its dangers.

Maree, meanwhile, was still unhappy about the way things were going with Frank. It was over but it wouldn't end. They were clinging on, arguing, fucking out of bitterness and fear.

In some ways, I envied them that.

Cynthia and I were fucking on something else, something much more gentle. It worked, but all we seemed to have now was affection. We lacked anger. We lacked confusion. And sex needed those things. It was another kind of death to accept it all, to be at peace.

Cynthia saw it. I couldn't keep up with her. I was saying no to her every so often, losing interest. And when she was away at work, I masturbated. I was dreaming about violence. About other women. About Rachel.

'We should go somewhere,' Maree suggested.

It was a little after midnight. The drinks were making us restless. We were on wine. Casks of Lambrusco. We discussed destinations. No one had any money. The only thing left seemed to be a drive.

'There's a little lake,' said Frank, 'about an hour from here.'

'What? You mean swimming?'

'We don't have to swim. We can just go and look at it.'

We agreed. Frank volunteered to drive. He was in a black mood. He wanted the speed. We took my car. We could've all fitted into Maree's little Fiat, but if you're going to be driving drunk and fast, the car might as well be a big one.

We drove. We were out of the western suburbs in twenty minutes and gliding through the hills. The road was dark, winding, shadowed with trees. We were in a forestry reserve. Fire tracks peeled off on either side. It was where people went to dump their unwanted cats and dogs. Bodies. We stuck to the main road and Frank let the Kingswood roll.

I was in the back seat with Cynthia and Rachel. The windows were down. The cool air was streaming in and the cask was going round. Frank let the car swing wide on the curves. The tires slid from time to time. Maree screamed in the front seat. It was better in the back. You couldn't see what was coming.

We made the lake in less than an hour. I peered out the window. There was no moon and no stars, only low clouds. They glowed orange, reflecting the lights of Brisbane.

'Frank,' I said, 'you didn't tell us there was a graveyard.'

'Didn't I?' He pulled up in front of the gates. The headlights shone over the stones. Frank stopped the car, left the lights on. We piled out and went reeling through the graves.

'A woman,' I said. 'There's gotta be a woman around here somewhere.'

I went from stone to stone, trying to read the inscriptions.

166

It was an old yard. I couldn't find any stones that had a date later than the 1940s. They all seemed to be male. 'I need a woman,' I yelled. 'Can anyone find a woman?'

I found a woman. She had died eighty years ago, at the age of twenty-two.

I fell on the grave. It was a rock slab, with deep cracks running up and down. I whispered into one of the cracks. 'C'mon babe. Let's go. You're only one hundred and twenty-two, you still got it.'

Rachel wandered over. 'That's sick, really sick.'

'C'mon Rach. She might even want it.'

But the stone was cold, and it was dark lonely night. I got up and let the dead lie.

We found a raised slab and sat on it, pouring the wine into some cups we'd brought along. I took my cup down to the water. The shore was muddy and tangled. I could just make out the top branches of drowned bushes, a few yards out. I rolled a cigarette. It wasn't a very good roll. Getting the filter in wasn't so easy in the dark.

I lit up. Rachel stood beside me.

'I think I'm drunk,' she said.

'There's nothing wrong with that.'

'I drink too much.' She had her arms wrapped around herself. 'I'm depressed.'

'Things aren't going well?'

'With what?' With uni? With life in general? Take your pick.'

'That bad.'

'I'm hopeless, Gordon. I'm so fucked up.'

'We all are.'

We stared at the water for a while.

I heard the car start up.

I spun around. It was reversing, throwing up dust into the headlights. Then it roared off, back up the road. Someone yelled out the window. It sounded like Cynthia.

'Hey,' I called, 'anyone left up there?'

No one answered.

'They'll be back,' said Rachel.

'Let's see if they left anything to drink.'

The cask was still on the slab. We sat down and drank a little. It was very quiet. For a while we could hear the car, but then the sound of it faded. There was only the wind. And the gravestones.

We sat on the slab.

'Don't leave me, Gordon,' she said.

'I'm not going anywhere.'

We drank.

Ten years before I'd dreamed of situations like this. 'Alone with Rachel in the Graveyard.' 'Rachel Getting Scared in the Graveyard.' 'Rachel Seeking Comfort from Gordon in the Graveyard.' 'Gordon Giving Comfort to Rachel in the Graveyard.' 'Rachel Being Very Very Grateful to Gordon . . .'

I said, 'Any men on the scene?'

'Who? *Me*?'

'Do you ever miss the sex?'

'I don't have much to miss.'

'What about what you had with Gerald?'

'It only happened a couple of times. At the end. When it was over. I loved him. I wanted to do it before he left.'

'Was it any good?'

'It was love.'

'What'd you do?'

'Do?'

'I mean, what'd you do? With Gerald.'

She laughed. 'None of your business.'

'C'mon, was it straight sex? Was it in bed, on the floor, did he tear your clothes?'

She was still laughing.

'Did he tie you up, did he fuck your arse?'

'Gordon!' she shrieked. 'Shut *up*.'

168

'What's wrong with it?'

'It'd hurt!'

'That's half the point, Rachel.'

We sat there. I thought about Rachel thinking about a prick up her arse. I thought about Rachel thinking that it'd hurt. I thought about Rachel thinking about *pain*.

Rachel said, 'I'm not necessarily against pain. I think I'd like to be tied up one day. I always thought that'd be fun.'

Jesus.

But we were sitting on opposite sides of the slab.

There was no way to reach across.

There was no point in reaching across.

'Death gets in the way of everything,' I said.

Later Rachel said, 'Can you hear voices?'

I listened. It did sound as if people were shouting, a long, long way away. I couldn't make out the words.

'Maybe the others are trying to scare us?'

'Could be.'

We waited. The shouting seemed to get closer, then it stopped. Silence. Rachel lay down on the slab. I looked at her in the dark. I drank my wine.

Then I could heard Frank yelling. 'Gordon! Rachel!'

I stood up. It'd come from up the road. 'What?!'

'Where the fuck are you?'

'Down here!'

We waited. I could hear voices. Frank and the girls. Eventually I could make out the three of them, walking down the road towards us.

'Where's the car?'

'I crashed it,' said Frank, 'not badly, but it's stuck in a ditch. We couldn't push it out.'

'Could all five of us get it out?'

'Maybe. It's not that far back along the road.'

Cynthia stared at Rachel and me. 'I thought you two might've finally got it together by now. I thought you'd be *doing* it.'

Rachel sat up.

'Me? With *Gordon*?'

We trudged back up the road. Maybe a mile along we came across the car. It was stuck nose first in a deep ditch. I crawled around it. The headlights hadn't smashed, and running my hands over the ground I couldn't feel any oil or water or petrol.

'Does the engine still go?'

'It does.'

'Okay.'

I got in and turned the ignition. It started. I revved the engine for a minute or so, listening.

'Rachel?' I said.

Rachel was probably the lightest of us. We put her in the driver's seat and the rest of us got in front of the car. Rachel engaged reverse. The wheels spun on the gravel. We pushed. The wheels gripped. The car rose back onto the road. Rachel gunned the engine. We loaded up. Frank took the wheel. I sat up front. The girls took the back.

'Okay,' I said, 'let's see how it goes.'

Frank pulled the column shift into drive and we started. We picked up speed. I was watching the speedo. Ten, twenty, thirty. The engine revved higher, then higher, then higher.

'Whoa,' I said. Frank slowed down. 'Are you sure you're in drive? Not second or low?'

He jiggled the column shift around. 'No. I'm in drive.'

'Try it again.'

He tried. By the time we reached forty the engine was screaming. He slowed down again.

'It's the transmission,' I said. 'We're stuck in first gear.'

'Fuck,' said Frank. 'I'm sorry, I'm really sorry.'

170

'Don't worry about it. It was due to go anyway.'

We crawled home. By the time we hit Brisbane it was almost dawn. The engine was overheating and the wine was all gone. We drove to Frank and Maree's house and parked.

'A cab,' I said to Cynthia.

We went inside and dialled. Frank and Maree went to bed. Rachel settled down on the couch. Cynthia and I went back outside and sat on the front steps. Cynthia nuzzled her head into my lap. I looked at the Kingswood. It was depressing. The only thing, perhaps, that I truly loved without question — and there it lay, dying in the cul de sac.

The taxi arrived. The driver was in a cheerful mood.

'Had a good night?' He had an Arabic accent.

'Not so bad,' I said.

'I love the morning!' He started humming.

The sun was rising now.

'What's your accent?' Cynthia asked him. 'It sounds Middle Eastern.'

'I am Persian.'

'Prove it. Sing something Persian.'

'I will.' He started singing. He wailed. I couldn't believe it. Five thirty in the morning and I was being sung to.

Cynthia leaned over. She unzipped me.

'Cynthia.'

'Shut up.'

She had my penis out and in her mouth. I looked at the taxi driver. He was singing, really singing. I looked out the window. At the sun rising, the early Sunday morning Brisbane traffic. I could feel Cynthia's head moving against my legs, but there was no sensation. I couldn't even tell if I was erect or not.

But the singing was fine.

Cynthia pulled her head up. I looked down and saw a

171

vague half erection. It looked tasty, like that. Warm and soft and suckable. Cynthia looked up at me and whispered, 'Can you come?'

'I don't think so.'

'Fair enough.' She lay her head on my thigh and took it back in her mouth, but didn't do much. Just held it there, rolling her tongue around. I still couldn't feel anything. I was too drunk.

'You like the song?' the driver asked.

'Yes. Do you know any others?'

'I do.'

He started up again.

Cynthia kept sucking.

The singing got us home.

TWENTY-NINE

That afternoon I called up Morris, from the Capital. He knew about cars. We chatted about life since we'd left the bottleshop. He was living on Social Security, the same as me. We agreed it was a good life.

Finally I said, 'I think the transmission on my car is gone. Could you take a look at it?'

He drove over, picked me up, and we headed out to the car.

'So you and Cynthia are living together now?'

'We are. It's good.'

'I've left Karen. I've just started up with someone new.'

'Really?'

'Her name is Hillary.'

'How old?'

'Sixteen.'

'Sixteen?!'

'She *looks* about twelve.'

'Jesus.'

'Take a look at my mouth, go on, look at it.'

I looked. His lips were scratched and puffed.

'She did that,' he said. 'She's an animal. On our first

night she tied me up and started whipping me. I've got cuts all over the place. I couldn't believe it.'

Neither could I.

Other men had it all over me when it came to things like that. I'd learnt that at the bottle shop. The staff had been exclusively male and all we'd ever talked about was sex. There seemed to be a lot it of going around.

And in various ways. One of my co-workers, a weightlifter called Arthur, was obsessed with sex in the cold. He lectured us at length on the topic. Had any of us ever been sucked off by a woman with icecubes in her mouth? Had any of us ever fucked in a freezer?

We hadn't

'It's great. The air's so fucking cold your prick's about to drop off, and then she wraps her mouth around it and it *burns*. Fucking amazing.'

'You do this a lot, Arthur?'

'Every chance I get.'

Morris and I made it to the Kingswood. There was a new dent in the right front panel, but otherwise it looked fine. Dents were no problem. They gave a car dignity.

I went and knocked on Maree and Frank's door. No one answered. Morris was on his back under the car. 'Look at this,' he yelled.

I went over and peered under.

'See?'

I looked. I knew very little about the underside of a car. I could see a hooked metal rod hanging down.

'This is the problem.'

He pulled it up, affixed it to a spot I couldn't see, and crawled out.

'That's it,' he said.

'What? It's fixed?'

'Sure.'

I drove home, tired and confused. I knew nothing about my car. I neglected it. I drove it badly. I let drunken fools do what they wanted with it. And yet it kept on going for me, mile after mile. Year after year.

It's love, I thought.

Again.

THIRTY

Fucking with Cynthia got harder.

There was less and less of me there. I went through the motions. Cynthia could tell. Sometimes she'd stop in the middle of sex and roll off me. She'd be crying. I didn't know what to do.

Then the Kingswood got stolen.

I went out one morning and it wasn't there. The day had come. It left a wide gaping hole in my heart, but I wasn't suprised. Cars got stolen all the time.

The loss was worse for Cynthia. It was her car as much as it was mine. Now she had to walk to work. Every night I walked up to the pub around closing time to meet her. I found it depressing. I took it as a sign. We'd lost our mobility. We couldn't get further away from each other than walking distance.

It was finally happening. We'd been together for four months. In all that time we'd barely been apart. I was faltering at last, running down. Life with Cynthia was good, it was better than anything I'd ever experienced, but things were starting to close in. I was all she had. Her family was two thousand miles away in one direction, her own friends six hundred miles away in the other. I couldn't replace them all. There wasn't enough in me.

And somewhere in my mind I was beginning to realise that I'd always assumed that she would *see* there wasn't enough. That sooner or later she would pack up and leave me. Go back to her real life in Darwin or Sydney. Write me letters and call me on the phone.

But there was no sign of that. She wasn't happy with the way things were going, but she wasn't going to leave. And I wondered how long I could go on fucking when the spirit was finally all gone, and Cynthia was still there.

Two weeks passed without the car.

Cynthia and I were lying in bed.

'Cynthia,' I said, 'I don't know if I can go on with this.'

'With what?'

'With us, the way we are now.'

'I don't understand.'

'I can't really explain. It's getting hard. Do you think we could stop fucking at least? For a while.'

'Jesus, Gordon.' She sat up. '*Jesus.* Don't say things like that.'

'I'm sorry. Look, I still feel the same about you. I'm not going to leave you or anything. I just need a break. From the sex at least. It's killing me.'

'Why? What did I do?'

'You didn't do anything. It's not you.'

'Just *tell* me. I'll stop it, whatever it is. It's because I'm so ugly, isn't it. Because I'm so fat.'

'Cynthia, no, you're not ugly, it's nothing like that.'

'Then what?'

'I'm just ... tired. I need a rest.'

'But why?'

'I can't say. I don't know. There's no reason for it.'

'Oh fuck.' She choked, lit a cigarette. '*Fuck*! It's happening again, it's fucking happening again. Just when I'm happy, just when I think I've really found someone, they start taking it away.'

'It's not over. It's not forever. I just need a while.'

'How long is a while?'

'I don't know.'

'You can't just say you don't know. You have to tell me how long. You have to tell me why.'

I wasn't sure what to say. It was a matter of self-preservation. I wanted her to stop re-arranging the way I sat. I wanted her to stop playing with my hair, opening my shirt. I wanted her to stop picking the blackheads out of my shoulders. I was sick of the mothering. I wanted her to let *go* for a while.

I said, 'I'm feeling owned, Cynthia. And I don't enjoy it any more.'

She didn't buy it. Cynthia wasn't into graceful acceptance of the truth. She got angry. She accused me of wanting other women, of playing power games, of being sadistic, of lying to her.

She said, 'Why all this sudden concern about sex? You said it never did much for you anyway. You said it didn't matter. And now you say it's not good enough?'

'I was wrong. It does matter. It's not right if there's no feeling there.'

'I don't care if there's no feeling. You can just fuck me, can't you? It doesn't take much, for chrissake. I'm easy to please.'

'How could you be happy with that?'

'It'd be better than nothing. I *love* you. You can't just take it away. You can't just say it's over. I won't let you.'

'Look. It's not over, Cynthia. I'm not going anywhere. I don't want you to go anywhere. I just need things to stop for a while.'

But it went on all night. Cynthia got frantic. Screamed at me. It was a barrage. There was no defence against it. Just a gut dread that told me not to give in. If I gave in, it'd only last another month, another two months, and then it'd be over. Really over. It'd turn into hatred.

I didn't want that.

Nothing was resolved. We slept and woke up and started again.

The days passed. Cynthia alternated between rage and depression. I went for long walks on my own. They didn't help. Long walks were a waste of time. Being on my own was a waste of time. I'd go back to the flat and it'd be like entering a boxing ring. We went round for round. Cynthia threw everything she could at me. I just put my hands over my head and took it.

In bed it was worse.

She clawed at my body, tugged at my prick. 'It's mine, it's mine. You're not going to take it away.'

'It's not yours, Cynthia,' I said. 'It's mine.'

We'd exhaust each other. Sleep. And then when she went off to work I dragged out the old porn magazines and masturbated. Once or twice a day.

Vass came to my door one afternoon. Cynthia was at work. I was watching TV, slumped in the couch.

He sat down and we talked for a while. He didn't look too good. The emphysema was bad. He rambled on about the women he'd known, the ones that'd destroyed him, the one that'd saved him, his wife, his children, the time Jesus Christ came to him in a vision.

I listened. I was looking into my own future again.

His talk ran out.

'How's that little woman of yours?' he said, finally.

'She's okay.'

179

'No she's not. I walk up and down that hall and I can hear you two at night. Something's wrong. Are you hitting her? I never thought you were the type for that.'

'Jesus, Vass, no.' I sat up. 'What makes you think I am?'

'I hear, I hear. I'm not as deaf as all that. I hear her crying, and I hear her saying, Stop it, stop it.'

'No. I'm not hitting her. I'd never do that. It's just that things aren't going too well at the moment. I think we might be breaking up. And Cynthia doesn't want us to.'

'Hitting is no good. It never is. You're a lucky man. You've got it all with her.'

'I know. It's just not working, that's all. But I'm not hitting her. Honestly.'

But I sounded guilty.

I felt guilty.

It got worse.

There was nowhere for Cynthia to go, nowhere for me to go. We weren't drinking, we weren't smoking anything, weren't taking anything, we weren't going out. There was only us. And Cynthia wasn't going to quit.

Three weeks after the car was stolen I was cooking dinner. Steak and rissoles again. Cynthia was sitting in the other room, watching TV. She'd been quiet for the last couple of days. Lying in bed. Staring at nothing. Scratching her face. Chain smoking. Not eating much. I couldn't rouse her.

I brought the plates out, steaming. 'Here it is.'

Cynthia looked at it. 'I'm not hungry.'

'You gotta eat, Cynthia.'

'What for?'

She got up and went and lay in bed. I sat down, ate my rissoles. I felt very, very tired. Then I got up, went into the bedroom.

She was smoking, her eyes were red, vacant.

I thought about what I was going to say. I thought I should be angry, but the energy wasn't there.

'Okay,' I said. 'I'll give it a try for a while longer. I can't stand this any more.'

She kept smoking.

I got up and went back to my meal. After a while she came out and ate in silence.

I looked at her. 'I can't promise anything, I'll just try, okay?'

She nodded. 'I'm going out for a minute.'

'Where to?'

'Just somewhere.'

She went. She came back about twenty minutes later with a carton of beer. Toohey's Old. Cans.

That night we got back to fucking. It was a decent, drunken attempt. If I was giving in to her, I thought, I might as well put my heart into it. For as long as I could.

'I love you, I *love* you,' she said, when it was over.

'It's a terrible sort of love,' I said. 'It's gonna kill us both.'

'I don't care.'

'It was only my first run, Cynthia. I'll try again.'

'I'll be ready.'

Next day, after Cynthia had gone to work, the phone rang.

'Gordon Buchanan?' a voice enquired.

'That's me.'

'Detective Terry Kindle here, Valley C.I.B. You reported the theft of a yellow Holden sedan, registration 467 NOS?'

'Yes.'

'Well, we've found it.'

'You're kidding!'

'We do find them occasionally, y'know. It turned up in a street in Albion. It's been sitting there for weeks.'

'How is it?'

'Fine. A few dents . . .'

'It already had quite a few.'

'Oh? Well, we've fingerprinted it, so you can come and pick it up if you like.' He gave me the details, I gave him my thanks, we said goodbye.

I put down the phone.

THIRTY-ONE

For a while, things weren't too bad.

If I was trapped with Cynthia, there was no need for it to be all pain. Just as long as I didn't struggle. She was good company. We got on well. It was only when I was very drunk, or sometimes when we fucked, that I understood how depressed I was.

I needed to be alone for a time.

It wasn't going to happen.

Cynthia's next period arrived. Her periods had been irregular ever since the abortion, but this time it was bad. Painful. The pre-menstrual cramps went on for days. And when the bleeding came it was black, clotted and dead. It was wrong. She was worried. I was worried. I kept my mouth away from it.

By that time I knew Cynthia's cunt almost as well as I knew my own prick. In fact, I knew it better. I'd never seen my penis from all the angles. That honour was Cynthia's.

She had even discovered a mole on the underside of my
balls. I'd never known it was there. It was *her* mole. Maybe
it was all hers. Balls, prick, the lot of it.

In which case, her cunt was mine. The whole thing, right
down to its dark and dangerous depths. I had four months
of exploration behind me. I'd stretched and pulled and
poked. I knew my way around. I knew how deep it was,
how wide it could go, how far I could suck the lips back
into my mouth before it really started to hurt.

Cynthia's cunt was my responsibility. I could tell when
something was wrong with it. And something was definitely
wrong with it.

It was my tongue that picked it up. It was two or three
nights after the bleeding had stopped. We were fucking
in the dark. I was down between her legs. My mouth was
latched on. And my tongue encountered lumps. Dozens of
them. The inside of her vagina felt like the sole of a
sandshoe.

I waited until after we'd finished. Then I told her about
it.

'Lumps?'

'Lumps.'

She sat up and switched on the light, then turned her
back to me and examined herself. 'Oh. Oh yuck.'

'What?'

'Look at this.'

She turned around and I got down between her legs. She
spread the lips. I looked in. The skin was spotted with what
looked like pimples. Small, white-headed pimples.

'Jesus,' I said.

'How far back do they go?'

'Far as I can see.'

She took her fingers away and lay back. 'What's *wrong*
with me?'

I didn't know.

I drove her up to Family Planning the next day. We went
to Family Planning for everything like this. They were free.
Cynthia wasn't looking forward to it.

'I *hate* vaginal examinations.'

'The doctor won't enjoy it either.'

'How would you know?'

'I know. It's all the doctors in the family. Between them
they've gone through hundreds of vaginas. When they were
interns it got so bad that they'd run screaming from any
woman with vaginal problems. There's a lot that can go
wrong with vaginas. They bleed, they stink, they exude
pus, they collapse, they grow tumours, they fall *out*.'

'Thanks. Thanks a lot. It's what I need to know. It's okay
for men. Men have it all hanging out, ready to look at.'

Which was true. There was only one risk with having
exterior sexual organs — they could be chopped off, or
crushed, or mangled. The family doctors had a lot of horror
stories there, too.

We reached Family Planning and I dropped Cynthia off at
the door. I parked and waited. She came walking back
along the footpath about half an hour later. She looked
upset. She was holding some leaflets. When medical clinics
or Social Security gave you leaflets, it was a bad sign.

I opened the door. 'What'd they say?'

'They think I've got genital warts.'

I started the car.

Cynthia lit up. 'I'm sick of this body. Pregnant. Diseased.
Why the fuck do I bother?'

'What happens now?'

'They'll burn the warts out.'

'Burn them?'

'With acid.'

'Christ.'

'It's painless. I'm not worried about that. I'm worried

about cancer. Warts can cause cervical cancer. They took some tests. I have to go back in a week.'

'Is it likely?'

'They took one look at my sexual history and freaked.'

'Well ...'

'When I told them about that last period they *really* freaked.'

'Yes, but ...'

'And when I told them I smoked, and took the pill, and spent half my life on cortisone, they fucking screamed at me.'

'Cynthia ...'

'I'm gonna die.'

'But what about me?'

'You'll have to get tested too, I suppose.'

'What can happen to a man with genital warts?'

'Cancer of the penis.'

'Oh my *God*.'

'It's a slim chance, I'll admit.'

We drove in silence.

She said, 'I don't think you should get yourself tested.'

'Why not? Cancer of the penis, Cynthia ...'

'They'll just tell you to start fucking with condoms. If I'm going to die I'm not gonna have my last few fucks with condoms. Wait till I'm gone. Wait till I'm dead.'

'What if you don't die?'

'Then wait till I *leave*. I refuse to fuck rubber!'

We got home and read the information. The virus was more or less harmless for men, as long as they kept an eye on it. Cancer of the penis was extremely rare. Women were the ones who had to worry. If Cynthia had been infected for long enough — several years — her chances of cervical cancer were pretty high.

Not that she was alone. The Wart Virus had once been a Notifiable Disease. The authorities had hoped to eradicate

186

it. The idea had only been abandoned after it was discovered that up to thirty per cent of the population were already infected.

We waited for the week to pass. From time to time Cynthia got scared. She could feel the cancer breeding inside.

'It's no surprise, Cynthia,' I said. 'Look at your life. Even if you don't have cervical cancer, you'll end up with cancer of *something*. You smoke too much, you drink too much, you take the pill, you eat badly, you don't exercise, you've fucked around all your life, you've taken too many of all the wrong drugs and far too many of the right ones . . . what chance have you got? Cancer of the breast, the lung, the cervix, the bowel — you're destined for them all. Not to mention heart disease, emphysema, liver collapse, renal failure and most certainly some sort of psychosis. Do you feel any better?'

'At least I'm not an asthmatic who *smokes*. You'll die long before I do.'

'Maybe. But I'll go in the middle of the night and I'll go quickly. It doesn't take long to suffocate. You're gonna suffer.'

The big day rolled round.

I said, 'I'll drive you down.'

'I'd rather go alone.'

'Okay. Fine.'

She left. I prowled around the flat. I felt guilty. Fuck, maybe she did have cancer. They'd rip out her cervix. They'd tear out her ovaries. She'd never be able to have kids. And we'd just got rid of one. She might even be *dying* . . .

She came in. I was watching TV. I looked up. I could see the news was bad. She had a cigarette in her mouth. She walked straight past me into the bedroom. I followed her in.

'What'd they say?'

It occurred to me that a high percentage of my conversations with Cynthia had been like this. Discussions about tests about her body. What'd they say? How'd it go? How bad is it this time?

She pulled on her cigarette, started at the ceiling.

'It's cancer.'

I sat on the bed.

'Cancer?'

'Cancer. I have to have an operation. They want to burn it out.'

'They *can* burn it out?'

'Yes. They said it was in a very, very early stage. They said they were sure they can stop it.'

'Well, that's pretty good.'

'Sure.'

She was pulling on the cigarette, staring at the walls.

I said, 'How serious is the operation?'

'I'll be in for two or three days. They knock me out, go in with the lasers, then keep me for a while for observation.'

'What about having kids? Did you ask them about that?'

'I did. They said it shouldn't affect it.'

I thought about that.

'Cynthia,' I said, carefully, 'I think that's not too bad. Considering.'

She lit up another cigarette.

'Easy for you to say.'

We lay there.

'When do you go in?'

'Two weeks time. The Royal Women's Hospital.'

'Public?'

'Public.'

THIRTY-TWO

For the next two weeks, Cynthia made me work. She was frightened. The knife was looming. Fucking was her only defence. It held back the fear. If she could fuck, she was still alive.

I did my best.

I appreciated the philosophy.

The operation came and went.

It was a moderate success.

They went in with the lasers and left an open wound on her cervix. The cancer was gone. They were quite sure they'd got it all. But then they gave her the bad news. Nothing and no one was allowed near her vagina for a month.

I found her sitting up in her hospital bed. She was angry.

'A month,' she said. 'A whole fucking month.'

'Cynthia, they saved your life . . .'

I, at least, was grateful.

To the doctors, to the cancer.

It was the break I'd been looking for.

But it was hard on Cynthia.

I was out of her reach and she knew it. She'd lost her grip, she'd been betrayed by her own body and there was nothing she could do. The cancer had scared her badly. She didn't dare take any risks, she didn't *dare* try to fuck me. The frustration drove her crazy. She counted down the days.

We existed.

It wasn't good, it wasn't bad. The luck was long gone, we were on our own. The times were quiet. We drank and played Scrabble. I could live with Cynthia this way. Possibly it was the only way I could keep living with her. All the problems were still there, but they were bearable. Sex was the thing that would kill us. It was only in bed that the balance fell apart, where it was all too naked and ugly to ignore. The possession and the hatred. The love and the manipulation.

And the scheduled Resumption of Fucking Day was closing in. I insisted we keep it to a month. A month exactly. I was playing for time. I had a taste of freedom. I knew, one way or the other, giving it up was going to be bad.

THIRTY-THREE

It was a Saturday night.

It was *the* night.

We were at a party at Molly's house. Everyone was there.

Cynthia was up as up as she'd ever been. She'd come through, she'd lasted it out. It was a triumph. In a few hours time I'd be hers again. I'd be under control. She moved around, talked, yelled, laughed. She was wild and beautiful. She was drinking fast.

So was I. I was depressed. I couldn't break out of it. I sat on the lawn and watched the crowd. Watched Cynthia. I didn't know what to do. The alcohol was bringing me down. I'd been drinking for the last three nights. Heavily. I was hungover and beaten.

Frank was with me.

There were still problems with Maree.

'It's getting worse,' he said. 'It's over, but we keep ending up in bed. And it's violent. It's hatred.'

I said, 'It's a lot to bear.'

'I don't know what she wants from me. She cries after the sex. But it goes on happening.'

'Why?'

'I don't know. I don't *know*.'

I looked at him.

Frank was a good man. I respected his opinion. He tried in a world where very few seemed to. But he was no better off than the rest of us. He was no closer to understanding.

He said, 'We don't compare to them, do we?'

'No.'

We sat there.

We drank. We watched the party.

We waited for our women.

Maree joined us. She was looking her age. Bony faced, tense. Then Leo came along. He produced a joint. It went round. I took a few deep pulls. It was good. It was strong. Cynthia came over. She sat down behind me and pulled me down into her lap. Her face hung over mine.

'My beautiful boy,' she said.

I stared past her, up to the sky.

I went upstairs to piss. I went in, shut the door, flipped up the lid, began. I looked around. The walls were covered with painting and writing. Circles and spirals and demonic signs. Poems. I read some of them. They were long and involved. They depressed me. Someone must have taken time to write them all up there. For a limited audience.

After I'd finished I wandered into the kitchen. Sophie was there. I hadn't seen her since the New Year's Eve party. She was inhaling from a large golden hookah pipe. She had two of the hoses in her mouth. Her cheeks sucked in around them. The cone was packed.

There were a few others around the table. One of them was Darren. He owned the pipe. I knew Darren. He was the supplier of most of the grass that I sometimes bought from Leo. Darren had his own plantation out in the mountains. He was a theology student. He had the shaman eyes.

Sophie finished her cone. She coughed up the smoke.

'Hello, Gordon,' she said.

I sat down. 'Can I have one of those?' I asked Darren.

He beamed. 'Certainly. *Certainly.*' He took the cone out, blew it clean. Then he rolled his fingers round in the mull bowl. 'Do you want it big or do you want it small?'

'Make it big.'

He nodded. He filled up the cone and packed it in.

Sophie was leaning back and looking at me with cool, distant eyes. 'How *are* you, Gordon?'

I said I was fine.

Darren was ready. He said, 'Be careful. This stuff will burn.'

I took the lighter. I slipped two of the hoses in my mouth, snapped the flint and held the flame over the cone. I began inhaling. The water bubbled. The smoke flowed through.

I coughed. He was right. The stuff was ugly. I went back to it, got a better run, finished the cone.

It swung into my head.

Sophie was still watching me. 'So, what d'you think?' she said. Her eyes were getting emptier and emptier.

'I think this was a mistake.'

My head spun. I felt ill. The world shrunk to a cocoon.

Sophie stood up. 'Come with me.'

I looked up at her. I went.

She took me to one of the bedrooms. I didn't know whose it was. Even with the light on it looked very dark. The windows were hung with heavy patterned curtains. There was a double bed secluded away in a cave between two wardrobes.

She closed the door.

I said, 'Whose room is this?'

193

She had hold of both my hands. She was pulling me over towards the bed. 'I don't know,' she said.

She kissed me. I kissed back.

'Do you want to make love to me, Gordon?'

Did I want to make love to her?

No. I didn't want to make love to anyone.

I wanted to go outside and lie on the lawn and wait until everything passed. Reality was slipping away. I wanted to go outside and lie on the lawn forever.

But we were pulling at each other's clothes. Someone turned on the stereo in the living room, turned it up loud. Then we were naked, kissing, rubbing. Sophie's body had changed from what I remembered of it. It was round. She was getting fat. Her breasts were round, her stomach was round. Her nipples had vanished. She was tall and ugly. I was tall and ugly. We were tall ugly giants. She was down around my waist.

I sat on the bed. She moved to the floor, knelt between my legs. I was already erect. Then I was in her mouth. I leaned back on the bed. My prick was miles away. It was a distant tower. She moved back up and we were kissing again. I felt sad. The kisses were cold. Our mouths were dry. I thought about heroin. I thought about the bathtub. It was all gone. I was never going to kiss like that again . . .

I found myself on top. I moved down. Sophie let her legs fall apart. I sank my face in. There was no hair. There was just naked skin and wetness. The slit was wide. I worked up to the clitoris and stroked it with my tongue. Sophie made noises. I didn't know what they were. I was lost. It was a dream. I brought up my hand and slid in a finger, then two. I fucked her with my fingers and my mouth.

She said, 'I want you in me.'

I remembered the wart virus. 'No.'

I stood up and went to one of wardrobes. I opened it. I

194

found a white tie. It was magical. Significant. A white tie. I went back to the bed. I looked at Sophie. I rolled her over. I gathered up her hands and bound them together behind her. I pulled it tight. Her shoulders arched. She closed her eyes. I rolled her back.

I kissed her breasts, her stomach, her cunt.

She was all flesh. It went on and on.

I stood up. I went back to the wardrobe. I found a scarf. The scarf was black. I wrapped it around Sophie's head, her eyes.

I saw a roll of masking tape on the desk. I picked it up. I came back and sat across Sophie's hips.

Her head moved blindly.

'What are you doing?'

I didn't answer. I couldn't find the edge of the tape. There was a long silent moment. The music had stopped. I found the edge, ripped a strip off. The sound was loud.

Sophie tilted her head up.

I took the strip and laid it down across her chest, in between her breasts. I pressed it flat.

'Oh,' she said. Quietly.

I peeled it off.

'Gordon . . .'

I took another strip. I laid it across her right breast. I pressed it down over the nipple.

I peeled if off, slowly. The nipple tilted up, swelled.

I unravelled yards of the tape. I wrapped her in it. Her breasts, her belly, her shoulders. I stretched it down her sides, onto her legs. Inside her thighs. Upwards.

'Not too close,' she said. 'Not too close.'

I tore off some more and covered her mouth.

She grunted at me.

Then I started peeling the tape away from her skin. I did it slowly. It pulled out hairs. She squirmed and made noises through the tape. I slid two fingers into her. Three fingers.

195

I held them there. She started fucking my hand. Her cunt clutched and pushed. Her body rolled. She pumped and pumped. The breath whistled through her nose. The sounds in her throat got frantic.

I took my fingers away.

I peeled the tape away from her mouth.

'Damn it,' she said. 'Christ.'

I climbed on top of her. My head was between her legs, my prick over her face. I nudged her mouth with it. She held her lips closed. I pushed harder. She opened up. I began fucking her mouth. I drove it in. She choked and gagged. I moved my fingers into her cunt. I jammed them deep. She kicked, struggled. I was crushing her, I was lying flat on her body. My prick was in her throat. Her teeth grated into it. I heard animal sounds. I fucked on. My fingers plunged in and out of her cunt. She was wet. She was slop. She was mud.

I came.

I took the blindfold off and untied her.

She didn't speak.

We dressed in silence.

I went back downstairs and sat with Cynthia and Frank and the others. No one was talking much. The party was already dying.

Maree was holding Frank's hand.

'Cynthia,' I said. 'Let's call a cab.'

We got home. Cynthia went off to the showers. I undressed. I lay in bed, feigning death. It *was* death. Cynthia came back. She took off the towel. She slid up next to me. Her arms went round my chest. She kissed me.

'I can't,' I said.

'What?'

'I can't do it, Cynthia. It has to stop. I don't love you.'

196

'*What?*'

'I'm sorry.'

'You don't *love* me?'

'No.'

'Oh my God. I can't believe it. I can't believe you're doing it *now*. I was so happy. All night I was so happy. All through the party I was thinking I could go home tonight and fuck you at last . . . and you're saying *no*?'

'It's wrong, Cynthia.'

'Oh bullshit.' She was choking back tears. 'Christ. The only thing that kept me going through the operation was you. I sat there in hospital and thought it'd all be okay because at the end of the four weeks you'd be waiting there for me. And now you're not, now you're fucking not.' The tears came.

I lay there. I didn't move to comfort her. I couldn't. I was evil. I was lying when I said I didn't love her. I did. She was the only person I loved, whatever love meant. But something somewhere was hugely wrong with me. I wanted her to go away.

'You can't do this, Gordon,' she was saying. 'You can't be so cruel. You can't *hurt* me this much.'

'I don't want to hurt you, Cynthia . . .'

'Oh fuck *off*! You're *enjoying* this!'

I rolled over, faced her. 'I am not enjoying this.'

'Then why are you doing it?' she screamed.

And there was no answer.

THIRTY-FOUR

It was on. For real this time. The same arguments, over and over, day after day. It was long and vicious and exhausting. We drank heavily. We screamed at each other. We were two stray dogs, battling it out to the death over the bones of love. Cynthia was the aggressor. She fought it hard and fast and with increasing creativity and desperation. The drinking spurred her on. Between the cortisone and the alcohol, she was uncontrollable. She screamed, cried, attacked me with her fists, knives, scissors. She meant to keep me or finish me off for ever.

My only goal was survival.

I didn't ask her to leave. I didn't have the power or the will for it. I'd made my one and only move. All I could do was ride the attack out and wait for her to tire.

Vass looked at me strangely in the hallways.

It was entertaining times for the old men.

From time to time I took the car and fled for a few hours. I didn't know where to go. I didn't want to see Leo or

Molly. Maree and Frank had their own difficulties. And Sophie was out of the question. I had only vague memories of what had happened at the party. It had the substance of a dream, a bad one. Where had all the hatred come from? But at least I finally understood one part of the situation. And fucking had nothing to do with it.

In the end I went and saw Rachel. She was good to me. I talked and she listened.

'You have to make Cynthia leave,' she said. 'Make the break. You're only making it worse for the both of you.'

It was sound advice. Useless advice. Rachel knew it. She had her own worries too. She'd started things up with a man and then he'd shot through to Sydney. People were making a mess of things everywhere I looked.

I went back to Cynthia. She was waiting.

'Where did you go?'

'I went and saw Rachel.'

'Did you fuck her?'

'I don't want to fuck anyone.'

'I'm not going to let you do this, Gordon. You don't have the right.'

It was true, I didn't have the right. But this time I had the patience, and Cynthia was slowing down.

Another week passed.

We weren't fucking, but we still slept side by side in the bed. There was nowhere else in the flat, only the couch, and it was too hard, too cold. It was worse for Cynthia. I had friends I could escape to, but there was no one for her. She called up some of her old people from Melbourne and Sydney, but they were a long way away. They couldn't understand. They didn't even know who I was.

We went out drinking on Sunday afternoon with Frank. He was depressed. It was over between him and Maree.

'I suppose I should be happy,' he said. 'I should feel like a butterfly that's just emerged from a four-year cocoon. But I don't. I feel like a moth. I keep flying blindly into lightbulbs.'

When the pub closed we caught a cab and had it drive by Frank's place. He was staying at his parents' house. It was his first night away from Maree. He got out.

Cynthia looked at me.

'I'm going with Frank,' she said.

'Okay,' I said.

She got out. Frank looked at her.

The cab took me away.

I arrived back at the flat. I was alone.

The house was quiet.

I went to bed.

Cynthia woke me up about midday. She was stroking my hair.

'I've been watching you sleep,' she said. 'You're still beautiful when you're asleep. I can imagine that you still love me.'

I curled up around her hips. She was warm.

'How'd it go with Frank?'

'It was good.'

'Do you feel any better?'

'A little. I feel sad. I think I'll always feel sad.'

We sat there.

For the next three days it was good.

The anger had run out. We were tired. It was over. And the love was still left there. Not enough, but some.

Then a letter arrived for Cynthia.

It was from the Tax Department. It was her refund. It was four or five months late. Four hundred dollars.

I asked her, 'What'll we do with it?'
Cynthia looked at the cheque.
She said, 'I guess I'll get a plane ticket.'

THIRTY-FIVE

I'd won.

THIRTY-SIX

Next day Cynthia rang around the airlines and booked herself on a standby ticket. It was due in two weeks. She was flying to Darwin. To her parents' place.

'Why not Sydney,' I said, 'or Melbourne? It's where all your friends are.'

'I don't want friends. I just want somewhere where I haven't got to worry about living, where someone will look after me. All I want is sleep. I don't want to work, I don't want to see anyone. I'm tired, Gordon.'

'I know. I'm sorry. It's been terrible.'

'You're not sorry enough. You'll never be sorry enough.'

The two weeks went by. Cynthia quit work. She called her parents. She went through all her clothes, sorting out the warm stuff. She wouldn't need it in Darwin. Darwin was never cold.

'If I leave some of this stuff here, will you look after it? Can you *do* that?'

I said I could.

'What if I come back, Gordon? I know you think it's over, but it's not over for me. I still love you.'

I said nothing.

'God,' she said, 'who's going to look after you? Who's going to pick your blackheads? You'll get sick. You'll get ugly.'

She was crying.

Her flight was on a Tuesday.

On our last Saturday night together we went out to see some bands that were playing at Easts Leagues Club. We'd spent the day trying to track down some acid. We wanted a big finish. One last time.

No one had any acid. Instead, we arrived at Easts early and concentrated on drinking. Drinking could be almost as good sometimes, if you did it right.

The support band started up. Cynthia lost herself in the crowd. I wandered around and drank and occasionally ran into people I knew. Suddenly there was Darren. His face was red and sweating and smiling.

'Hey man,' he said.

'You're tripping.'

'Yep...'

'Where'd you get it?'

'There's a guy here, selling.'

'Is he still around?'

'I don't know. Look, I've got one tab left. I've already had four.'

'Four?'

'I know. I'm losing it. I'll sell you the last one.'

'The thing is I need two. One for Cynthia.'

'I've only got the one. Just take it yourself. She won't even know.'

'She'd know. I couldn't.'

'Wow. That's dedication.'

'It's caution.'

'She wouldn't do the same for you. She'd take it.'

'Maybe. I can't, though.'

'Well, I'll look around for the guy, okay? If I see him I'll come get you.'

'Okay. Thanks. Very much.'

He made off. Four tabs. He looked like he was about to die.

I wandered on, found a table down near the back and sat on it, watching the crowd. Cynthia was in there somewhere, up the front. For a support, the band didn't seem too bad. Fifteen or twenty minutes later they were finished and Cynthia came back through the crowd. She saw me, came over.

'I just saw Darren up the front,' she said.

'Yeah?'

'He offered me a tab. Twenty bucks.'

'What'd you say?'

'I said yes please. What else would I say? But then he said no, he wouldn't give it to me. He said I should talk to you.'

'I think he was just trying to prove a point.'

She looked at me. I didn't explain.

Ten minutes later Darren showed up with the dealer. We bought our tabs and settled into the night.

The acid was good, and so was the music. Loud and hard and purging. Cynthia disappeared up the front again for most of the night. I prowled around the back, getting off on the crowd, watching them sway. I could understand their movements, I could grasp the mass consciousness that drove them. But I wasn't part of it. I was elated and alone. I would always be alone.

Then the band wrapped it up, the crowd screamed and the lights came on. Cynthia fought her way back. Her eyes were wild, she was wet with communal sweat. 'Why's it over?' she yelled at me. 'Why is it fucking over?'

'I am only one man, Cynthia,' I said. 'I have no say in this.'

She was pure hatred. 'Get away from me!' And she was off again, darting across the floor. She was crazy. I went after her.

We caught a bus home.

There were no seats. Cynthia and I stood in the aisle and raved at each other. She was angry, I was angry, we weren't even hearing each other. The acid was peaking. Looking out the window I couldn't see where we were.

Cynthia screamed, 'This bus is taking us to HELL!'

People looked at her.

'This bus is full of SHITHEADS!'

People looked away.

Cynthia was genuinely scared. 'Where are we, Gordon?'

'On our way home.'

'Don't *lose* me, okay.'

'I won't.'

'You know what you are?' she said, profoundly.

'What?'

'You are a mild person.'

'Is that good or bad?'

'It's nice. You're nice.'

'That *is* bad.'

'No.' She sounded weary. 'In the end, nice is all you want.'

We got off in the Valley and walked home along Brunswick Street. We stopped off in a bistro for coffee, then hamburgers and chips and coke. We hadn't eaten for what seemed a long time.

Leo and Molly were waiting for us in the flat. They were drinking and smoking. Molly came up and looked in my eyes. 'You guys are tripping!'

'Yes, but it's no good without alcohol.'
Fortunately we had plenty.

Around five a.m. Leo and Molly got tired and set up a bed
on the carpet. Cynthia and I went to our own bed. We
weren't tired, the acid probably wouldn't let us sleep for
hours yet. We sat on the bed. Cynthia attacked my zip and
got my penis out.

I was listening.

'They're *fucking* in there,' I said.

Cynthia listened too.

'Are you two fucking in there?' she yelled. 'It sounds like
you're fucking!'

There was no answer. The noises stopped. We looked at
my penis. Her hand was playing with it, it was growing.
It'd been a good night. It was no time to bring it all up
again. It wasn't worth the pain. And Cynthia would only
be with me for three more nights . . .

'Okay,' I said, 'jump on. Let's do it.'

She started tugging off my jeans.

We made it noisy. We threw everything into it. All the
hatred and sorrow. All the violence we had left.

And it was good. We knew what to do. We fell out of the
bed, fucked on the floor, pumped and squeezed and pounded
each other, contorted, climbed back into bed, bit, strangled
. . . and in the end, I was on top. Her legs were up around
my shoulders. 'I love you,' Cynthia screamed, 'God I fucking
love you.'

I came. I collapsed over her. I didn't say anything. I
couldn't say anything. I bit into her neck. We held each
other there. My prick shrunk away. Pulled out.

I rolled off.

'Did you hear that?' Cynthia yelled, for Leo and Molly.
'Even the mild one can make more noise than you!'

'Keep it down, Cynthia.'

But she was laughing. 'The mild one, I called you the mild one, didn't I. Mild One, I think I love you.' She kept on laughing. We both laughed. It was true.

Leo cried out from the next room. 'Will you shut the fuck up.'

But we couldn't.

Not yet.

THIRTY-SEVEN

The next afternoon was bad. I woke up to asthma and vomiting. Cynthia was no better. Drinking was the only solution. We picked up a carton of beer, a cask of wine. Cynthia paid. Her tax cheque was dwindling away, but she only needed two hundred and fifty dollars for the flight. She'd make it.

Leo and Molly didn't seem much better. They stayed on, drinking with us. We all felt very low.

Molly said, 'We heard you two last night.'

'You were supposed to,' said Cynthia.

'You were faking it, I know. Sex is never *that* good.'

'It wasn't the sex, Molly.'

Molly didn't understand Cynthia. She didn't understand love. Neither did I. Molly and I would've been a far better match. We were both cold and self-absorbed. We had nothing to give. It'd never happen.

We drank all afternoon, watched TV, listened to records. Cynthia's mood declined. She wanted us to be alone. It was our second-last day.

We didn't eat. No one was hungry. Leo and Molly wouldn't leave. Eventually it was night. Cynthia hadn't said anything for hours. I watched her. I knew she would want to fuck me again. I knew I wouldn't be up to it. The night before had been good, but if we tried it again, tired and drunk and depressed, it just wouldn't work.

Around midnight we finished off the last of the drinks.

Cynthia sat down next to me. She said, 'I'm going to bed. Are you coming?'

'I don't think so. Not yet.'

She stood up. 'Fuck you, Gordon.'

She went into the bedroom. Leo and Molly and I sat there for a while. We didn't say anything. I knew Cynthia was waiting, they knew Cynthia was waiting. In the end I got up and went in to face it.

She was in bed, smoking, staring at the ceiling. I undressed, climbed into bed.

She said, 'Will you fuck me now?'

'No, Cynthia. It wouldn't be any good tonight.'

'I don't believe you. Last night you wanted it and even though I didn't, I went along with it because I love you. It *hurt* me last night, Gordon, and you didn't even notice. And now *I* feel like it and you just say fuck off, Cynthia, not tonight. How can you do that?'

I lay there.

Cynthia sat up. She started hitting me. Hard. Bunched up fists. A few blows caught me round the head before I got hold of her hands. 'BASTARD!' she screamed, 'BASTARD BASTARD BASTARD.'

'Cynthia . . .'

'GET OUT OF MY BED. GET THE FUCK OUT!'

'Okay, Cynthia, okay.'

I let go of her hands. I stood up. There was a glass Coke bottle on the bedside table, full of water. She picked it up and threw it at me. Hard and straight. I ducked. It caught me squarely on the top of head. Whang. I fell over backwards, hit the floor.

It hurt. My skull was ringing. There was water all over me. I felt the top of my head. I looked at my hand. There was blood on my fingers.

I got up again.

'Are you satisfied?'

'No!'

I put on my jeans, then a shirt. I felt my head. Blood was seeping through the hair. I could feel a big round lump with a split on the top of it. I went out into the living room. Leo and Molly were lying on the floor. They looked at me. I went out into the hallway and down to the bathroom. I ran water over my head, looked at it in the mirror. I couldn't see anything. Too much hair. I needed a haircut. Blood was trickling down my cheeks. I wondered if I was concussed. I help up a hand, counted the fingers. They were all there.

Leo came into the bathroom. 'What happened? You okay?'

'I'm okay. Cynthia threw a Coke bottle at me.'

He examined the top of my head. 'Jesus, it's split open.'

'I don't think it's that bad. There isn't much blood, and I feel okay.'

'This might need stitches.'

I felt it again. There really wasn't that much blood.

'It's okay. Honestly.'

'You might be concussed.'

'I'm an expert on concussion. I know I'm not.'

'I should ring your brother. The doctor.'

'Don't. It's late. I don't need him.'

'I'm calling him. What's the number.'

'I don't remember. Maybe I *am* concussed.'

'Bullshit.'

I gave him the number. He went off. I washed my head again and went back down the hall to the flat. Leo was hanging up the phone.

'He's on his way,' he said.

I sat down, poured myself a glass from the dregs of the

wine, and turned on the TV. Things didn't seem too bad. My head felt swollen and vague, but it didn't hurt any more.

We sat there. Leo and Molly didn't say much. It was awkward. I felt my head from time to time. The bleeding had almost stopped. Joseph arrived and looked at it.

'It's nothing,' he said. 'Just a little cut. Why'd you get me over here for this?'

'I'm sorry. It wasn't my idea.'

Just a scratch. Where was the poetry in that? I began wishing that Cynthia had knifed me, cut my throat, gashed my stomach, hospitalised me. It might've balanced things up. She was right. I was a bastard. I was no good.

Joseph left. Leo and Molly called themselves a cab. Then I was alone. The alcohol was all gone. I watched TV.

Cynthia came out, wearing one of my shirts. She didn't look at me. She went into the hall. She came back a few minutes later. She was holding an empty beer bottle. She threw it at me. This time she missed by a good yard. She went into the bedroom. Came out again.

She sat down next to me.

I said, 'My head's okay. Joe came over. He said it was nothing.'

She was staring at the screen.

'What?' she said.

'My head. You hit it with the Coke bottle.'

'Did I?'

She was out of it, completely crazy. I'd been a fool even getting into the same bed as her.

She said, 'Are you gonna fuck me, then?'

'Christ, Cynthia, no.'

We watched TV. She reached out and took my hand, put it between her legs. I didn't move it. I was tired of it all. I was full of hate. Not necessarily for her. She wasn't even conscious, the Cynthia I knew was miles away. But the

212

hate was still there. I couldn't bring myself to help her. After a while she took my fingers and placed them against her cunt. She started moving them. I didn't pull them away. I kept my eyes on the screen. She rubbed my hand up and down. She jammed it against her clitoris. She grunted, worked. Then she quickened, pumped, came. I took my hand back.

I didn't look at her. I was still watching TV. Eventually she got up and went back into the bedroom. An hour or so later I did the same. She was asleep. I undressed, climbed in carefully and curled up beside her. She stirred. 'Gordon?' she whispered.

'It's me. It's okay. I'm here.'

She sighed, leaned into me.

God, I thought. Jesus fucking Christ.

I kissed her.

THIRTY-EIGHT

Someone was knocking on the door. It was morning. I got up, wrapped a towel around my waist and answered it. It was Maree.

'Are you okay?' she said. 'Leo called me this morning and told me what happened.'

'I'm okay. It's only a bit of a lump.'

'I'm worried about you, Gordon. Cynthia might've killed you.'

'I know . . . but it's not her, it's the alcohol and the cortisone, they drive her crazy. It's my own fault. I should've kept my distance last night.'

'You can always stay at my place if things are that bad.'

'Thanks. But she goes tomorrow anyway.'

'Are you going to be okay?'

'I will be. Really.'

We sat down. Cynthia came out. She looked terrible. Red-eyed and raw-skinned. 'Good morning,' she said. Her voice faint and whispery. 'Hello Maree.'

'Hello Cynthia,' Maree said. 'You okay?'

'No. I feel lousy. I think my voice is going.'

We made tea, drank it. Maree left.

Cynthia winced when she tried to speak, but she got it out. 'What was Maree doing here?'

'She was worried about what you did last night.'

'Why? What did I do last night?'

'Don't you remember?'

'No?'

'You threw a Coke bottle at me. It split my head open. See? Joe had to come over and check it.'

She looked at my head. 'Oh . . . I did that? God. I'm sorry, Gordon. I don't remember.'

'It's okay. It's my fault anyway.'

'Yes. It is. But I am sorry.'

'I know.'

I felt as much love for Cynthia in that moment as I ever had, even in the good times. It was strange and confusing. But when a woman loved you enough to want you to die, it was hard not to love her back.

The day passed quietly. Cynthia's voice faded away. We did the rounds of all our friends so that Cynthia could say goodbye. It was a gloomy progression. Cynthia could barely talk. None of us were drinking. There was no joy. We came home and went to bed early. We couldn't sleep, and we couldn't talk. We held each other. Around dawn, we fucked, just the once, very softly. Then we got up, dressed, and drove out to the airport.

THIRTY-NINE

Cynthia was on a standby ticket. She would only get a seat
if one of the booked passengers failed to show up. Cynthia
wasn't worried. She said that there were always a few that
didn't make it. But she had had to arrive about an hour
and a half early and check in at the desk. We were faced
with all that time of saying goodbye, when there was no
certainty that she was even leaving.

We checked in, then moved to the bar. We had a beer
each. Cynthia was very quiet. She wasn't interested in
drinking. We went and sat in a couch in the departure
lounge.

She started crying.

'I don't want to go.'

'I know.'

'How can you let me go?'

'I have to, Cynthia. We'll kill each other if you don't.'

'I know, I know. But I'll be so lonely.'

'I'll call. I'll call you tonight.'

'You'd better write to me. I want at least one letter a
week, Gordon. You owe me that.'

216

'I know. I will.'

'I don't care what you write. Anything. Just do it, okay?'

'I will, honestly.'

'I thought it was going to go so well. I really did.'

'It was, Cynthia. For a while there.'

'Then what went wrong?'

'It was me, not you.'

'You were so nice to me. I know I've been a bitch lately, but you *were* nice to me. You never tried to hurt me. And even in bed. You don't have any talent there but you tried, you really tried, I love you for that. I love your little penis, the way you poke it around. I love your eyelashes . . .'

I held her. I was struggling with tears. Please God, I thought, let her leave today.

Ten minutes before departure time we moved to a seat near the desk. The attendants called her name. She went up, talked to them, came back. 'I'm on,' she said.

They started calling the flight. We went over to the gate. Two hostesses were taking tickets. We stood there, not knowing what to do. It was over, it was really over.

Cynthia was crying again 'Goodbye. I love you.'

I was numb.

I said, 'I love you too.'

We kissed, held each other.

'You're going to let me go, aren't you? You really aren't going to stop me.'

'No. I'm sorry. I'm not.'

She dug her head into my shoulder. 'Oh God, oh God.' I held on. 'I wish I'd had the baby,' she said. 'The only reason I didn't was because I didn't want to lose you, and now I'm losing you anyway and I've got nothing to remember you by. What am I going to do?'

There was nothing I could say.

They called her flight again. It wasn't the final call. We could've stayed there longer. Another ten minutes. But she

217

pulled away. She picked up the bag she was carrying on. It was full of books.

She looked up at me. Lost. Betrayed. I felt pain come howling up from somewhere deep inside. She turned away. The hostesses took her ticket. They looked at it, passed her on. She went to the door. She looked back one more time. Then she was gone.

I choked, I started to cry. I sat down. I couldn't stop the crying. It got worse. I put my hands over my face and sobbed. I was helpless. I didn't know what it was. Relief. Horror. Love. It went on and on, getting louder and more agonising. This is it, I thought. This is the breakdown, you've fucked things up completely this time.

Finally it stopped. I took my hands away. I sucked in the air and looked up. The two hostesses were watching me. They lowered their eyes. I stood up. Started walking. I thought — this doesn't make sense, this doesn't make any *sense*. A man and a woman come to the departure gate, they cling to each other, they kiss, they cry, they say they love each other . . . and then she goes. And he lets her. Where was the reason in that? Where was the understanding?

I found the car park, found the car. I sat in it and started crying again. Painful, noisy crying. A plane roared, flew over, turned across the city. It might've been hers. I didn't know. I stopped crying. I put the keys in the ignition. The car wasn't the same. There was a great empty space in the passenger seat where Cynthia had been. I started up and drove. I was alone again.

FORTY

I didn't go home. I went to Molly's place. Darren was there. I purchased another tab of acid. Then I went home.

I opened up the flat and took the tab. It came on quickly, the room swung in. I sat in the flat for the rest of the day, watching television and drinking cask wine and letting the acid run. Then I dialled Cynthia. After ten, when the long distance charges had dropped. It rang. Then it was picked up.

'Cynthia?'

She said, 'My love.'

Next day it was time to face some realities. I went down to the STD clinic. It was in an old building on the quieter end of Adelaide Street in the City. The sign outside said Special Clinic. I went inside, walked up the stairs and gave my name at the desk. Then I sat down to wait.

There were three other men there. My fellow diseased. My fellow *male* diseased. The women's waiting room was somewhere else. It made sense. The sexes were embattled enough as it was.

I read some leaflets, some magazines. I thought about the warts. There were no growths on my penis, but I was sure to have the virus. It was my first sexual disease. If that wasn't a sign of manhood, what was? I should've felt *good*. The waiting room was an initiation chamber for *men*.

I didn't feel good. I was sad. I felt like a fool. They called my name and I got up and followed the doctor in.

My doctor was a woman. She sat me down and asked me what the problem was. I told her about Cynthia and the warts.

'Okay,' she said, pulling out a form, 'I'll just get some details.'

'Fine.'

'How many sexual partners have you had over the last twelve months?'

'Three.'

'Use condoms?'

'No. Not with Cynthia.'

'Uh-huh. Ever used intravenous drugs?'

'A couple of times. Not lately.'

'Did you share syringes?'

'No.'

'Any homosexual experiences?'

'Barely. Just the once.'

'Any anal intercourse?'

'No.'

'Any anal intercourse with your female partners?'

'Yes.'

'Any idea about their sexual history?'

'In some cases, prolific.'

'Had any sexually transmitted diseases in the past?'

'No.'

'Any current symptoms that you might think are due to a sexual disease?'

'No.'

'Do you want an AIDS test?'

'Should I?'

'You could be at risk. It couldn't hurt.'

'Okay.'

And there it was. My life.

'Okay. Take off your pants and lie on the table.'

The doctor turned away to a table of instruments. I pulled down my jeans. There it was, the organ in question, my penis. Retracted and wrinkled and tiny and pink. I tweaked it a couple of times. It didn't relax. It knew what was coming.

I lay down.

She came over, pulling on a pair of thin plastic gloves. She took my prick in one hand, bent down over me and scrutinised it. The gloves felt cool. I put my arms behind my head, stared at the ceiling.

She was twisting it around, looking from all the angles. Then she started on my balls, rolling them, squeezing them, lifting the sac. 'Have you always had this mole?'

'Apparently.'

'Has it changed shape lately?'

'Well, I don't really see it that much.'

'You should keep an eye on it. Use a mirror.'

She stood up. 'I can't see any warts. What I'll do now is douse your penis with vinegar and then look at it under a UV light. That should show up any warts that are too small for me to see. They're like that sometimes.'

She went over to the table and came back with some strips of tissue soaked in vinegar. 'This'll feel cold,' she said. She wrapped them round. She was right about the cold.

'I'll have to leave it like that for a while.'

We waited.

'So what do you do with yourself, Gordon?'

221

'Nothing. I'm unemployed.'

Silence.

I said, 'This must be thrilling for you, day after day.'

'Well, at least I'm on men today. Men are a lot easier.'

'That makes sense. Does it get busy?'

'Sometimes. Not today. Mondays and Fridays are the big days. Friday everyone comes in to make sure they're okay for the weekend, then Monday they all come in again to make sure they're okay *after* the weekend. They don't have a clue.'

We waited again.

Then she took the wrapping off. She pulled the lamp down over my hips and switched it on. The plastic fingers took me again. Probed, pulled.

'Ah-ha.'

I looked down. 'What?'

'Here's a little one. See?'

I looked. My penis had grown a bit. She was pointing to an area about halfway down the shaft.

'I can't see anything.'

She peered at it again. 'It is only a small one.'

'What now?'

'We'll get rid of it. I'll dab it with some acid. It'll turn black after a couple of days, then drop off.'

'Drop off?'

'It won't *hurt*.'

She went off, came back with a small bottle and a cotton bud. She dabbed the wart with a clear cold liquid. It didn't sizzle, it didn't burn.

'Now,' she said, 'this one will fall off, but you'll have to come back regularly for check-ups. You'll be infectious for about a year, so if you do have sex with anyone, you *must* use condoms.'

'I don't think it's likely to happen.'

'Even so, don't forget.'

222

'I won't.'

'Okay. Now we'll test for all the other diseases. Syphilis, gonorrhoea, herpes, a few more of the regular ones. Okay?'

'Okay.'

She went back to the table, picked up a scalpel and a small, sharp hook.

She held them up. She looked at me.

'This might hurt a little.'

'Hey. No one told me there'd be *hooks*.'

'Ah. Well, there has to be *some* pain for the men. We have to be fair, don't you think?'

She pried open the eye of my penis, and sank the hook in.

After she was finished I went back into the waiting room to wait for the results. My prick was stinging. Cynthia's revenge. The doctor hadn't even noticed the tattoo, right on the head: 'Property of Cynthia Lamonde. NO TRESPASSING.'

It was an unworthy thought. I deserved more than a stinging penis. A stinging penis was something to be amused by. I thought about Cynthia's cramps after the abortion, about the black clotted blood. There was nothing funny there. I read some more magazines. After about twenty minutes the doctor called me back in.

'All clear,' she said. 'Nothing but the warts.'

'Good.'

'Of course the AIDS results will be a couple of weeks yet. You have to come back then for your first check-up anyway.'

'Fine.'

I went back into the street.

FORTY-ONE

I walked back home, sat down. Vass came in. 'You hear what happened to Bill?'

Bill lived in the room next to Vass, across the hall from me.

'I was drinking with him up at the Brunswick. Just sitting there, drinking. Then I could smell shit. I said, "Bill, can you smell shit?" And he was white as a ghost. It was him. His arsehole had ripped open, just ripped right open! There was shit all through his pants. I called up an ambulance. The manager threw us out. Told us never to come back.'

So much for a warty penis.

'I didn't think that was possible,' I said, 'to just rip open. How is he now?'

'Dunno. The ambulance took him off. The poor bastard stank.'

'So why'd it happen?'

'He said he hadn't had a shit for weeks. I think he must've just burst.'

'Jesus.'

Vass was looking around the flat. 'Where's the little lady?'

'She's gone. Gone for good. She flew to Darwin yesterday.'

'Aaah. That's a terrible thing . . .

'Yes, it is.'

'You okay?'

'I'm okay.'

Later that afternoon I called up Rachel.

'Has Cynthia gone?' she asked.

'Yesterday.'

'How are you?'

'Not too good. I think I had a nervous breakdown at the airport.'

'I heard about the Coke bottle. Cynthia was crazy, Gordon. She had to go.'

'I know. But it wasn't really her fault. I mean, I was fucking up her life, she had to do something. Love isn't rational. Listen, are you doing anything tonight? Could I come over?'

She hesitated. 'I really should be studying, but okay.'

I hung up and drove over. I picked up a cask of red on the way. She looked at it when I arrived. 'Planning a big night?'

'I have to celebrate. I went to the STD clinic today. I've got genital warts.'

I filled up her glass, filled up my own. I sat on the couch, Rachel sat on the floor.

'Genital warts?'

'Cynthia gave them to me. She'd had them so long she developed cervical cancer. They cut it out in hospital.'

We drank and talked. It was a stable, sane conversation. Rachel was good for that. And I liked watching her, listening to her, hearing what she thought about the world. We talked about men and women. About what went wrong between them. Rachel traced all her own disasters with relationships back to a lack of understanding. She wanted to understand people, she thought it was important. I wasn't so sure. In the end I preferred to be mystified.

Rachel herself still mystified me. She wasn't like Cynthia. Cynthia had impressed me, amazed me, but on a certain level I *understood* what she was doing.

We turned on the TV. Rachel stopped drinking after four or five glasses. I drank on till one or two in the morning. Then Rachel said she was going to bed. She asked me what I was going to do.

'I can't drive home. Can I crash here?'

'I'll get you a mattress.'

'Thanks.'

She produced the mattress, set it up on the floor with some sheets and a pillow. I was drunk. I stood up and said goodnight. I kissed her on the forehead. It was the first time in my life that I'd kissed her anywhere.

'Rach,' I said, 'do you ever get lonely?'

'All the time.'

'Look, if you ever want someone to sleep with, I mean, just to *sleep* with, to lie in bed with, I'm available. It's nice to sleep with someone, and wake up with someone. People should do it more often. You know what I mean?'

'Thanks, Gordon. I know what you mean. It's nice of you to say that.'

I didn't know what I meant. It'd just come out. It was the pain. I was lonely already. But Rachel was never going to say yes to me, no matter how nicely I put it.

Still, she was nice enough to me in the morning. She didn't feel like studying, so we went for a drive out around the bay. Sandgate and Redcliffe. We walked along the beach,

226

around the shops. She talked about her course, about what she thought she could do with it. I listened. Administrative Sciences meant nothing to me, but I was interested because it was what *she* was interested in.

We drove back to her place. I pulled up outside.

'Thanks, Gordon,' she said. 'It was a nice day.'

'Yes. I enjoyed it.'

'I might see you over the weekend.'

'Okay.'

She got out. I drove home.

I had drinks with Frank that night. I told him about the genital warts. I told him about the hook. He was appalled. He knew he had to get himself tested too — he and Cynthia hadn't used condoms.

We were in a bar in the Valley. Frank was buying. I didn't have the money. I wouldn't have now, without Cynthia. Sooner or later I'd have to get a job. I wasn't sure I was even employable any more. The idea of work depressed me greatly. It wasn't just the hours, it was having to work for someone else, to act as if I gave a damn about their business, their customers, their money. I didn't think I could fake it any more.

Frank said, 'What are you gonna do? Write?'

'I can't write, not anything that'll sell. I think an institution is my only chance. The army, a hospital, a religious order ... somewhere where they feed you, give you a bed, keep you alive. It'd be enough.'

That night I sat down and wrote my first letter to Cynthia. It was long, emotional, drunken. Next morning I sent it off without rereading it. I couldn't even remember what was there.

This was Friday. I went down to the post office and mailed it Express Courier. I'd promised Cynthia I'd get it to her by

227

the weekend. Monday would have to do. It cost me seven dollars. That night I called her. I spent a long hour listening to her cry and argue at thirty-seven cents a minute.

I said, 'I can't afford these phone calls, Cynthia.'

'I don't *care*. I can't make it if you don't call me.'

She wasn't enjoying Darwin. It was hot, the house was too small, her parents were oppressive, there was nothing to do, no one to see. I told her about the warts. That cheered her up a little. She asked me questions. What had I been doing? What was I wearing? How was my penis?

I answered, but it was unwilling. I was feeling trapped and hateful again. She was right, it wasn't over. I loved her, I wanted her to leave me alone. If there was some way I could stop calling, never speak to her again. But there wasn't. I couldn't do it. It was bad now, but it'd get better. Something could be saved. Something had to be saved.

I mentioned that I had spent the day with Rachel.

'*Rachel?*' cried Cynthia. 'Oh shit. Of course. I'm out of the way now. You can fuck your little goddess at last. Christ, Gordon, she's so dull! You don't have to settle for shit like her!'

'I'm not going to be fucking Rachel, not even if I wanted to. And leave her alone. You don't know her.'

'Sure. She's *frigid*, Gordon.'

'Cynthia, stop it.'

'Why should I? What the fuck do you care?'

It went on. I suspected it'd be going on for months, years. I'd always be paying for it.

At thirty-seven cents a minute.

FORTY-TWO

I didn't see Rachel that weekend, but she rang me the week after that. Her exams were over and she was going home to spend the weekend at her parents' farm. No one else would be there. The rest of her family was holidaying at the coast. She wanted to know if I was interested in coming along. Just for a break.

I was.

I said, 'We can take my car.'

'I'll pay for some of the petrol.'

'Don't worry about it, Rachel.'

'I didn't ask you along just for the sake of a free ride, Gordon.'

'I know.'

We drove out on a Saturday. Her parents' farm was at the eastern foot of a mountain range that arched out into the wheat plains from the Great Divide. It was a forty-minute drive from Dalby. The mountains were low and rolling, bald and grassy in some places, heavily rainforested in others. Her parents' fence line followed the boundary of a national park. They ran cattle. I'd been there only a couple of times before. Short visits. When Rachel and I were at school.

I liked the mountains. They were modest and lonely and no one bothered with the national park much. From the top of them, looking west, with binoculars, you could just make out my own parents' farm, maybe thirty or thirty-five miles away, out on the plain.

We drove around for the morning and then stopped off for a late lunch at one of the small local pubs. There was no one else in the bar. We drank, talked, watched the odd car go by. Towards dark we picked up some drinks and drove on.

Her parents' house wasn't so different from my own parents' house. Large and ugly, bits tacked on here and there as the family grew. But the farms themselves were different. Cattle compared to grain. I knew nothing about cattle grazing, except that it seemed a harder, poorer life than grain growing. And things were different for Rachel, too. I was the ninth child out of ten, she was the first child of eight. She could ride a horse. She could round up livestock. All I'd ever learned to do was drive a tractor. To watch the world crawl by at three or four miles an hour. They were import-ant things to remember about each other.

Rachel cooked dinner. We sat out on the back verandah in the cane armchairs and ate and drank and looked up at the hills. It was calm. Cynthia and the flat and Brisbane seemed a long way away.

'It's a pity I hate all this now,' said Rachel.

'You do?'

'It's not the farm itself, it's the attitude. My parents, my family. They don't understand what I've been going through in Brisbane, or what I want to do. It's so incomprehensible from the point of view of life out here.'

'Indeed it is.'

230

'What is it they get from this sort of life, anyway? What do they *want* from it?'

'Just survival, Rachel. That's what it always comes down to, in the end.'

'I don't believe that . . .'

'No, I was talking from a personal perspective.'

She looked at me.

'I can't believe that either. You couldn't be content with that, Gordon. Just having existed for sixty or seventy years.'

'It won't be that long.'

'You didn't always think like that.'

'No, I didn't. Or maybe I did. It's hard to tell, looking back, what I really believed.'

'You should read some of the old letters you wrote me.'

'God, no. All that love in them, Rach. No wonder you told me to stop it.'

She didn't answer.

I asked, 'Are you embarrassed by it, these days?'

'You mean by me and you? No. I never understood what you were going on about. I certainly never felt the same. And for all that you kept telling me that you loved me, you never actually said much. You never do. I don't know if you know this or not, but you don't express your emotions very well. You act decently enough towards the people you care about, sometimes, but you don't *tell* them anything.'

I looked at my drink. I hadn't expected this.

I said, 'Speech is such a definite thing.'

'So?'

I thought for a long time, staring at my drink.

I started again. 'Maybe it's a matter of sincerity. I'm never that certain of anything I feel about a person, and talking about it simplifies it all so brutally. It's easier to keep quiet. To act what you feel. Actions are softer. They can be interpreted in lots of different ways, and emotions *should* be interpreted in lots of different ways.'

231

'But people are never going to understand you.'

'People are never going to understand you if you tell them things, either. It'd be even worse.'

She shook her head.

'It's been weird,' she said, 'watching you go through the women. They get so infatuated with you. I don't know why.'

'You know me better than they do, that's all.'

She was staring at me.

'You do have a certain sort of look, I suppose.'

'It's not the way I look. It's more to do with the fact that I don't represent any sort of threat to anyone.'

It was an important statement. What I meant was that because I had no particular life or commitments of my own, I was never going to threaten the life or commitments of anyone else. It could be a frightening thing, looking at how a possible relationship might change the way you existed. In that respect at least, I was a safe option.

Rachel was looking away to the hills again.

'I don't know about *that*,' she said.

Around midnight we went to bed. Rachel put me in one of her brothers' bedrooms. I didn't kiss her goodnight and I didn't make any offers. It was a cool evening. I curled up in the single bed and thought about Rachel, curled up in her single bed. I thought about her body, the way it would curl. It was a solid, angular body. It was almost sexless. But it did something to me.

It was excitement and sadness.

I'd seen her bedroom. There was a jar of Vaseline on the bedside table.

They weren't noble thoughts, but they were still sad.

What did she do, I wondered, with that Vaseline?

Next day Rachel saddled up her old horse and went riding. I didn't like horses. Large animals in general. I had no sympathy for them, or for people who liked them. I watched her move up the hills. It looked awkward. A little stiff. She hadn't ridden for some time. She disappeared.

I didn't know what I'd hoped for from the weekend. Depression settled.

Things were back to normal.

FORTY-THREE

Rachel.

Again.

I couldn't stop thinking about her. Once we were back in
Brisbane I travelled over to her place every few days, to get
out of the flat. Life was slow. I was sleeping fifteen or sixteen hours a day, staring at TV. I needed the conversation.

They were strange days. I didn't understand why I was
there, what it was I wanted from Rachel. I understood that
she wanted nothing from me but friendship. I understood
that all I could do was hurt her if I pushed it further than
that. And I understood that she didn't even have any of the
qualities I was attracted to in a woman. Lust or greed or
impatience. She was sympathetic, she was sincere. It was
all wrong.

And I had nothing to offer her. She told me about her
men. They weren't anything like me. She talked about the
love, she talked about the sex. She discussed it all in
emotional terms. What the love meant. What the sex meant.

I didn't care what the sex meant. I only wanted to know
what happened. If she enjoyed it, if she came. I watched

her talking and I thought how wide did she open her mouth to fit his penis in? Did she even do that? What *did* they do? How often? Where? How did she undress? How did he undress? Did they do it fast, did they do it slow? What noises did she make? What did she say? How did they sleep when it was over?

I imagined Rachel naked. I masturbated over it. I wrote poems about her. It depressed me, disgusted me. I couldn't keep away from her. I even tried to sort out the attraction, rationalise it the way Rachel herself might have, but there were no answers. When I was away from her I could make judgements. I could see the impossibility of it all. But once I was with her again, once I could see her, smell her, listen to her voice, it all slipped away. Something unnamable took over. Something deeper than reason.

Reason said I should have stayed with Cynthia. Cynthia was everything Rachel wasn't. It was obvious Cynthia was right for me and I was right for her. And yet it still hadn't worked.

Then it was a Sunday night. Rachel, Frank and I were drinking at the Queen's Arms. Things were pretty slow, the crowd was small, but we were drinking steadily enough. We were talking about Cynthia. The bar staff, all her old workmates, kept coming over and asking me how she was.

Frank had to work next morning. About nine he called a cab and left. Rachel and I drank on. When the bar closed, we began walking home to my place. We were both drunk.

'Gordon,' she said, 'I think you should stop talking about Cynthia. You should stop calling her and stop thinking about her. You're never going to get over her if you go on like this.'

'I don't think it's really up to me. Anyway, I need the phone calls to Darwin. They're difficult, but they're important. It's something to do with sanity.'

'How?'

'Because *Cynthia* has sanity. It's not obvious, but if I really think about her behaviour, it makes sense. I can't say that for anyone else I know.'

'She was crazy, Gordon.'

'No. She just understands some difficult things.'

'Like what?'

'Like nothing bad should *ever* be accepted gracefully.'

'Bullshit, Gordon. She's four weeks out of your life and you've already forgotten all the reasons why you hated her.'

She was wrong. I hadn't forgotten.

About a block from home I stopped off at a takeaway to order a hamburger. Rachel wasn't hungry. She said she'd walk on and meet me back at the flat. She'd kept that old liking for walking the streets alone at night.

I waited five minutes or so for the burger. Then I started off. Halfway there I looked up a side street and saw Rachel wandering along the footpath. I called out. She turned around and came back.

'Help me, Gordon,' she said. 'I'm lost.'

I put my arm around her. 'Where were you going?'

'I don't know, I don't know.'

We made it home. We sat in front of the TV while I ate. Then I said, 'I'm going to bed, Rachel. You can have half the mattress, if you want. I'll drive you home in the morning.'

She thought about it. 'Okay. Thanks.'

We went to bed. Normally I slept naked. This time I put on some shorts. Rachel took off her jeans and lay down next to me.

We talked for a while. We were very close, our hips were touching. Rachel rolled towards me and put her head on my shoulder.

236

'Rachel, I don't think you should do that.'
'Do what?'
'Touch me.'
'Why not?'
'I want more from this than you do.'
She took hold of my arm. She was quiet a long time.
Then she said, 'Don't be too sure.'

I thought, Oh my God.

I couldn't think of anything to say.
I kissed her.
She kissed back.
It was The Miracle.

Our mouths worked open.
I thought, I'm kissing Rachel, I'm kissing *Rachel*.
And it was good. I couldn't compare it to kissing Cynthia, or to kissing anyone. I couldn't even remember what anyone else had been like. This was ten years of fantasy and repression coming true. This was frightening. This was Rachel, this was Rachel's *mouth*.

We rolled together. I was erect, but I didn't press it against her. I was convinced that whatever Rachel was doing with me, it had nothing to do with my penis or my warts.

I ran my hands along her sides, along her T-shirt. Rachel was tall. Her sides were long and smooth. They curved out with her hips and then . . . then I was at the end of the T-shirt.

I slid a finger under the hem. I thought, She can't want this, *surely* she can't want this.

She didn't stop me. I moved my hand under. I was touching naked skin. Her stomach. It was hot, soft, dry. I moved my hand up. We weren't kissing any more. I was lying

237

on my side. She was lying on her back. I was running
my hand across her stomach. Upwards. It was happening.
And Rachel . . . I wasn't sure *what* she was doing. Maybe
nothing. Maybe she was just lying there, waiting.

I was at her breasts.

If you don't stop this now, Rachel, I thought, if you don't
stop this now . . .

Her breasts were small. With my other hand I raised the
T-shirt to uncover them. It was dark in the room. I couldn't
see anything, but my hand was there, and the tips of my
fingers. I found a nipple, rolled a finger around it, across it.

She made a sound.

She said, 'I want you to touch me, Gordon.'

And I was.

Touching *Rachel*.

My brain wouldn't accept it. It was worse than I could
ever have imagined.

I was kissing her breasts, *Rachel's* breasts, sucking them,
catching them between my teeth. Her hands, *Rachel's* hands,
were on my back, in my hair . . .

Then my hand was moving down again, along *Rachel's*
side, over *Rachel's* hip, *Rachel's* panties, along *Rachel's* leg,
back up again, along *Rachel's* thigh, down inside to the flat
stretch of her panties, across it, feeling that it was wet,
Rachel was *wet*, then down along the other thigh, back up
again.

Then my fingers were under the hem of her panties, into
her pubic hair. It was thick, curled. Then on through the
hair, down, under the stretch of elastic. The hair gave out
and then there was just skin. A fold that opened into
Rachel's cunt. *Rachel's* cunt. And Rachel's cunt was warm
and wet and open, just a little. I was running my fingers
around the edges, up to the clitoris. It hardened, moved
under my finger.

238

And Rachel was making noises and pushing against my hand.

Then I was kissing her breasts again. Then sliding down her chest, hooking my hands under her panties, pulling them down. Lifting her hips. Pulling the panties over her ankles.

And then my head was between her legs.

Vaginas.

There were several billion of them out there in the world. Women were raised with them, examined them, got used to them, knew about them. But men, what could men do? What could they ever hope to understand? Vaginas were baffling. They spent most of their lives closed up and unthought of, but they were never still. They sweated and moved. They suffered disease, hid disease, harboured disease. They grew stale, smelt terrible, contracted so that not even a finger could get in, expanded so that a baby could get out. They tore open, healed, had spasms, itched, bled, passed urine. They took pleasure, took pain, lubricated, didn't lubricate, stretched over the years, lost shape, had large lips, had no lips, had hair, had no hair, had depth, had curves, had lumps and creases and folds.

And they were part of a *woman*. And if something happened to a vagina, it happened to a woman. And anything that a man did to a vagina, he did to a woman.

But a man could never know exactly what it was he was doing.

When he found himself there.

I nuzzled my way in. Rachel's legs fell to the sides. She smelt light, good. She smelt like Cynthia. She was wetter, though. Cynthia never lubricated very well. I ran my nose up and down the slit, breathing on it, wondering what it felt like for her. I knew it was unhealthy to breathe into vaginas. I didn't know why. I pushed out my tongue, ran it around the rim for a while. My mouth slotted around it perfectly. The lips of Rachel's cunt were small tight ridges, smooth and uncomplicated. I moved my mouth up to where the lips joined and licked the spot until I had her clitoris exposed again and swollen. I squeezed my hands under her buttocks. I lifted her a little. Settled down to it with my tongue.

I didn't expect it to work. It wasn't like anything else, other times and other women. I had no confidence. Not when it came to Rachel, not like this. And confidence was everything. I developed a rhythm with my tongue, up down, up down, treating her clit as if it was a nipple. Rachel pushed with her hips, pulled back, made noises, ran her hands through my hair. My tongue began to ache. Maybe it was working, maybe it wasn't. I was worried about Rachel. Oral sex could be such a horrible thing for the one who had to receive it. It wasn't like fucking. There was the terrible onus of having to enjoy it.

Maybe she wasn't enjoying it? Maybe she wasn't enjoying it at all? Maybe she was just trying to, for my sake, and the longer my tongue licked up and down, the worse it became. The worse it became for us both. Maybe it was failing. Maybe I'd go on until my tongue couldn't take it any more and I'd pull away and she'd make uncertain movements and say something like, 'That was nice'. And we'd be left with it. That word. Nice.

And this was it, this was all there was. I knew we weren't going to be fucking. I knew I wouldn't even be fucking her with my fingers. This was all we were going to have.

But then it *worked*.

Rachel's breathing deepened. Her hands in my hair grew distracted. Her legs tightened around my head and began to quiver. She gasped, hissed, jammed her cunt in my face.

And she came. My mouth was full of saliva, juices. I had to swallow to avoid gagging. I drank her in. Her thighs were slippery with it.

'Stop stop stop,' she said, tugging at my hair.

I stopped.

I rose up and kissed her mouth.

She kissed back.

She said, 'I can't believe this.'

'Neither can I.'

'I feel terrible. I used you, Gordon.'

'Rachel, I *want* you to use me.'

She was quiet for a while. 'I've had dreams, y'know, about what it would be like to sleep with you. After all these years.'

'Where they good or bad dreams?'

'I don't know. I don't feel the same as you do. I'm not in love with you. You seem to think I'm some sort of perfect person. I'm not.'

'I know. I don't know what it is. But I know it isn't the same for you. It's okay.'

'I can't do anything for you. I mean, sexually.'

'I know. It doesn't matter.'

'Yes it does.'

'Okay, maybe it does, but not at the moment. Did you enjoy it, Rachel? I mean, if you didn't, you should tell me, and I won't do it again.'

'I enjoyed it. I don't fake things, if that's what you mean.'

'I suppose I do.'

'Don't worry, then.'

We dozed. Later we woke up and started again. This time it didn't work so well. She moved and made noises and pressed, but there was no conclusion. I lifted my mouth away. I used my fingers, tried to move one deeper in. Her cunt closed up. I stopped.

I lay down. I was erect. I had been, off and on, for the last couple of hours. My shorts were wet.

We dozed again. Rachel rolled away from me. I curled up against her back. She tensed. Moved away. Dawn came around and we were both awake. I was staring at her shoulder blades. It was a long, straight, narrow back. She turned over and looked at me.

'I think I should go.'

'Wait a while. I'll be sober enough to drive you home in a few hours.'

'No. I should go now. This is all wrong.'

'Why?'

'It just is.' She was up now, dressing. I watched her.

I said, 'I'm sorry. I didn't mean to force anything.'

'Don't apologise. I wanted you to do it. That's why I feel so bad now. It was manipulation.'

'I don't care.'

'I do.'

She finished dressing.

I said, 'Could I come round tonight?'

'Gordon, this can't happen again.'

'How will you get home?'

'I'll walk. I need a walk.'

And she went.

I lay there for a long time, not knowing what to feel. Her smell was still in the room, on my fingers. Finally I masturbated, thinking about her, about the way she'd come. Then I came. Then I slept.

FORTY-FOUR

I spent the day in the flat. I kept smelling my fingers. I told myself it was obscene, ridiculous, unfair to Rachel. She'd been nice to me the last few weeks, treated me gently when I needed it most. The last thing she deserved was for me to be fixating on the smell of her vagina.

But it was a smell that wouldn't go away. I made sandwiches, ate them, I drank some wine, smoked cigarettes — and it was still there. Between asthma and hayfever and smoking, my sense of smell wasn't even that good. I was hallucinating. My mind was doing dangerous things with what had happened.

I'd seen Rachel at a costume party once. She'd dressed up as Joan of Arc, and even though her body was all wrong for it, somehow she had looked right.

I thought about that, looking at my fingers.

Rachel called about nine that night.
'How're you feeling?' she said.
'Not too bad. How about you?'
'Terrible. I have to explain things, Gordon.'
'Well . . .'

'I'm sorry I rushed out this morning. I was confused, I needed to be alone.'

'It's okay. How do you feel about it now?'

'I don't know.'

'I don't want to pressure you, Rachel. I enjoyed it. I'd love to do it again. But not if it's going to drive you crazy.'

'I don't know, I just don't know. Maybe I *should* try things with you. We've been spending so much time together anyway. I've enjoyed it. And the rest of it, I mean emotionally, and in bed too, might come after a while.'

'Yes, it might.'

'I'll have to think about it.'

'Okay. I'm certainly prepared to wait.'

We talked a little more, then hung up.

I poured myself a glass of wine. So I was still in with a chance. At what I didn't know — but it didn't matter. Anything would do.

I poured myself a glass of wine and dialled Cynthia. We talked for half an hour. It went well.

I didn't mention Rachel.

It wasn't until the end of the week that I saw Rachel again. We went to a party, then back to her place. There was a cask of wine in the fridge. We poured glasses. We sat on the couch and watched the late night music videos for a while. We were holding hands. She had long, beautiful hands.

'I've been thinking, Gordon,' she said.

'And?'

'And I think we could try it for a while.'

'Good.'

'I'm not promising anything . . .'

I thought about kissing her. It was the right time, but I preferred to let moments like that pass. We didn't move. We held hands.

244

We leaned back on the couch, her head was on my shoulder. I ran my hand through her hair, kissed it. She turned up her head . . . and there it was, we were kissing. I was kissing Rachel for a *second night*. Life was full of the impossible.

We got up and went into her bedroom. We lay on the bed. I undressed her slowly. I unbuttoned her shirt, took it off. I kissed her breasts through her bra. She had told me once that she was the first girl in her class to develop breasts. She was ten and a half, it was two years before I fell in love with her. I unhooked the bra, took it off.

She started tugging at my shirt.

I took it off, I took everything off. I was erect and the tip of my penis was wet. I kept it away from her vagina. I moved in with my mouth. I worked and sweated. My tongue ached, cramped. I persevered and finally it all seemed to work.

'You're very patient,' she said, afterwards.

'It does get to the tongue after a while.'

'I know. I have the same problem with my finger.'

Rachel?

Masturbating?

She was right. I didn't know her or understand anything about her at all. I still thought of her as some kind of virgin saint. It was a mistake. Of course she thought about sex, of course she masturbated, of course she drank, swore, procrastinated, fucked up her life like anyone else.

But it was strange. There was something in her that seemed to reject all those things. She lacked a certain sympathy for people who let their lives get out of control. She didn't like Cynthia because Cynthia was crass and lazy and a slave to her own cunt. Rachel didn't appreciate just how sex and self-indulgence could completely take over. Even I understood that. Sex appalled me, disappointed me, depressed me, but I knew it had *power* over me, all the same.

245

Only heroin seemed capable of engrossing me more, and heroin was sex anyway. But the urge to fuck was the one thing for which I could pardon anyone, anytime, for anything.

Maybe that's what I was after with Rachel. Maybe I needed to prove to myself that she wasn't any different from the rest of us. To prove that her cunt could over-ride her reason. I wanted to see what lay under all that self control.

Other men had been there. Driven her there.

It was my turn.

We started up again. At one stage I was on my stomach and Rachel was astride my hips, massaging my back. It didn't feel right, not for me, not for her. Her hands didn't suck up my flesh the way mine sucked up hers. My body was just a body — a large, round, ungainly body at that. She went for thin, bony men. And there wasn't enough love between us to surpass the physical. I rolled her off me, sought out her cunt again with my fingers.

Then I was astride her. My fingers were rolling around her clitoris. She was stretched out below me, moving and breathing and building up. I took her hand and moved it down. I placed her index finger on her clitoris, placed my own finger on top of that, then moved them both, up and down, side to side. Her finger took over. I lifted mine away. I watched her do it to herself. Her finger moved quicker and in a different pattern to the way I'd been doing it. She spread her legs. She worked at it. She was coming while I looked on. I couldn't stand it any more. I dived back down, applied my tongue, finished it off. Then I started up again, very softly.

I could've stayed there, implanted to her vagina, for hours. I wanted *this* to be Rachel. It didn't matter if it was the whole truth about her, or any of the truth. I could believe

246

it. I chose to believe it. This *was* her. My mouth was wrapped around the straw that led to her soul.

I took my mouth away.

We looked at each other.

'Lie on your back,' she said.

I lay back. She crouched over me. I was alarmed. I hadn't been expecting this. Her hands moved around. Finally they found my prick. It was lubricating, wet. She rolled her palm over the tip, moved her fingers down the shaft. I was close to panicking. RACHEL WAS TOUCHING MY PENIS! The sensations were very light, she wasn't using any pressure, but her hands were *there*. They were long and cool and excruciating. Then she moved down my chest.

I lay quite still. I didn't know what to do. Her hand was still moving. Up, down. Her head dropped. She kissed the insides of my thighs. Then she moved upwards. Her face hovered over my erection. I could feel her breath. I was terrified. What was I going to do? The Virgin Saint was going to suck my prick. It was conceptually incomprehensible. It wasn't part of the plan. It was wrong. God, I couldn't come in her *mouth* . . .

Her lips still hovered, just a few inches above. They were open. They were ready. She was watching her hand as it moved.

She looked up at me.

'I'm sorry,' she said, 'I can't help thinking.'

'Yes?'

'About the warts.'

'Oh.'

Her hand stopped.

She took it away.

Later that night I tried it with my fingers again, just in case. She was wet. She seemed to like it as long as my fingers only moved around the rim. I coaxed a finger in, rolled it around gently, pulled it back, pushed it forward, very slow, very rhythmic. She moved with it, but I couldn't tell in exactly what sense. I concentrated, put all my mixed up longings into that finger. After a minute or two, I said, 'Is this hurting?'

She sighed.

'It doesn't hurt, but it doesn't feel right either.'

I withdrew the finger. 'I'm sorry.'

'No, it's okay.'

Next morning I woke to hayfever and asthma. Hayfever was a fairly constant problem with me. Cynthia wasn't the only one with allergies. In my case, antihistamines usually helped. I was on about eight or ten milligrams of antihistamines a day at that stage. I was allergic to all the things I liked — nicotine, alcohol, dope, dust, wool, cheese, tomatoes, Chinese food . . .

I didn't have any antihistamines with me. I got up, gasping and sniffling and clutching my sinuses. I went and sat in the bathtub. I ran the shower over my head. This cure took a lot longer, but it often worked.

I sat there until the hot water ran out. Then I lay in front of the television and put a handkerchief over my nose and mouth — that sometimes helped too. Some time later, towards noon, Rachel came out wrapped in a towel. She said good morning and looked at me.

'You look sick.'

'It's only hayfever. It'll go away.'

She was concerned. 'When you were asleep last night, I listened to your chest, it sounded *terrible*.'

'I know. I shouldn't smoke.'

She went off and showered. Then she came back and went into her bedroom. Her bedroom door was right next to the television. She left it open. I watched. She took off the towel, stood naked looking about the room for clothes.

248

'What're you doing today?' she asked me.
'Nothing.'
'Any ideas for breakfast?'
'Anything to eat here?'
'Nope.'
She found a bra, put it on. Then some panties. Then she came and stood in the door. 'There's a deli in Paddington . . .'
I looked at her. I was all fucked up. It was like I was looking at the Mother of God in her underwear.
I blew my nose.
She got dressed.

My car was outside her place. We got in, drove to the deli and bought ourselves breakfast. It wasn't very good. There was nothing to say. We knew everything about each other . . . we'd grown up together, known each other half our lives. The only things we didn't know about each other were sexual. And in the early, hungover, post-sex afternoon, what was to say even about that?

After lunch I dropped her home again.
All I had in mind for the afternoon was a beer or two and the Saturday afternoon game of Rugby League — and Rachel didn't follow the football. Not many women I knew did. Maybe it was too obvious for them. A symbol of male preoccupations. Violence, strength, pointless skill, war.
Cynthia liked the League. She didn't follow any particular team, but there were some she hated. Some of the Sydney teams. Canterbury. Balmain. I felt largely the same way. Brisbane was my home, after all.
Balmain were playing that afternoon. I watched the game. Balmain lost in an upset result to a bottom of the ladder side. I called up Cynthia.
'Did you *see* that?'
'See what?'

'The game! Balmain went down!'

'So?'

'What's wrong?'

'How's Rachel?'

'She's okay, why?'

'I *know* about it, Gordon, you *fucked* her. You couldn't even wait a month after I'd gone.'

'Cynthia . . . I was going to tell you.'

'She's ugly, Gordon, she's ugly!'

'It's not like that, we aren't having sex, we're just in the same bed . . .'

'Oh God.' She was sobbing. 'Do you think that makes it any better?'

'How did you know?'

'It doesn't matter. Anyone but Rachel, Gordon, anyone but her.'

And suddenly I was angry. Tired. She was thousands of miles away and she still wouldn't let me go.

I said, 'Cynthia, you have to stop this.'

'I can't. I love you!'

'That's not enough . . .'

She stopped crying. She sniffed. 'Okay. Fine. So what's she like to fuck, then?'

'I told you. We aren't doing that.'

'Oh, so you both just lie there in bed getting off on conversation? What the fuck is wrong with you?'

'Cynthia . . .'

'Oh, sorry, I forgot about this Great Love of yours. So what is it, you haven't actually stuck it in yet?'

'I'm not going to.'

'Well what d'you do, then, suck each other off?'

'Cynthia, you don't want to know —'

'I want to know!' And then, quietly, 'I have to know.'

And I had to answer. I owed her that.

'I do things to her, that's all. She doesn't touch me. It's weird.'

She started laughing. She sounded insane. 'You do things to her? Fuck, Gordon, that makes me *sick*!'

I said, 'Look, it's none of your business any more.'

'Oh bullshit. Bullshit bullshit bull*shit*!'

She slammed the phone down.

I hung up my end.

I thought about calling her back, I knew she wanted me to.

The time passed.

I didn't call. The phone didn't ring.

FORTY-FIVE

I bought a pack of condoms.
  Ultra Forms, economy pack.
  Thirty-six of the things.

I went drinking with Frank again, in one of the Valley
pubs.
  I said, 'I've bought thirty-six condoms.'
  'That's quite a few.'
  'I might need them.'
  'You and Rachel?'
  'I don't know.'
  'Do you think she wants to?'
  'I don't know.'
  'Do you want to?'
  'I don't know.'
  'I see.'
  'It's not healthy, Frank.'
  We drank.
  Frank said, 'It's just sex, Gordon.'

I went over to Rachel's place a few nights later, on a Friday. We planned to spend the weekend together. I took the condoms with me. They disturbed me — nothing was clear — but they were necessary. Rachel met me at the door. She poured me a wine and we sat down on the couch. She talked about her week. There was nothing to say about mine. We held hands, got our legs tangled up, started kissing. It was good. This much was natural. I was Making It On The Couch With Rachel.

'What's this?' she said, digging into the pocket of my shirt.

'I'm not sure you want to know.'

She took out the condoms. It was a big, big box. And there was a tube of K-Y as well. It didn't look good.

She examined it all.

'Think you're gonna get lucky, huh?'

'It's got nothing to do with luck, Rachel.'

'It won't be tonight,' she said, 'I've got my period.'

'Is that supposed to bother me or you?'

'Me.'

'Oh.'

And it was gone again.

She was untouchable.

We drank for a few hours. The alcohol confused the issue. Probably it was our only hope. Certainly it was my only hope. I didn't know *what* Rachel was. We started kissing again. It wasn't the same. All my preoccupations about her came flooding up. We couldn't just fuck. I wasn't there for sex or love. I was there for adoration. Self-abasement. The impulses were all diseased, rooted in darkness.

I got her shirt off and I'd tugged her bra down under her breasts, forcing them up and out. I got down on my knees on the floor, between her legs. I worked on the button to her jeans.

253

'No,' she said.

The button was undone. I pulled down her jeans. Pulled down her panties. The string was there. I tugged the tampon out.

'Gordon, *don't* . . .'

I moved between her legs.

Her cunt was there, where it always was. I could taste iron and sweat. I sucked it in, rolled my tongue against the clitoris. It hardened. My chin was dug into the couch. This was all I was, a mouth and a tongue. A slave. Whether she wanted it or not. *I* was the slave to *her* cunt. It was all wrong. This wasn't the way to her soul, anyone could see that. Her soul was somewhere else, somewhere where I'd never find it. Another man would be the one for that. I didn't care. I could live without her soul. All I wanted was this.

And maybe she wanted me. Just a little. Some part of her responded. Not a good part, but it was still her. Her legs relaxed, spread. She lifted her hips. Her cunt molded around my mouth. I stroked and stroked. Then she was coming. I looked up. Her head was arched back. Her face was contorted. Noises were coming from her mouth. It was ugly. It was pain.

Then it was over. She wouldn't look at me. I stood up. I took her hand and led her into her bedroom. She lay down. We didn't speak. I took off my clothes. I was erect. I walked back into the living room, got the condoms and the K-Y and went back. Rachel had rolled onto her side, facing the wall. I sat down beside her.

I said, 'Rachel, can you do this?'

I watched her back.

'No,' she said.

I put the condoms on the floor.

'Why can't you wait until I've sorted out what I feel?' she said. She was crying. 'Why can't men ever *wait*?'

254

I said, 'Rachel, why did you choose tampons over pads?'
She rolled over. Stared at me. 'What?'
'I was just wondering . . .'
'What the fuck does it matter?'
'I don't know.'
She rolled away again.
I watched her for a while. I looked at the condoms and the K-Y. At the floor, the walls, the ceiling.
My erection went down.

FORTY-SIX

We didn't speak a great deal the next morning. Rachel was distant, moody. Around midday I packed it in, drove home and went back to bed.

The phone woke me about seven that evening. It was Rachel. She said, 'We have to talk, Gordon. I'm not sure about things any more. Can I come over?'

'Sure. I'll come and pick you up.'

'Thanks.'

'It's okay.'

I drove over, picked her up and drove back. We stopped along the way for a cask of rosé. We sat down on the couch and drank a few glasses, but it wasn't very good. Rachel was uncomfortable.

She said, 'I don't think it's going to work.'

I was ready for it. I said, 'I understand.'

'I just don't feel the same as you do, Gordon. It's not going to change.'

'I know. I'm sorry.'

'Don't apologise. I wanted to try things out as much as you did. I don't know what I thought would happen, but obviously it's not going to . . .'

'It's okay, Rachel. I'm glad we got as far as we did. But if you don't feel right about it, then we'll stop. I can do it. My feelings towards you aren't exactly healthy, but they're not uncontrollable.'

She looked at me. 'That's one of the problems. I don't understand the way you feel about me. Not exactly healthy? What am I supposed to think you mean by that?'

'I don't really understand that myself . . .'

'It annoys me, Gordon. How can I sort things out with you when I don't even know what you see in me? What *do* you see in me?'

It was the question I'd been dreading. I stared at my drink. Nothing I could say was going to be right.

I said, 'You have presence.'

Sure enough, she got angry. 'That's pathetic. It's bullshit. *Presence*? What's that supposed to mean? Is it my company you like? Is that what you mean? Is it what I say? Is it what I do with my life?'

'No. Those things don't seem to matter.'

'Well, how do you think that makes me feel? If you don't like me for my company, for what I am and what I do, then how can I feel that you're attracted to me at all?'

'But I am. At least, all the things you talk about and all the things you do become important to me because they're yours.'

'But otherwise they wouldn't matter at all. You don't agree with me, or share any interests with me, do you?'

'I guess not . . .'

'Then what sort of understanding could we ever have? I mean, what've you really got to *offer* me in a relationship, Gordon?'

I was sitting forward on the couch. I was staring at the

floor. I'd been cornered, I knew it. Everything she was saying was right. She'd stripped all the magic away.

I said, 'Nothing.'

And it was true. I was empty-handed. I had no life to share. I had nothing to offer but endless spare time and a cruel, mindless devotion. Some women might've considered that, but not Rachel.

'Nothing,' she said. 'Great. That's just great.'

We didn't say anything for a time. I finished my glass and poured another.

Finally she said, 'I don't want to hurt you, Gordon, you're important to me, but what are you doing with your life? You can't develop a love with someone unless you know what you're doing yourself. Do you know what you're doing?'

'No.'

I was beaten, I was tired of questions. I *did* know what I was doing. The problem was that the knowledge was deeply unconscious, it was a premonition, it was a gut-level instinct. I knew I had to stick it out with this life for *some* reason, some important reason.

'Is it the writing?' Rachel asked. 'Is that it?'

'No, I don't think so.'

And that was true, too. Whatever it was, it wasn't the writing. It wasn't anything external at all. It was something profoundly internal. Something to do with simple survival. With existence. I wasn't even close to knowing. But in some way, what I was doing — wandering around this way, month after month, wasting my time, my health, my money, going nowhere, seeing nothing — somehow it had a purpose. My life as a whole felt right, as much as all the individual pieces of it looked wrong.

But I couldn't say any of this to Rachel.

We sat in silence. We drank. We watched TV. The TV, at least, had a lot to say.

258

About midnight Rachel said she was tired and was going home. I looked at her.

'You can have half the bed, just to sleep.'

'I should go.'

'I can't drive you, I've drunk too much. And you can't walk now, it's too late, and you can't afford a taxi...'

'I know, I know ... Okay. I'll stay.'

She went in to bed. I had another drink, then followed her in. She was lying under the sheets, fully clothed. I undressed, climbed in. She wasn't asleep.

'You could take off your clothes,' I said.

She looked at me. She was unhappy. 'What do you want me to do, Gordon?'

'I don't know. Sleep with me? Just for the sake of it? It's good to have sex with *someone*.'

'I could sleep with any number of men, if sex was what I wanted. Why should it be you?'

And there was no answer.

She was crying.

I said, 'I'm sorry.'

'No. It's okay. I don't hate you, Gordon, I just don't understand you.'

I got up again, went back to the couch. I was tired. It was all over already. The grand obsession and fantasy had flared and died. And I was letting it go. I wasn't screaming at Rachel, I wasn't going to fight her over it, I was going to accept it gracefully. I didn't have the sort of strength that Cynthia had. The effort would only depress me. I knew I would lose.

So I drank until all the wine was gone. Then I went back to Rachel, and the bed.

I woke to find her face resting against mine. I looked at it. It wasn't a good face, up close, in the morning. There were the pimples and the gum in the eyes. But it was Rachel and it was the end of a lot of things. I kissed her. She stirred, opened her eyes, and kissed me back. Her breath was warm. Stale. Mine was worse. The kiss didn't stop. It was happening one last time. We pulled off her clothes and I was down in the heat between her legs. It would always be there. For whatever reason. The flesh of Rachel's cunt was the mystery incarnate. And it folded itself around my mouth, and it pulled, and it took everything I had to give . . .

'I'm sorry,' she said, 'that time it *was* just for the sex.'
    'I know. It doesn't matter.'
    'It's the last time.'
    'I know that too.'
We got up, dressed, and I drove her home.

FORTY-SEVEN

I went back to the poetry. I wrote about Cynthia. Love poems, sex poems, hate poems. There didn't seem to be anything to say about Rachel. I put the poems into the letters to Cynthia, sent them off. On the phone I told her how things had turned out with Rachel.

'Good,' she said. 'You deserve it, I hope it hurts.'

But there wasn't much real hatred left in Cynthia. The phone calls were getting better. She liked the letters, liked the poems. Some of them hurt her, some of them had nothing in them but disgust at what she was, but I sent them all. It was a matter of honesty. And she seemed to understand. But she didn't write back. She said *that* would take time.

I spent several very quiet weeks. I saw Rachel a few times. It was okay. I saw everyone. I went out for drinks, drank alone, but nothing much seemed to happen. Social Security sent me my money. The house was quiet. Vass was thinking of moving out. There was a woman who wanted him. A woman with long golden red hair and a pet dog and a house of her own.

I told him he was lucky. I told him he was a fool if he didn't go. I flicked through the porn mags and masturbated and dreamed of sex. I didn't want to be alone.

I received a phone call. It was from Sophie. She'd heard it was all over between me and Cynthia. She was having a party.

I went. It was a Friday night. Sophie lived in a block of small brick flats. There were about twenty people crammed into her living room. Office workers, factory workers. A good crowd. Sophie took me in and introduced me round. I ended up talking to a woman called Susan. She lived in the flat next to Sophie's.

She said, 'Sophie tells me you're a writer. Is that true?'

'No. Not really.'

'Good.'

I liked her. She was short and wide, with bobbed blonde hair. Huge eyes. We talked and the party went on around us. Sophie joined us from time to time. In the end it was just the three of us, sitting around the table, drinking. It got later and later. Susan grew quiet. Sophie talked and talked. I could see what was going to happen. Finally Susan said she was going to bed. We all said goodnight. Susan left. Sophie went off to the toilet. I ran into the hall and knocked on Susan's door. She opened it.

I said, 'Can I call you tomorrow?'

'Sure.'

I ran back to Sophie's flat, sat down again. Sophie came out. We talked for a while longer. Then she took me into her bedroom.

We lay down, started kissing. It felt good, there was plenty to like about Sophie, but my heart wasn't there. I was thinking about the warts. About other things. We stopped.

Sophie said, 'You certainly spent a lot of time with Sue tonight. I thought something was going on.'

262

'It was. I should warn you, I like her. I'm going to call her tomorrow.'

'*What*? Christ, why do you always say things like that?'

'Sorry. I didn't want to lie about it . . .'

'Well, why don't you go next door now?'

'Because I'm with you.'

'Well, *why* are you with me? Why are you telling me this?'

'I'm sorry.'

'Forget it, just forget it.'

The mood was broken. There was no getting back to it. I didn't know why I *was* there. But Susan didn't seem any better as a solution. The question itself was too vast. In the end I slept. Alone, on my side of the bed.

When I woke up it was late and Sophie was gone. I dressed and then knocked on Susan's door. There was no answer. I walked back to my car and drove home.

I called Susan that night.

I said, 'How about drinks?'

'I don't think so, Gordon. I've been talking to Sophie. She's really pissed off. You hurt her last night. She's not as tough as you think.'

'Yes . . . I know that.'

'Anyway, she's a good friend of mine, and I don't think it'd be worth all the hassle.'

'I see.'

'Maybe later.'

'Sure.'

'I'll see you round, Gordon.'

We hung up.

FORTY-EIGHT

I fell ill.

It was the weather maybe. It'd been cold and wet for about a week, and I'd been walking in the rain, sitting around in soaked clothes.

It was a mixture of things — asthma, the flu, a chest infection. My respiratory system was a mess. The only things that helped were nicotine and alcohol. I spent several days in the flat, drinking the occasional glass of wine and smoking and coughing up mucus. I seemed to have it under control. At least it didn't get any worse.

Another invitation came through. This time it was for a party with all the old staff members from the Capital hotel. It was Morris who rang me. He was still bumming around, living on the dole. He'd broken up with his sixteen-year-old. I told him that for me, too, the good life was long gone.

The party was at Carla's place. Thursday night. Carla wasn't a barmaid any more. She was running deliveries around town for a courier company.

I went along. I wasn't feeling well. I needed it.

It was a cocktail party. The idea was for everyone to bring along a different bottle of spirits. I dropped into a liqour barn along the way and picked up the cheapest bottle of gin I could find. Eleven dollars ninety-nine. Off-loaded subsidised surplus from Hungary.

Carla had a nice house. She shared it with her brother and her fourteen-year-old daughter. There were maybe thirty people there. Thirty bottles of assorted spirits. My gin was bottom of the range. There were a few good bourbons, a few good liqueurs. Carla's brother had plenty of dope to smoke. And in the living room there were four people crouched around something I'd only ever dreamed about seeing. An industrial-sized cylinder of nitrous oxide. It was all going to be okay. I liked the company. They'd been good people to work with and they were very good people to drink with. No one was going anywhere. They had no money, no plans, no ambitions.

I drank down a few cocktails. The decent stuff was going first — Benedictine, Cointreau, Tia Maria, Wild Turkey, Midori, in assorted combinations. I started feeling better. My breathing lightened up. I had a few puffs on one of the joints going round. I sat down at the nitrous cylinder and waited my turn.

Carla tracked me down.

'Morris wants to fuck my *daughter!*'

'He's like that with kids . . .'

'I'm worried. She's in love with him.'

'Have you told him that?'

'No. Should I? Would that stop him?'

'No. That would be the worst thing you could do. That would make him really go for it.'

'She's only fourteen.'

'He's done it with fourteen-year-olds before. Fourteen-year-olds have *asked* him to do it with them.'

265

'I'll tear his balls off.'

'No. Morris is a good person. If someone's going to do it to her it might as well be him.'

'Gordon!'

'Don't worry. He won't do anything. He just likes to talk about it.'

'What have you been doing with yourself?'

'Nothing.'

'I hear you and Cynthia were living together.'

'Yes. We were. She's in Darwin now.'

'Who left who?'

'It was a mutual decision.'

'Anyone else?'

'Not really. I was in love, but there's no point thinking about that . . .'

'You sound very sad.'

'I am.'

It was my turn at the nitrous. It was hard to suck much in. My lungs felt fine, they just couldn't handle any volume. Then it was Carla's turn. We lost it for a few minutes.

Carla was thirty-five or thirty-six. Long black hair. Strong. I liked her. She had always been good to me, all those years at the hotel. I could never quite tell if she wanted anything to happen between us. I could never quite tell if *I* wanted anything to happen between us. Either way it never had.

I asked, 'Anyone special for you?'

'Oh, I've got a boy, he keeps me going, but he's in Sydney right now.'

'The young ones are what you need.'

'An old one is what *you* need.'

'I think you're right.'

'Cheer up, for Christ's sake.'

'You're right. I will.'

I did, for a while. I left the nitrous and went back to drinking. It was going down seriously, round for round, on the back verandah. I joined in. Morris was there. I told him about Carla's daughter. He said he was aware of the situation.

'Are you going to try anything?'

'Carla would kill me.'

I descended into drunkenness. I smoked my way to the end of my pouch of tobacco. I started bumming cigarettes off the others. I could barely taste them. I hated ready-made cigarettes. Unless they were Winfield Blues. Cynthia's brand. No one had any Winfield Blues. I smoked whatever I could get, one after the other.

The cocktails went on. We got down to the bad stuff. They were mixing vodka and gin and crème de menthe. It was horrible. We forced it down. A rumour went round that someone was putting dishwashing liquid in the drinks. It could've been true.

About one or two in the morning I wandered back into the living room. Things were getting blurred, bodies were staggering around. I had another go at a joint, sucked on the nitrous. It didn't seem to have any effect. There was a stack of videos in the corner. I started going through them. Carla joined me.

'We need some porn,' I said. 'Is there any here?'

'I dunno if that's what we really need, Gordon . . .'

But there it was, on the bottom of the pile. Every house has one somewhere.

'I'm not gonna watch that,' Carla told me.

'Fair enough.' I slid it in, turned it on.

Carla left.

The crowd in the living room didn't take to it. They thought I was trying to get an orgy started. They picked it to pieces.

'This is gross.'

'Look, it's not even erect!'

'It's fake, it's fake!'

'He's not gonna make it, he'll never come like *that*.'

'This is *sick*!'

They demanded I turn it off. I didn't. I was enjoying it. They were missing the point. This was good.

I tried to explain. There was a right way and a wrong way to watch movies like this. The wrong way was to sit back and make comments about the inanity of it all. Any fool could do that. The purpose of porn was to accept it all and learn. To go beyond the terrible acting, the film quality, the editing, the plot, and get into the bodies themselves. The bodies were the important things. They were real. The people were real. They thrust and bounced and the raw flesh gurgled. You could see what humanity was all about.

'Porn videos,' I told them, 'are a chronicle. They're a testimony. Watching them, you get to the very essence of mankind's age-long struggle with credibility.'

And it was a struggle mankind was likely to lose. The reaction of the living room crowd made that clear to me. The fucking distracted them, enthralled them, disgusted them. Someone shouldered by me and turned it off.

It was time to go.

I found Carla and said goodbye. She asked me to call her one day. I said I would.

I passed Morris in the doorway. He was leaning over Carla's daughter. The daughter was beautiful. Her eyes were wide. She was what Carla had been, twenty years ago.

Outside it was raining again.

I walked out into the street, down to the main road, looking for a taxi. There weren't any. I started walking home. I got there before I saw any cabs, two hours later, and fell into bed.

268

FORTY-NINE

I woke early next afternoon.

I was dying.

This was it, I'd gone too far, my lungs had had enough. I couldn't breathe. The asthma had me. There was no air. Every time I tried to inhale all that came was pain. I sucked at the Ventolin. I coughed and shuddered. Nothing went in. I was over the edge, I was going.

I sat on the bed for a long time, hoping it would pass. It didn't. I needed a cigarette. There was no tobacco in the flat. I was thankful for that, otherwise I would've tried and it would've been the end.

Instead I got up. My vision went red, faded. I swayed. There was no oxygen in my brain. I waited until it passed. I went and showered. I didn't feel any better. I sat in the flat for another hour. Nothing improved. I became deeply annoyed. My body was letting me down. I wasn't going to make it on my own. I was going to have to seek *medical help*.

I dressed and drove up to the Royal Brisbane Hospital. There was nowhere to leave the car except a multi-level car park. Two dollars fifty an hour. I couldn't afford this. *Damn* the lungs.

I walked very slowly across to casualty, then up through the long waiting room to the nurse's desk. She looked up.

I said, 'I'm having an asthma attack.' It was barely a whisper. There was death in my throat.

'Right,' she said. She took me straight through to the consulting rooms. She left me in one and went off for the doctor. I felt gratified. I was a serious case, they were rushing me through.

The doctor came in, a young woman, a resident. She looked at me. 'How long have you been like this?'

'A few hours.'

She shook her head, started some tests. She listened to my lungs, took my blood pressure, got me to blow into a machine that registered my lung capacity. It hurt to blow into anything. The needle went up, went down.

'How's it look?'

'Forty per cent,' she said.

'That's bad?'

'That's terrible.'

It felt about right.

'I'm going to have to admit you,' she went on. 'I don't think you can treat this at home.'

'I'd prefer to, if I could . . .' I was thinking of the car. Two fifty an hour.

'No.' She took me into another room and asked me to undress. I did so and she gave me a robe. I put it on and lay down on the table. She put a mask over my face, pumped oxygen and Ventolin through it. Then she inserted a drip into my arm, injected several drugs through it, attached a saline bag. Then she took a blood sample and left me there.

I still couldn't breathe, but I wasn't worried about that now. It was out of my hands. The system was taking over and for once I was glad.

270

Another nurse came in and started taking my details down.

'Do you smoke?'

'Yes.'

'With asthma like this?'

'I know. I suppose I should stop.'

'The doctors are gonna scream at you.'

I was beginning to feel like a fool. Tobacco was necessary, but this would not be a noble way to die.

She went away. The doctor came back.

'You smoke.'

'Yes.'

'Christ . . .'

She checked some things, left again. A man came in, a wardsman. He put me on a trolley, and wheeled me off to another room where I had my chest X-rayed. Then I was wheeled into the hall. He said I'd have to wait there until I was assigned to a ward.

I was there for an hour or two. I was near the entry bay for the ambulance patients. I sat up and watched the casualties roll by. There were some sick people. Broken legs, blood, screaming, broken backs. What was I doing there? I didn't even feel sick. I just couldn't breath.

Finally another wardsman came for me. He took me up to my ward. It was a long crowded room, about forty beds. One end male, the other end female. Everyone seemed to be very old and very sick. There were cries of pain. Hands writhed above sheets. A lot of the patients looked catatonic, lying on their backs, open-mouthed and vacant. It was my fourth time in hospital and I'd never seen anything like it.

A nurse and the wardsman conferred, then he wheeled me down to a bed. I got off the trolley. I said, 'What is this place?'

271

'This is ward 2D.'

'Ward 2D?'

'It's the end of the world.'

'Oh.'

'It's the worst ward in the hospital. It's where they send all the old people. The ones who won't ever get better but who aren't quite ready to die either. The ones the nursing homes refuse to take.'

'Why am I here?'

'They couldn't fit you anywhere else. The hospital is always packed on Friday nights.'

He went off and I settled down. On my right there was a thin old man with huge ears. His feet had been cut off. He was rubbing his left ear and staring down at the bandaged stumps. On my left was another old man. He was asleep. A large clear tube ran out of his stomach. It went up to a bottle on the wall. The bottle was full of grey, bloody pus. I listened to the moans, the wailing, the terrible old voices. The wardsman was right. The place *was* the end of the world, it was purgatory. No one there was ever going to leave alive.

I couldn't sleep. I didn't know what drugs they were dripping into me, but they were doing something. I was high. It was like acid. Around eleven they turned all the lights off and I sat there hallucinating. The beds were moving, the old people were getting up, tottering around, pus gurgling in the tubes.

I dozed. I heard voices in my mind. The catatonics were talking to me. Their spirits were restless and trapped. The voices ranted about colours and brightness and pain. A female voice started yelling that she was not going to leave, she was not going to *go*. I woke up. There was a cluster of nurses down around one of the beds on the women's section. She's dead, I thought, she's *gone*.

I was right. The nurses drew all the curtains around our beds. Then I heard them wheel her out.

'Why do you close all the curtains?' I whispered to the nurse when she opened mine again.

'We don't want to upset anyone,' she whispered back.

But the ward was awake now, the old people knew.

By the next morning I was feeling more coherent. The consultant came by on his rounds. He examined me, listened to my lungs, made me blow into the machine again. I hadn't improved.

He said, 'I think you'll be here for a few days.'

'Oh.'

'You're a smoker aren't you?'

'Yes.'

'Well, you're a fool. Did anyone tell you the results of your blood test? It was appalling. If I'd been here last night you would've been in intensive care. You could've very easily *died* yesterday.'

I looked guilty. I felt guilty.

'I will tell you this only once,' he said. 'If you keep smoking, I wouldn't give you fifteen more years. Stop!'

I said, 'I will.'

Two days passed. It wasn't too bad. After the first night it was even good. My breathing gradually relaxed. They brought me three decent enough meals a day. I was being looked after. It was what I'd always wanted. I stayed in bed. I slept, read newspapers, stared, thought. On the second day I got up and wandered around the ward. I watched the old people slipping away. Some of them could still talk. Their conversation was full of memories.

My only worry was the car. It was clocking up all that money. A nurse had told me that they only charged a maximum of eight dollars a day, but still, I was going to have to ring someone, let them know, ask them to come and take it away. I didn't want to have to do that. I thought about who it would be.

I thought, Rachel?

I thought, Maree, Frank, Leo, my family?

But I dreaded talking to any of them. They cared. They'd come and visit, they'd abuse me about the smoking, they'd be nice to me. I was embarrassed enough as it was.

On the third day I finally went out to the phones in the hall. They were both occupied. I sat down. I still wasn't sure who I wanted to call. I thought it would be Rachel. I wanted to see her. I missed her. I missed her company. I hadn't been expecting that.

Some patients came out of the ward across the hall. A man and a woman, both young. I'd been told that the ward across the hall was the psych ward, the locked ward. So these were some of the crazies. They looked it. They were beautiful. They had thin faces and short cropped hair and dark eyes. And they were smoking, lounging up against the walls. The smoking confirmed it. Only the insane were allowed to smoke in hospitals. I watched them do it. Lifting the cigarettes, drawing it in, letting it go. It hurt. It was going to be hard. They saw me watching, looked me over with their distant, arrogant eyes. They were lords, they were gods, they had it all and they knew it.

What was I?

I was an asthma patient.

I knew who it had to be. I got up to the phone, put the money in the slot and dialled STD to Darwin.

Cynthia answered.

I said, 'I'm in hospital, Cynthia. The asthma finally got me.'

'What?' She started laughing. It was rich, loving laughter. 'Oh my poor, poor baby,' she said. 'You're sick? You're really sick?'

'I am.'

'You don't know how *good* that makes me feel.'
It was what I needed to hear.

In the end they kept me there a week. I rang Frank. He
came and took my car away. Rachel visited several times.
She sat on my bed and we talked. It was good. The others
dropped through. I got better.

It was Friday afternoon again when they sent me back
out. They gave me several bottle of pills, warnings and
instructions, and I caught the lift down to the street. I
stood on the footpath in front of casualty. I felt fit and
strange. It was the real world again. I looked at the waiting
line of taxis. Then I started walking home.

FIFTY

For the first time in several years, I was entirely healthy. Over the next few days I did not drink and I did not smoke. I woke up in the mornings and felt good. I could breathe. No coughing, no wheezing, no hangover. I could walk for hours . . . and nothing happened. No pain, no attack.

I was untouchable, uncorrupted, pure. I had conversations and I was aloof to everything anyone said, anything *I* said. My voice seemed to have deepened from some of the drugs. I was still on high doses. I spoke with wisdom, authority. I'd been close to death. I knew it all.

But then I came off the drugs.

I felt strange, restless, uncomfortable. I longed for nicotine but that was gone forever. I couldn't look anyone in the eye. Conversations alternately disgusted or frightened me. I was incapable of dealing with people.

Then, after a few more days, that passed too.

And it was just me again.

Alone.

It was time to go back to the STD clinic for the results of the AIDS test.

The waiting room was a little more crowded this time. I sat and read the magazines. They were the same ones I'd read the last time. I moved around in my seat. I felt loose-limbed and aroused. I had an erection. It was the women in the underwear advertisements.

A doctor, a man this time, called my name. I followed him into one of the rooms. He sat down, I sat down. He took out my file and read down through it.

He looked at me. 'Warts, huh?'

'Yes.'

'Just the one, I see. Did it fall off?'

'It did.'

'Noticed any more?'

'No.'

'Well, take off your pants and we'll have a look.'

I looked at him. 'I'm here for results of an AIDS test.'

'Oh.'

He went back to the file.

'Oh, yes. Here it is. Negative. Didn't anyone tell you?'

'No. They didn't.'

'Well, there you go. Negative. Positive news, huh?'

He laughed.

I stood up and lowered my jeans.

After the clinic, I made my way to a barber.

I looked at my long, lank hair in the mirror.

'Cut it off,' I said.

A few days later I was sitting in the flat. It was a Friday, early afternoon, two weeks after I'd left hospital. I was watching television. The weekend was looming. I had some money. I didn't know what to do with it. There didn't seem any point in going out. There was no one I wanted to see. Nothing new was going to happen. We'd exhausted it all.

The phone rang. It was my brother Stephen. He managed

a section in the public service. I never had learned the name of it. He said, 'I might be able to get you a job, if you want one.'

'What doing?'

'Well, just shit in the mailing room. It'd only be temporary. Three or four months. You interested?'

'I'm not sure. Could I call you back in a while?'

'Okay. Only make it this afternoon.'

'I will.'

I hung up.

I looked around the flat. I thought about things. It was almost nine months since I'd been employed. Did I want to go back? Was this life working or wasn't it?

I didn't know any more. The old certainty was gone.

But a job, a *job*? Surely work wasn't the answer. Things weren't going too well for me at the moment, but surely the rest of society didn't have it right either, did they?

After a while I picked up the phone. I rang Carla's number. I thought she'd probably be out, driving her deliveries around. But she wasn't.

'Gordon? I didn't think you'd call.'

'I was wondering if you had any plans over the weekend?'

'Nothing much. What'd you have in mind?'

'A few drinks, maybe.'

'Sure. Look, come over tonight if you want. There'll be a few of us around. No cocktails, though, just wine.'

'That sounds fine.'

'What've you been up to anyway? How'd you pull up after the party? You were really out of it when you left . . .'

'I know. I didn't pull up too well at all.'

'No one did. There really *was* dishwashing liquid in some of those drinks.'

'That explains many things.'

'I know. I'll see you tonight, then?'

'Okay. I'll be there.'

I put the phone down.

The afternoon was still waiting there. I got up. I put on some clothes and went out. It was a warm, sunny, winter's day.

I walked to the nearest corner store. I had eight dollars. I stood at the counter for some time, looking at the shelves. The attendant waited. I thought about him. He looked about my age. *He* was working. *He* could take it. What was different about me?

I looked at the shelves.

I thought, *fifteen years.*

Then I asked him to give me a pouch of White Ox tobacco. And, with it, two packs of cigarette papers, a bag of filters and a box of matches. He handed them over. He put his hand out for the money.

Eight dollars was just enough.